CW00405317

Megan Taylor

How We Were Lost

FLAME
BOOKS

Flame Books Limited, England

www.flamebooks.com

This edition published in 2007 by Flame Books
First published in 2007 by Flame Books

Printed in England by CPod Ltd

Cover Illustration and Design © Nikki Pinder, 2007
www.nikkipinder.co.uk

Layout & Typesetting by REPUBLIKA D&MPB, Italy
www.rdmpb.com

ISBN 0-9545945-8-4

For Ann Taylor, our courageous, lovely and inspiring Mum.
With love forever.

One

They've been missing since Wednesday. Two young girls, holidaymakers, who disappeared from West Beach some time between three-fifteen and five. They're about the same height, these girls, with the same brownish-blondish hair, but it turns out that they're friends, and not sisters like I thought.

"Best friends," the policewoman says. "Ordinary children, like any of you."

Her words don't seem to go anywhere. They hang over us, settling with the dust motes in the hall's heavy air. The smell of wood varnish and school dinners mixes with our Juicy Fruit breath, our cheap, sharp perfume, and the thickening undercurrent of sweat. For the moment, everyone's sitting motionless, transfixed. Nobody's scraping their chair legs, or talking, or passing little, psychotic notes. Nothing moves except the fly crawling sluggishly from one closed window to another, and the policewoman up there, on the stage. She's bobbing up and down, fussing with a flip board, attempting to angle its metal feet around the dips in the sagging, wooden floor. On the first page, in gleeful bubble writing, is the phrase 'PLAY SAFE'. Just behind her, the stage curtain flickers. There's a long silvery ripple, but nobody comes out to help her, not one of the teachers, and by the time she's finished setting up, you can *feel* how hot she is. Her face is blazing, she's blinking fast, and when she takes off her jacket there are sweat stains growing like blue flowers on her shirt.

I look away then, to a splodge of biro on my pleated lap, to the long brown scab on my left arm. At the start of this endless assembly, it was me up there. The entire 'achievers' group were forced up those narrow wooden steps to collect certificates, so I know all too well how it feels to hear the self-conscious shuffle of your own footsteps echoing in your ears. To have the heat pressing in on you from the yellow windows, while all those eyes stare up at you, straight into you, locking you in place...

"Tara and Stacey," the policewoman announces. Despite myself, my head goes snapping up. I'm gawping again, along with everyone else. I can't help it, she's turning the page and *here they are.*

Our famous Missing Girls.

Right away, the little Year Sevens in the front row are sitting up taller. They're craning forward as if expecting the girls themselves to appear from the folds of the sun-bleached curtains, like elaborate magic tricks or confessional TV; *"surprise!"* But, of course, we've seen it all before. The girls are still in their Guide uniforms. They're still looking up into the camera, with their arms linked and their hair neatly brushed. Their mouths are still pinched open in obedient good-girl smiles. It's the same picture that's been on television and in the papers, the same faces taped up in shop windows and tied to lampposts; slapped on leaflets and shoved through our doors. But although this image has been everywhere, (even floating among the firework-patterns behind my eyelids before I sleep), I can't stop staring.

And I can't stop thinking the same old things. Once again, I'm noticing the way that one girl is slightly prettier than the other, even though she has more freckles. And I'm thinking how the not-so-pretty girl's eyes are smaller and darker, and perhaps more knowing, than her friend's. For the hundredth time I'm wondering if, even as she beamed, some secret part of her somehow suspected that this picture would end up in a school assembly or screwed up on our doormat, or on the streets. And that, one day, she'd have a title.

'MISSING', it says in giant letters, overhead.

The policewoman rubs a hand across her throat. "You're sensible kids," she informs us. "And I'm sure you're already aware of everything I'm about to tell you, but today I want you to really listen. To really *think*. From now on, I want each and every one of you to *play safe*."

She reaches up for the next page and the Missing Girls vanish in a fresh twinkling of dust motes. They're replaced by line after line of that same bold bubble writing, and at last the policewoman can relax. Her hand moves from her neck to wipe her shining forehead, and then back again, and she smiles and blinks as if surprised, relieved that she's reached them at last, her *'Play Safe Rules'*.

"Rule Number One," she begins, "stick together, in groups of three or more. And always tell your parents and carers exactly where you're going and what time you will be home. That's Rule Number Two..."

And all around me now, the atmosphere is changing, relaxing. The Year Sevens have slumped down again into their seats and when one of the boys at the back of the hall boots the chair in front of him, several other boys start to laugh. The girl sitting next to me has pulled a purple gel pen from her bag and is writing something urgent on her best friend's fake-tanned hand. Only a moment ago, they'd all looked so rapt, so serious; I should have known it couldn't last. *Balloon heads*, I think. For a few seconds, the Missing Girls had made them forget the clear blue sky outside and the heat in here, the fact that today is the last day of term. Not anymore. Their excitement is back and it's more intense than ever. You can feel it thrumming like strings beneath the sudden flurry of coughing and muttering, cutting like cheese-wire through the murky greenhouse light. Suddenly everyone's itching to get out of here. Everyone, but me.

"Number Three. Always plan your journeys in advance. If you're using public transport, check the timetables, and if you have a mobile, keep it topped up and with you at all times."

I run my right hand over my left arm, find the edge of the cut where the scab's grown thickest and test it with a nail. I think about the Missing Girl's classmates back in London or Bristol or wherever it was they came from. I imagine gaggles of uniformed girls weeping, mourning, suddenly too scared to hang around outside. But perhaps they're not like that. Maybe they're more like the people all around me, *"ordinary children, like any of you."* Perhaps they don't feel anything at all.

Over at the windows, the fly is following himself in ever-smaller circles around a single smeary pane. He's like a ripple in the sepia glass, his own sad shadow. You can't see the playground beyond his small black body, or the sunshine, or the sky. There could be nothing out there, no one at all.

And suddenly there doesn't seem enough air in here for all of us. There's too much sweating. Too much skin.

"Steer clear of wooded areas and waste-ground," the policewoman says, "even in broad daylight." I raise my right hand to wipe my forehead. Where I've been scratching at my scab, there's a kind of cocoa powder trapped beneath my nails.

"Beware of derelict houses, building sites, the caves down on the beach." She blinks. The air between us is shimmering with dust. The fly continues to go nowhere, drawing spirals on the glass, and for the thousandth time I'm wondering where the Missing Girls could be. Whether they're holed up somewhere, hiding, or if someone's hidden them. Are they imprisoned, scrabbling at damp stone walls, at darkness? Are they crying? Screaming? Or buried already? What does it mean to be so lost?

And then I'm thinking about my mother, although I know I'm not supposed to. I'm thinking about gaps and Missingness. The space where someone's gone.

I dig my fingers into my arm, and try to block out everything except the policewoman, her hand a spider at her throat. Nevertheless, now I've started, I can't stop wondering; where my mother is, who she is, *if* she is, at all.

"Remember," the policewoman is saying, "it's not just

bad men out there. There are bad women too." And now I'm the one who's lost.

*****

It's last Wednesday (sometime between three-fifteen and five) and the girls are bounding up the steps that lead to West Beach. They're whispering and giggling and rolling into one another as they climb. When they start to run, their hair rises in brownish-blondish strings and you can see red blotches, picked gnat bites, dotted among the sun cream behind their knees. Between their swimming costume straps, their shoulder blades are gleaming. Two sharp little sets of honey-coloured wings.

At the top of the cliff, the ice-cream van is waiting. Everything's just as it always is on any July day when the sun's out. There's a queue, with parents shouting, nailed to the spot, while their little kids run everywhere, banging plastic buckets on the dusty ground or chasing one another in circles between their mothers and the bin. The bin is overflowing - it's always overflowing - with Coke cans and lolly wrappers. The rubbish at the top is alive with wasps, and there are more wasps floating just above it, six or seven at least, looking bigger and darker against the empty sky than they really are. Not that the children care. The wasps are just something else to scream about, not a real reason, surely, to feel afraid.

And those brownish-blondish girls are no different from anyone else. They're just as ordinary, as innocent. They don't think to look beyond the ice cream man and wheeling toddlers. They can't see past the wasps, which, they are convinced, are buzzing slowly closer... For a long time, they're not going to notice the woman who is watching them. The woman who is already stepping neatly from the driver's side of a long white car. This car is tucked closer to the railings than the rest. It's parked at an angle, beside a row of gleaming motorbikes. There aren't many trees or bushes up here and beyond the roof and that clean white bonnet the sea is just a peaceful silver square. You can't see the swimmers from this distance. You can barely see the waves, they're only scratches every now and then, rips letting in light.

The woman is short and blonde with rosy cheeks and a tanned and crinkled cleavage. She's wearing white - to match her car, I think; a sleeveless blouse and a flimsy, floating skirt. She doesn't bother wearing shades and her eyes are as clean and open as the sky. As she moves quietly around the car, her edges soften. She's rimmed with gold. She doesn't look like a woman who is planning anything and yet... She's tugging at the chrome handle on the shining white back door. She takes a small step away, but leaves it gaping. Standing open. It's an invitation, like her smile, her clear blue eyes. Except inside there's only dark.

"Now, what we don't want you to do is worry," says the policewoman, and I come jolting back to her, to the room, with my heart banging and my hands locked tightly together, my fingers slippery with sweat.

The daydream's the same, just as powerful as when it came to me almost a week ago, when those girls' freckled, smiling faces were first brandished on the news. It's that last image that won't let go of me. The pale, blonde woman with her small white smile, and her car, so bright it's dazzling, but already spilling shadows from the back...

Returning to the school hall is a shock, like stepping from our sunlit garden into the darkness of the house. Everything looks hazy and slightly too big or out of place. My head's thumping, hurting, and for a moment, it's all the practical, solid things that aren't quite real. I want to cover my eyes with my hands, but I don't. I hold myself still. If I don't move and I don't think, everything will be all right. After a moment, I take a deep breath and look around slowly, carefully, giving the stage, the walls, the kids around me, a chance to slide back into their rightful places, their proper shapes. The fly, I notice, has found some energy from somewhere. He's hovering about a foot from the burning glass now, rising and shrinking as he buzzes back and forth, still relentlessly searching for a crack, a gap.

I turn back to the policewoman. She's rubbing pink circles into her neck again, while intoning her age-old warnings about lifts and gifts and strangers. I listen politely, from a distance. I even nod. I'm going to be ok. The girl sitting next to me jabs my shoulder. She's whispering in hisses, but I ignore her, like I ignore the mobile that's started bleeping at my back. Nothing bad is happening. I'm in school. I'm in assembly. It's the last day of term. It's very hot, *that's all*.

But then I look down and I see that it's not just sweat caught like glue between my fingers. Somehow I've torn my scab right open, I've gouged it out and there's mess, blood, everywhere. My left arm is stained down to my wrist and the fingerprints on my right hand are shockingly defined. There's a pattern like crushed berries on my skirt. I reach under my seat for my bag, a tissue, anything. I can clean it up, I tell myself. It's nothing. *I'm still ok,* but the girl sitting next to me is leaning over. She's *staring*, and other girls, from the row in front, are craning around. And I can't seem to find a tissue, can't even get the zip to open on my bag, and out of the corner of my eye, I see that the fly is growing desperate. He's started to hurl himself against the window and every time that small black body hits the glass, I feel the thud right through me, starting just behind my eyes.

Two

"Jesus," says Diana. "What happened to you?"

She's sitting at the kitchen table, clutching a cup of coffee, surrounded by her stuff. She takes a long wincing sip as she waits for me to answer, steam curling up beside her dense black hair, but she doesn't take her eyes off me. I have no idea what she's thinking. Despite the fact that we share a room, it feels like days, weeks, since we last spoke, and beneath her steady gaze I start to fidget, winding the long canvas strap of my P.E. bag round my left arm between my elbow and my wrist. The strap covers the cut quite effectively and I managed to wash most of the blood off in the school toilets but, glancing down, I see there are still distinct blotches on my grey cotton skirt, and a shadowy handprint pressed against my thigh.

I look past Diana, to the saucepans in the sink and the pool of crumbs leaking out beneath the toaster. I want to talk to her, I do, but what is there, really, that I can say? As pleased as I am to see her, I think about turning, running back outside, to where the sun is shining and the trees are green and the sky is chalked with gulls. But between the front door and me, our hallway is filled with dark, fuzzy shapes. I know they're just our coats, bags and discarded junk, but from where I'm sitting, they could be anything. However bright it gets outside, our hall is always dark. There's a narrow window above the front door at the end, but between the frosted glass and cobwebs, the light down there gets smudged away to almost nothing. A square of smoke, that's all.

"Well?" Diana says. I know she won't come right out and ask me twice.

I think about telling her that I may be going crazy, that I'm scared, except that now of course, I'm not. Now I'm just stupid and exhausted, having worked myself into a state. Again. I slump into the spare chair opposite and put my face down on the table, rubbing my cheek against the warm, dark wood. I don't need to look up to know that my sister's eyes are rolling, that she's about to turn away.

The table smells sweet in the way that mouldy fruit smells sweet. I think of all the things we've spilt here and barely bothered to clean up. Grease merging like plastic with the varnish, milk creeping into the gaps and tiny, peeling splits; fur growing secretly inside. But it doesn't bother me, not really. I stay exactly where I am, breathing it all in and staring down my nose to the things Diana's gathered to pack into her bag. There are her sunglasses and her mobile, her purple lipstick in its purple velvet case. There are her cigarette papers and an open packet of Amber Leaf, spilling tobacco in wispy shreds across the table. My eyes widen;

there's a miniature bottle of 'Bells', half-full, which vanishes as she lifts it. I wait for the chink, the careful glug, as it slops into her coffee, and then I'm sitting up, belatedly protesting.

"Diana!" I say. "What are you doing? Rene's going to kill you!"

There it is again, the eye-roll. On anyone else it'd be annoying, but Diana's beautiful so she gets away with it. She gets away with most things. As if to prove my point, she finishes licking down the roll-up she's been making and sticks it dead in the centre of her violet lipstick smile. Even my sister's not usually this blatant, drinking *and* smoking in the house. It isn't even night.

"Diana," I protest, "what's going on?"

It's her turn not to answer now. She just looks at me with her huge, wet, silent, movie-star eyes, their edges clumpy with mascara. She tilts her head and the tiny hairs on her cheek turn gold, and then vanish. After a moment, I hear it, coming from upstairs. Crying. And I wonder how I didn't notice it before. It's a ragged sound, a high-pitched loop. It goes on and on and on.

The Missing Girls' mothers, that's who I think of first. For days, they've been on television, sitting behind an enormous desk, doing press conferences, appeals. They're about the same size as each other, the same age; they're both softly spoken and polite. They take it in turns to speak and then to cry.

"*Please*," one or the other of them always says. "If anyone has any information, anything out of the ordinary they saw or heard last Wednesday - anything at all, however small - please, please make that call." Their faces are pasty against a wide beige background. They have those same folded arms, the same eyes even, dark and beaded and squashed into their faces like raisins in dough. Like their daughters, you could easily mistake these two for sisters, though it's funny, because they look nothing like their girls.

Across the table, Diana doesn't blink. From the ceiling, there are footsteps, the floorboards whinge, and then there's a series of loud, unglamorous snorts as someone blows their nose savagely, repeatedly. I imagine tissues being wrestled by the fistful from the box. Of course it's not the television. It's nothing to do with search parties or rewards or remembering our prayers.

"Aunt Rene?" I say.

And still Diana doesn't blink, or nod or look away, but nevertheless I understand.

For a moment, I'm dragged back several years, to the times when Rene's migraines were a regular thing, and Diana and I would scuttle about, waiting for Dad to throw us a look if our dolls or cars or felt-tip pens so much as scraped, so much as tapped, against the floor. Except, sometimes, for a dare, we'd creep off to Rene's room to watch her lying on her bed. I remember how she always seemed to lie in exactly the same way, with her shoes off, but fully clothed, a wet white flannel pressed across her eyes. Beneath this blindfold, her nose looked even bigger and more beaky than it usually did. Her mouth was always gaping wide.

As I sit here, staring at Diana and listening to the crying overhead, Rene's mouth - *like that* - comes back to me so powerfully that I can clearly picture the lines like cuts at the corners of her lips and her faded lipstick too. The stains on her back teeth. Most of all, I remember the black hole that was her throat, and how Diana and I would tiptoe right up to the bed to peer at her, to peer inside. She was so still that she looked dead, like the picture in Diana's Disney book of Snow White in her glass coffin, (except Rene was never beautiful enough to be Snow White, Rene was more like the shrivelled-up witch version of the Wicked Queen). On several occasions though, Rene would surprise us. She'd sit up smoothly as we gazed at her and pull the flannel from her face. I'd always jump, but Diana would be cool (she's always been so cool). She'd pretend that we were only there to see if Rene wanted anything. Rene never replied. Her eyes, I remember - dramatically exposed as the flannel dropped - were small and pink and yet somehow so startling I'd often wonder what she'd been doing behind that blindfold. Surely she hadn't been crying under there? Of course, I'd never ask this question out loud, just as Dad would never quite put into words his opinion that Rene's 'migraines' might not actually be anything physical. He'd never explicitly state such a thing, but nonetheless he let it be known, through hints and sighs and those quick sad shakes of his head, that her pain might have more to do with something else, with absent Uncle Pete perhaps, or even us. But surely Rene *crying* wasn't possible - not our Aunt Rene - and yet... Her eyes were pink. Her eyes were small... Never once though, did we see any actual tears. Never once did we hear her sobbing.

"Diana," I say, "what have you done?"

In one motion, my big sister stands and sweeps everything, shades, mobile, lipstick, tobacco, from the table into her bag. "Get changed, Janie," she says. "We're getting out of here."

Walking into town, despite Rene's weird reedy crying and Diana's cigarette and scaring myself half-silly back at school, I somehow decide that everything is secretly all right. It's as simple as this; the day's got even warmer, the sky even bluer and I'm almost feeling normal ~ whatever normal is supposed to mean. It's like the crying, especially, hasn't happened, or that its just another one of those things - my things - that I've made up. For the minute, it's easy to tuck it all away with the lid pressed closed. Everything's simple: I'm out with Diana, my sister. My cool, beautiful sister.

As we walk she doesn't speak, but I don't mind. For now I'm happy, scuffing down the centre of our empty, dusty road, enjoying the whirr and whisper of sprinklers from behind our neighbours' clipped clean bushes and the deep green smell of their gardens, so peaceful and well-tended, so different from our own. Because we're at the top of the hill, there's the relief of a breeze. I watch it play with Diana's hair as she descends ahead of me; rippling colours - a bronze, and then a burnt crimson - moving through the black. I shiver. The breeze keeps pace with us, rolling through the bushes as though an animal, some kind of big cat, is lolloping just inside. There's light like tiger-eyes between the branches. I'm blank, not worrying. Gulls wheel and wail overhead and the sand on the road grows thicker, puffing up around our heels.

Gradually, the town creeps up on us. It closes in; all

cobblestones and balconies, cool dark alleyways, pub signs. And then, too quickly, we're in the midst of it. There are too many cars parked nose to tail down narrow roads. Too many tourists, swinging by with lilos and body boards and countless carrier bags of sodden towels and tourist-tat. Everyone's dressed in pink or white or lemon yellow, their summer clothes like more empty wrappers cluttering our town. As we walk towards them, they raise their sweaty, sunburnt faces and let us through. It's Diana they're looking at. They can hardly help it (they're tourists, sightseers, after all), but then again, being beautiful, neither can she. And she doesn't look back at them, my Diana, not once. Not even when we pass a group of lads in vests and boots, their biker jackets like beetle shells sucking up the sun. They shout across and I'm pretty sure that one of them is the latest boyfriend, Carl, but Diana, unhearing, just keeps on marching past. *My* sister, I think, bowling happily along inside her shadow. She's tied some kind of paisley hippy scarf over her shorts, and you can't help staring at her bum and legs. Especially the legs. They're long and toffee-coloured; they stride so easily away. The fringes on the scarf rise and fall with a delicate, dark ripple for every bouncing step. Everything about Diana is beautiful today; from the faint, silvery scattering of childhood scars on her left calf - like ghostly fishes - to the little blue flower tattoo floating high up on her back... It's been ages, months, since Diana's taken me anywhere. What, I find myself wondering, have I been doing all this time?

As we walk along the High Street, she's reflected in the windows on both sides. I'm surrounded, safe, so that when we pass the estate agents where Rene sometimes works, my aunt slides into my mind, but then straight out again, and when the MISSING posters appear, I'm able to look at them quite calmly, quite casually, as if considering the girls' pretty, freckled faces for the very first time. Even when Diana leads me up past the arcades, towards the steps that lead to West Beach, I'm ok. I don't tug at her arm and pull her back or even ask her where we're going, or why. I don't speak at all and when a girl about the same age as me - as them - comes strolling by, I turn my face away. I'm careful not to look. Or think.

The beach is packed. I keep my head down, like Diana, as we pick our way over soft white lolly-stick legs, and craters dug out like graves. The breeze has dropped and the air is dense with the smell of sunscreen. Everywhere, ahead of us, the waves crash in and hiss back. The sea warps the view like a funhouse mirror, stretching and shattering the bobbing shapes of swimmers and all the little shining toddlers who fill up their buckets or shout at the bubbles in the rushing, breaking tide. I watch the surfers, further out, as they glide and bump and fall, as they struggle, wobbling back up on to their feet. Gulls swing past us, shouting as they sail through the blue before diving down for sandwich crusts and bits of washed-up crab. Between their wings and all that glinting, secretive sea, the light is buttery.

Diana leads me round the cove, towards the furthest cliff. We clamber over the broken old sea wall and across the little rocks and pools where some of the smallest children play, fishing with nets and buckets or simply lying there, staring, on their flattened bellies. The smell of seaweed grows thicker as the pools get deeper. There are long, bubbling ropes of it everywhere, green or brown, with hair, and air pockets in rows like tiny jellied eyes. I feel the barnacles biting through the bottom of my shoes and I realise that I haven't been this way for a long, long time, not since winter when the world was grey and empty and I had to battle the wind to fetch my friend Laura's stupid Labrador back down from his climb. At the base of the cliff, a little way up its red clay face, there are a series of little crimson caves. Their shadowy entrances are spaced evenly apart and they look lived in, welcoming, except they're not - the broken rocks along the bottom here are treacherous. You have to constantly watch where you're stepping. Sometimes the tourists don't and there's an accident. Last year a teenage boy broke his ankle, getting it wedged between these rocks. He'd gone to the caves to drink beer one night - this is one of the places that the older teenagers go - and slipped on his way back down. He must have been the last one there because no one helped him, no one found him, until morning. Snivelling like a baby, the coastguard said.

But then, there are always stories, every summer. I remember hearing something once about a woman, (a tourist of course), a mum off exploring with her young kids, who tripped exactly where she shouldn't have. The tall, jagged edge of a rock went right through her, they said. It came out the other side. *Impaled*. It makes you think, doesn't it? However quickly they covered their faces or ran, her kids would be seeing that forever, every time they shut their eyes.

"Get a move on," Diana calls. She's way ahead of me, already sitting in the entrance to one of the smallest caves, her toffee legs dangling at my head height, ankles swinging in the sun. Her heels make a soft scuffing sound as they beat against the rock. Awkward, grunting, I scramble up after her. I try to hurry, imagining what I look like from behind, my bony bum a comedy prop, poking at the air. But, on her ledge, Diana watches me from behind her roll-up and her lighter, and she doesn't even smile. As I scramble up beside her, it creeps over me for the first time that maybe something is really wrong, properly wrong. After all, I remind myself, Rene was crying, actually crying, and the pair of us just walked away.

"Diana," I say.

"Shut up," she replies, "shut up!"

Her eyes are black and shining. *Don't you cry too*, I think. I don't want to look at her now. Whatever's wrong, I'd rather keep it bound up tight. I can't stand to see her cry. I blink past the sea, *too bright*, to the beach beyond the rocks. But over there, everything's too busy, too noisy and too colourful. I lean back, resting on my elbows. There's a great, dark soot stain overhead, spreading around the edges of the cave's red mouth. They've had fires in here, I think. Diana's eyes keep pulling at me. I go on staring at the ripples of red rock above our heads, at that sugary black stain, but there's nothing I can do to stop her speaking. After all, that's why we're here, and you can tell from the way she's sitting with all her things spread out again, that she's been here before, perhaps often, and probably because she's been forbidden... And now I'm wondering what else they do in here, Diana and her friends, apart from lighting fires and drinking, when there's no one else to see.

"Guess what?" Diana says. Her eyes have hardened now. Black plastic buttons. She sucks in smoke.

"What?" I think I've said it, but the sea's got louder, so it's difficult to tell. Diana's smoke comes out again, in expert little rings.

"Shit," she says. "I'm pregnant."

For a minute there's nothing, nothing at all and then the beach rushes back, and all of a sudden it's inescapable, deafening; the waves and shouts and reeling kids. The screaming of young girls.

The sheer sound of it all rolls over us, a separate tide, filling up our cave. We sit beneath it, frozen. Then Diana's phone goes off, that stupid tinkling ringtone and she draws one leg up and back to kick out hard. Still tinkling, it skitters off, spinning away into a mound of ash and cans and broken glass piled up where the cave goes narrow, becoming just a hole.

"Shit," I say, just like Diana, but I can't reach over to her. I can't take it in, and then as soon as I try to, I don't believe her. Not a word. She's always flying ahead, jumping to conclusions; panicking. *Over-active imaginations*, Rene would say, the pair of us. Everything always has to be a drama. And I'm angry now because Rene's right. Smug Rene with her stupid tears, what's she got to cry about, anyway? But there's this hot feeling in my own eyes now and the skin around my mouth feels hooked and stretched... But it's not because I think Diana's pregnant - I don't believe that for a minute, not for a single second - it's because the proud, safe feeling I had walking down through town with her has been wiped away. Completely. There's a space there now, and she's let everything back in.

Diana's hiding her face, her head is bent into her knees and she's crying intensely. No muffled, snorting, Rene-tears for her. Each sob, each yowl, comes bowling back at us, echoed by the rusty walls, but still the beach is louder. And before I can stop myself, I'm squinting, with one hand raised against the ocean's glare. I'm looking and looking, and sure enough, they're there. Girls like me, like *them*, lying on towels or slumped in deckchairs, wearing shades and hissing headphones clamped around their skulls. I watch as they lean forward so their mothers can rub more sun cream on to their backs, or else they run, forgetting themselves, like children. They tumble, shouting and laughing, headfirst into the sea. And I tell myself to stop looking at the beach, that these are other girls, not them, and all the while Diana's hands are opening and closing in her hair. Her hair is all over the place, a black cloud, shaking with the shoulders underneath. But all I can think, all I *keep* thinking, is what if the Missing Girls *are* here after all? What if they're hiding by not hiding, mingling with the crowd... In many ways, wouldn't that be the most perfect way to disappear? After all, perhaps nothing bad has happened to them. Maybe they have just run away. It's a possibility. They could have had a plan. They could have hidden a pair of rucksacks among the rocks the night before so that they could slip away quite innocently, in their swimming costumes, the next day.

And now, looking across the crowded beach, past the surfers peeling on or off their wet suits, past the older men sipping cans, it's easy to imagine how those brownish-blondish girls might have done it. It's easy to picture them struggling frantically to squeeze their damp legs into their stiff jeans, hopping like gulls between the deckchairs, across the sand. Their eyes flashing like polished spoons as they wait to get caught with their trousers round their knees. But because it's so busy, no one would catch them, no one would notice. They might have even started to giggle, but by the time they're finished, they'd be serious again, silent. They'd stalk off towards the steps with their baseball caps pulled down low, covering up their eyebrows as if they're spies.

And this time when I imagine them climbing out of here, I picture their rucksacks jolting at each stone step, while their humpbacked shadows flutter easily away across the rocks. And all the while, down here, back on the beach, everything would just carry on as normal. Like it is today, like it is down here every single sunny day, forever. There'd be these same wide women flapping the wasps away as they pack up their blankets and sandwich bags and children. At the edge of the sea, the toddlers would go on playing where the surf is grey and gentle, while further out, the sunlight smashes into the water filling it with so much silver that it hurts your head. So beautiful. But those girls wouldn't have looked back to see it and nor would anyone have glanced up to see them go. There'd have been no one to follow the rhythmic slop and shuffle of their flip-flops and the dusty marks they left behind. It would be just them up there, I think, *just them and me*. We're the only ones who're really here.

"Janie," Diana says. "Janie!"

I make myself turn back to her. She thinks she's pregnant, I remember. Pregnant. But it means nothing to me. It's like the names the policewoman gave my Missing Girls - Tara, Stacey - the words are meaningless. It's their faces that get at you, the faces that are everything and everywhere...

Feeling slightly sick, I want to lean over to Diana now, to touch her and comfort her, no matter what she's doing all this for, but before I get there, something new catches my eye. There are black shapes, bin-bags, where a stranger's dumped their rubbish, just below us, to the left. The bags are caught among the rocks, half-floating in the pools. I realise I've been smelling them for quite some time. It's a sticky, background smell that coats your throat, like things soaked up by sawdust. My heart is beating fast, then faster. You can clearly hear the flies.

"For fuck's sake, Janie," Diana says.

I make a grab for her at last. But it's too late, she's already disappearing. In one smooth movement, she's turning and rising up away from me. And just before she jumps down from the ledge, she looks back at me over her perfect shoulder. Then rolls her eyes, disgusted.

Three

It's been going on for hours. By the time I've sloped in from the beach, Diana's probably been back ages and Dad's home too. They're in the kitchen, along with Rene, talking together in loud, sniping whispers that somehow seem to grow louder, less whispery, with every step I take away from them. I climb up through the rings of shadow on the stairs, concentrating on making my own movements as quiet and cat-like as I can, pressing my toes down carefully and then my heels. Toe, and now heel, I think, toe, and now heel, while my hand brushes lightly over the cool, smooth rail. As I climb, I watch the hallway below me through the banisters, picturing the kitchen door opening and a head poking out. A white face, blinking up at me with dark distracted eyes, calling me down. But the kitchen is the last place I want to be right now and when I reach the landing, I feel like a little kid again, I'm so relieved. It's like playing 'What's the time, Mr Wolf?' or not stepping on the pavement cracks or on three drains in a row. I practically run into Dad's study, and when I've shut the door I lean my back against it, pressing my palms, my shoulders, the top of my head, into the deep lined wood. But I can still hear them in the kitchen. Not the words, not the insults, but the tone. Angry and accusing, going on and on and on.

You can't escape anything in this house, but I try. I always try. If only I could call Laura (my best friend, my only friend), it would all be much more bearable. I could slip away to her house and we could put on her mum's old Blondie album, like we did one time, near Christmas. We could dance that stupid dance again, swinging our arms, shaking our hair out, Pogo-ing around her small neat living room. We'd scatter the cushions from the sofa and sprawl amongst them when the songs were done. And when we were no longer pink-faced and giggling, when we'd finally got our breath back, perhaps we'd talk. Perhaps I'd find a way to tell her about the Missing Girls and me; how I can't get them out of my head, how they're always with me like lucky stones inside my pocket that I can't stop turning over and over. I'm scared to hold them and I'm scared to put them down. But Laura's not here. She's been gone a whole fortnight already and she won't be back till the autumn term. She's spending the whole summer in Florida with her dad while I'm stuck at home on my own.

I turn on the computer, self-consciously singing and half-humming under my breath, trying to remember the words to 'Atomic' in the right order while I sweep a pile of Dad's students' unmarked papers from his bashed up leather chair. Dad's study is a mess. There are piles of paper everywhere; they're on top of the monitor, gagging out of the printer,

25

wedged between the books that line the shelves. Some of the stacks have started growing dust, a fine grey silk that you almost want to touch. But when I bend over the nearest furry pile, I see that it's full of hair (cat hair, maybe?) and I pull my hand away, sending the nearest heap slithering, in pieces, to the floor. And behind it, as if waiting, there's a photo of Diana.

I'm surprised to find her here. We don't really do pictures in our house, not like the grinning-laughing-family-holiday shots that plaster Laura's walls. We have some, of course. There are several embarrassing school portraits in the dining room and one of Rene out with her workmates, grinning desperately from beneath a stupid Santa hat (that you just know has been jammed on to her uptight head by someone else). On the mantelpiece in the living room, there's a lone picture of Dad shaking hands with a man in an important looking suit, and a couple of baby and toddler shots of Diana on the coffee table, but that's it. That's all; there aren't any of me when I was that small, and nothing of our mother, of course, since she left when I was three years old... None that I'm allowed to look at, anyway.

I pick up this picture of Diana and blow it hard, feeling the dust itching and squirming in my nose as I hold it right up, before my face. She stares straight back at me; young, but not a little girl. Ten, I think, perhaps eleven? It was taken when she was just beginning to grow up, but before she dyed her hair pitch black or started growing breasts. In my hands, she's blonde, unchanged; it's the way that she still looks to me in dreams. She's disgustingly fresh-faced, clear skinned, smiling. A dazzling, riveting Hollywood smile, even way back then. And her eyes haven't changed at all. They're just as glittering and fearless and as I gaze into them, I can't help thinking how much more confident and in control Diana looks than the girls in the Missing posters, even all those years ago. She's playing to the camera, I think, playing a part ("I'm pregnant"). She looks a lot less real.

The monitor flashes blue and I throw Diana back down, facedown, among Dad's things. I fumble for the mouse, searching the screen for an email from Laura, a way out of here, a distraction, but like yesterday and the day before, like every day since she left, there's nothing. I refuse to give up though. I stay where I am, clicking 'Send and Receive' every ten seconds or so. And I'm still singing, I'm still humming, still tapping at the keyboard, when Rene comes to the bottom of the stairs, to scream at me to get down, *right now*, for dinner. And so they knew that I was up here all along.

I've barely sat down at the table when Diana rises, shouting, and goes flying from the room, turning her back and her swinging black hair on us all. *Bang!* The dining room door slams and Dad flinches as though it's his knuckles that have been wacked.

"I don't know why I bother," Rene says. She's still holding her cutlery in front of her face and it's as if she's addressing the piece of uneaten potato on the end of her fork, instead of talking to us. Both Dad and I are happy to go along with this idea. We stare at the potato, (which happens to be pretty similar in shade and texture to Rene's actual face - pale and powdery-yellowish), and neither one of us replies. Rene's loaded the make-up on tonight, perhaps trying to hide the stains and blotches from this afternoon's tears, but it hasn't really worked. Her eyes look small and very pink against that dusty skin, her eyelids weighted. Migraine eyes, I think. Her mouth stretches and puckers and then stretches once again, but there isn't any sound. Mute, she shakes her head and rises. She picks up her plate, piled with untouched casserole, and for an instant I imagine that she'll throw it. I picture it exploding in vivid white chunks, a horror film handprint of meat and gravy sliding in streaks down the opposite wall... But instead she simply swipes Diana's plate up too. The steam from both uneaten meals merges and rises together. Behind it, Rene's crisp white blouse billows and sinks with her short fierce breaths.

"I don't think I can do this anymore," she says.

And it's funny because that's just want Diana yelled before she tore out of the room. Except Diana said fucking.

"*I'm not fucking doing this.*"

Then *don't*, I'd thought. *Please stop.*

Now, plates in hand, my aunt goes rushing out too, but unlike Diana, who went pounding up the stairs, Rene stops abruptly in the hallway. I can see her just beyond the open door, the thin shadow of her sensible skirt, and her stiff white blouse, the back of her hair somehow as impossibly neat as the front. She clears her throat. The steam's still rising from the plates she's carrying. It drifts back to us in tatters.

"It's at times like these that a girl needs her mother," she says.

She says it breathlessly, but casually, as if she might just be talking to herself, except, of course, she isn't. There's a pause in which Dad and I don't look at one another, and then the kitchen door slams open. Dad flinches on cue. I stare at his big bony hands, while on the other side of the wall Rene clatters saucepans together and then starts crashing cupboard doors. When she scrapes the plates clean over the bin, there's a nails down a chalkboard kind of sound, and I grit my teeth, thinking only of teeth and not of nails, or screeching knives or anything else.

Now it's Dad's turn to stand up. He isn't waiting for Rene to come back, for her to say another word. But he isn't giving up his dinner either. He picks up his plate and stalks away with it, into the living room. And so I'm alone again, abandoned among their dirty glasses, pushed back chairs, and the atmosphere they've left behind, like the whole room's got a headache, like the air is pressing in. Even the cat's gone. Usually he's under the tablecloth, pouncing on our scraps and then growling as he chokes them down, but tonight he's nowhere to be seen. From across the hall, the television blurts into life - chiming advert voices giving way to the earnest pulse of music at the beginning of the news - and after about ten seconds of out-staring the empty spaces at the table, I get up and join my father on the sofa.

We don't talk about what's happening. Instead we sit side by side with our plates burning on to our knees and watch the news. Rene comes and hovers in the doorway, but we pretend that we can't see her. And I think how, these days, it's mostly in silence that Dad and I seem to understand each other best. It's in silence that we're united, protected. When we're quiet like this, concentrated, it's like there's a barrier around us, a wall that he has taught me (wordlessly, naturally) to build. From our shelter we don't have to pick up on the way that Rene's fingers are crawling over and over themselves and we can pretend not to notice her pursed, pale mouth, the *unfairness* of it all that comes blazing from her eyes. We are perfectly oblivious, innocent, even. Safe.

We focus on eating and listening to the frowning, lip glossed news reporter. After a while, my Missing Girls are back. They flicker across the screen, doubled in the lenses of Dad's glasses. They're smiling and glowing, pink and blue and white and even gold. Same Guide uniforms, same freckles, same brownish-blondish hair. A fresh appeal for the same information, it's like something from a dream.

The casserole smells of burning plastic and moves around our mouths like glue, but we keep on eating, eating and listening obliviously, until every little lump of it is gone. Then Rene takes a heavy step into the room and for a minute I'm afraid that we won't be able to ignore her this time, that she'll say them again, those unspeakable words: *it's at times like these...*

Well, it's too bad, Aunt Rene, I'm thinking. *Too. Bad.* I won't look at her. I rest one hand against the side of my face as if I'm wearing blinkers like a horse. Directly in front of me, the television flashes, jumping through a series of pictures of our town; the bus shelter and the High Street, and then an ancient winter storm shot of white waves smashing down against the rocks.

"And so the hunt continues" we're told. And Dad takes off his glasses and rubs a thumb across his nose. He sighs. I take a chance, I drop my fingers and glance back towards the doorway. Already, Rene's gone.

Diana's asleep when I go upstairs. She's lying on top of her covers, snoring gently, sleeping deeply, though she's still got her sandals on and it isn't even night yet, not really. Through the open window, the wide, weighty branches have softened and greyed, but the sky itself is still lilac and every now and then there's the white ghostly flicker of a seagull, coasting back and forth between the trees. I go right over to my sister's bed and stare down at her, thinking how young she looks when she's asleep - younger even than in Dad's picture - despite the way her mascara's spread and the fact you can see her twisted bra strap, slipping down one arm. I bet even I look older than Diana right now. It's the way she's sleeping, curled up with both fists against her mouth, and it's her skin, and the perfect curve of her cheek beneath those fists. She looks warm, unreal, almost edible. *Baby-soft*, is what I'm thinking. You can't really see her stomach. It's hidden behind her thighs and bended knees, but from what I can make out, there's nothing different about her shape, there's nothing new to see. However long and hard you stare at her, there's no way you can imagine that she's pregnant, though I try, I really do, but all that I can picture is a small black space inside of her. And besides, I reason, wouldn't I know it? Wouldn't I sense it, feel it somehow, if this baby-thing were real? Even when I was quite small, I understood when something was upsetting Diana, eating away at her, and she always looked after me in that way too. It wasn't just the big-sister practical things - making my packed lunches, tying my hair, and dropping me off at school, - she'd also hunt me out if I was lonely; pull me into bed with her when I had a bad dream or woke too early, with the sky still dark outside. All too clearly I can conjure up that icy dash over to her side of the room, the relief when she hauled me in beside her. I remember how everything about her seemed warm; her skin, her cheap flannel nightdress, even her smell. A smell like hot bread or little yellow cakes. Something soft and sweet and freshly baked.

Now, through the bruised, tender light, I reach out for Diana as I've reached out to touch her a thousand times before, but this time, my fingers stop. They hover just centimetres from her curved hip, her packed-up stomach. I gaze back over to the soft, dumbly sweet expression on her face, balanced amidst that mass of coarse black hair. And *what are you playing at?* I wonder. *With this whole baby-thing, what is it that you want?*

My arm falls heavily back down against my side. I'm standing stiffly, but a part of me is so tempted to crawl into bed beside her, to feel the cool cotton gliding down around me. The press of her brown skin.

But then I'm hearing Rene's words again: *it's at times like these...*

I rub my fists against my eyes. What's the matter with everyone? Why can't everything just keep on going in its boring, thoughtless way? But it's not just Rene. It's me; it's those Missing Girls again, messing with my head. Until they disappeared, I didn't think about our mother, not day-to-day, not really. I was so young when she left that, unlike Diana, I have no memories of her. No knowledge and so no pain. On the rare occasions when she did cross my mind, (usually because someone at school had said something or asked something, or innocently *assumed*), it did sometimes occur to me that there might be this little hole in my life. But it was always something tiny. Small as a bullet hole, only not nearly as dramatic. More like that fleeting nanosecond of darkness when you blink and for just an instant, the world is gone.

Diana's drifting away from me. Those Missing Girls... It's all mixed up. I pull a hair from my mouth and run my hands across my face. I realise I'm exhausted. And I'm backing away from Diana and her rumpled bed, when I suddenly remember the box of pictures she used to keep hidden underneath it. I narrow my eyes at her sprawling legs and fallen covers, at the bottom sheet crumpled like newspaper under her heels. I stare into the thicker dark beneath her mattress and wonder if it's still there, that metal box, the one I opened, just that once, a long, long time ago. I was very young. Too young. Try as I might I can't recall a single thing about the photos of our mother, or the papers stashed inside. All I can really remember is Diana's anger - a surprising thing, back then.

"*If you ever touch that box again, you'll shrivel up and die.*" And after that, she bought a padlock.

Beneath me, within pinching distance, her head rolls gently on the pillow. Even now, I wouldn't dare go near that box, even now I couldn't ask about our Mum. My brain's aching and my bones feel tired. *I'm like an old, old lady*, I think, stumbling back to my side of the room, my skinny feet catching in the litter of clothes and magazines, scattering a trail of silver bangles on the floor. I undress quickly in the long mauve shadows and throw myself into my cold and messed up sheets. I don't want to think anymore, *I don't want to know* like I've *never* wanted to know...

Immediately, sleep's grabbing at me, pressing down with sandy fingers, but I don't let myself sink away with it, not yet. For a little while, I lie there staring back across our floor, the layers of mess, towards Diana. I can't stop thinking about photographs and secrets. About the darkness rolling like water beneath my sister's bed.

Four

We're out on the heath together, amongst its prehistoric dips and sudden chunky rises, though I don't remember the grass ever looking quite this pale before. The sun has bleached it almost white and it stretches out as far as you can see, whispering and rolling all the way to the blue horizon. Up close, it's not so soft. Up close, it's stiff and brittle. It reaches up beneath my skirt, poking my calves and scratching my knees. It rubs the backs of my thighs like toothbrush bristles. Standing beside me, the Missing Girls are looking pretty messed up. Their Guide uniforms look glued to their shoulders and ribs, sticking to their sunken little stomachs in broad black patches. Against the dark blue cotton, it's difficult to work out for certain what these patches might be. They could be mud or blood, or only water. But their faces look puffy, bruised maybe, especially around their mouths, their bitten lips. Their eyes are definitely wrong. Their pupils are huge, black and glassy; and they look like they are about to pop right out of their faces like cartoon eyes, as they stare across the grass.

"There," says one of the girls, "over there." And then they drop to the ground, taking me with them. We're crouching like rabbits in the dirt, and still it takes me a minute or so to understand we're hiding. I follow the girls' gaze through the long grass to a small group of grown-ups shambling out of the bushes and creamy scrub beyond the furthest dip. Like the grass, the grown-ups don't seem quite real. They're more like ghosts, grey shapes against a clean, deep snow.

I'm in the middle. The girl on my right has her elbow in my ribs; on my left, the other girl's thigh is squashed against my own. Huddled this close, I can't help smelling them; they smell the same. Like the dirt beneath us, and of something sweeter, tackier, like Coca Cola. I look down at their shoes.

The hum of adult voices grows louder. They're coming closer. The noise they make breaks up now and then, becoming smaller sounds that might be actual words. I feel my heart slip and then start banging again, faster now - too fast. *Are they calling out our names?* Over our heads, the grass rocks back and forth carving small white scratches in the blue silk sky.

"It's all right," says one of the girls, the prettier one. She's the one in charge, I think, and so it's crucial to listen very carefully to what she has to say. She places one hand on my shoulder, reaches across me and puts the other on her friend's. We lean in close.

"They can't hurt us," she whispers, "not unless we want them to." And then I remember that this is a game, that's all. It's a game I used to play a long, long time ago, back when Diana was my world. "Now do what I say. Lie down." And we do, the other girl and me. We do it straight away. From crouching, we push forward on to our knees and then stretch out together in the grass. The prettier girl, still squatting, reaches down to clutch my leg above the knee. "Lie still." I realise that my leg is jumping, twitching, beneath the thin pressure of her dirty nails. I make it stop. "Good," she says. "That's right."

And so we lie there, motionless on the dusty ground, as the prettier girl moves away from us, and then stands up. As she calls the grown-ups over.

I fall out of the dream like stepping off a curb into a great, dark rush of nothing. For a moment I'm not here, not there, not anywhere, and I sit up straight in my bed with my eyes wide open, searching the pale shadows for something to hold on to.

Diana, I think. But I can't hear Diana breathing. Diana isn't here.

Through the gloaming, I see how the window's been pushed open to its widest, but I knew she was gone even before I glanced over at the glass. I knew it in the very instant when I woke, in that emptiness. It's still not properly dark so I can't have slept for long. It's probably only minutes since she left, less than an hour certainly, since she scrambled quickly and silently away. She didn't take much with her. As far as I can see, it's all still here - magazines, the path of bangles shining softly, the clothes piled on the floor. Nothing's been disturbed.

I count the bangles backwards, trying to slow my breathing at the very same time. Telling myself *she'll be back soon,* while in the half-light my chest is small and flickering like ancient film, caged in beneath the thick black fishbone shadow surrounding my ribs.

I resist the urge to rush over to the window, to stare out into the night. Instead I make myself lie still, un-twitching. I don't even glance at her empty bed. Instead I try to breathe deeply. I watch the shadows on the ceiling drift and part and smudge together once again. Somewhere, on the road beyond our dark, dark garden, an engine rumbles past and if you listen really hard, there's the sea too. It always sounds much closer in the night. *Hush, hush, hush* it murmurs, like the swish of bone-dry grass.

I bend the damp, fusty pillow round my ears. I will not panic. But already, I'm gazing back towards the window. Already, the lilac sky is changing. And as I watch it filling up steadily with waves of gentle black, the realisation floods through me all over again: my sister's out there somewhere. Diana's gone.

Five

It's a golden morning. I wake to light pouring through the open window with the sweet blowsy scent of fat pink flowers and dew-wet grass. On the floor by my bed, the clock radio is jabbering.

"Forces from as far a field as Gloucestershire and London have joined up with local police in the ongoing search for Tara Matlock and Stacey Hughes. In a statement issued last night, Chief Inspector Jackson, in charge of the case, urged the public here to remain vigilant despite an official widening of the search area."

"We refuse to give up hope," the policeman declares; though the report then goes on to consider the time that has passed since the girls went missing and the possible effect on tourism for years to come. There are sound bites from local business people, adding layers of practical concern to the general anguish. Then a replay of an interview with the ice-cream seller who may have been one of the last people to see the girls last Wednesday.

As he breathes heavily into the microphone, telling us all over again how he can't honestly be sure whether it was *those girls* he saw between three-fifteen and five, I picture him as he looked on the television news. I see his large red head again. The stubble, like salt flakes, that was ground across his chin.

"It's been non-stop," he says. And besides, as far as he's concerned, girls that age all look the same. At least the pretty ones do, the fair and freckled skinny type with brownish-blondish hair. I've heard all this before, of course. Nevertheless I listen carefully, taking in the uneven rumbling of his tone as much as the words. And then I'm sitting up carefully too, cupping my elbows as if they're made of glass, two fingers on the new soft scab running down my arm. I don't want to knock the fragile idea that's blossoming inside me, the idea that's taking shape while the ice-cream seller rambles on. The thought that's growing stronger by the second, becoming a conviction. A certainty, almost.

That, perhaps, it is up to me to find those Missing Girls. That it's me who will bring them home.

Sunlight flashes across the bangles on our floor and everything's buzzing. Along with birdsong, the morning's filled with the sound of bees. But there's another buzzing too, a fizzing in my heels, my calves, my thighs. Electricity races along my bones like tiny, chasing fairy lights. It's this hope, this new belief. It makes me want to run.

The room flickers and I jump up from the bed to see a bird floating outside the window, calling and calling as he blocks out half the sun. For a moment he looks black and huge and then he's gone and the brilliant yellow morning rushes back.

With the sun on my shoulders, I start kicking clothes about, hunting for shoes. It's all starting to make sense. The dreams, the beach, the whole reason why those girls have been haunting me. I now know why I can't shake off their faces, those Girl Guide smiles, why they won't let me go. It's nothing to do with Diana or Rene or my long lost absent mother.

It's because I'm meant to find them.

On her side of the room, from beneath a mound of covers, Diana makes a soft scoffing sound, which isn't quite a snore. She's hunched small and turtle-like, in the middle of her bed. She's drenched with light ~ not that she'd know it. She's somewhere far away from here. I turn hastily away from her, shaking my head, my lips curling in disgust. I'm not worrying about Diana anymore, that's another thing I'm deciding. From now on, she can take care of herself. She came back in the early hours, just as I knew she would, as she always does, rustling branches and snapping twigs, swearing as she heaved herself up the swaying apple tree outside, and over the sill. Usually that's when I can shut my eyes and burrow deeper beneath the duvet, when I can finally get some sleep, but last night she just slumped right there on the carpet beneath the window, so of course I had to go to her. I don't know what she'd been drinking but she smelt sharp and syrupy, like an open tin of pears.

"Get up, get up," I whispered. "You can't sleep here." And when I finally managed to haul her to her feet, with my hands clamped beneath her armpits, her head knocked so heavily into mine that I staggered back a step or two and nearly dropped her. And her hair was everywhere, in my face and in my mouth, greasy and synthetic tasting. All that dye. Her hair smelt of tinned fruit too, so sweet, but also like thick black bonfire smoke. We rocked together for a moment before I was able to push her over on to her bed, before I dumped the pile of sheets and clothes on top of her.

Well, I've finished with her now. I'm done. I pull on jean shorts and baseball boots, start throwing clothes into the air behind me in the search for a clean top. From today on, I tell myself, I've got bigger, more important things to worry about than Diana and her dramas. I pick up her tie-dyed vest and pull it on. It hangs off me like a sack and stinks of her white musk perfume, but I don't care. Nothing matters except for the Missing Girls. That moment when I'll bring them home.

I can picture it so easily. People everywhere, clapping, cheering. Reporters shouting questions, camera flashes in our faces, microphones jostling the air. *A hero's welcome in the heart of town*, that's what the headlines will say and the TV and radio reports - and look! Here come the Missing Girls' mothers, they're rushing forward, colour erupting in their pale pastry cheeks at last, and over there, emerging through the rows of reaching hands and beaming faces, will be the policewoman from school.

I make the fantasy stop, a part of me aware that I'm standing, grinning like an idiot, in the middle of the room. I know that it won't really happen like that, that it won't be that simple, that the girls might not even be alive. Yet there's a soothing, warm-milk feeling sloshing about inside my stomach that I don't want to give up. I keep it with me as I stride out on to the landing, and when I hear Rene start shouting, my first instinct is to hang on to it even tighter. I even manage to hold on for several seconds after Rene's shouts have turned to screams. But then the screaming takes over everything. It empties me; my head, my stomach, and especially my legs. Ridiculously, as if they could save me from falling, I press my shaky fingers to the wall. The sound seems to be coming from just outside the house, so what I should be doing is dashing down the stairs, bursting through the hall and straight out of the front door, but I can't. Instead I'm fumbling my way across the carpet, and then slipping and stumbling into the clean, blank bedroom opposite our own, Rene's room at the front of the house. It's the one with the clearest view, but even once I'm inside, I don't run. I creep instead. I creep, almost shyly, over to the long, mirror-like windows, hoping that by the time I've started peering out, the noise will have stopped and there'll be nothing left to see.

But there she is. There's Rene, standing right below me, in the drive. She's screaming still. She's roaring. Though, from this angle, I can't see what she's screaming at, or who. As far as I can make out, she isn't being attacked and her zippy little red car's right there, just a few feet away, if she needs to make one of her zippy little exits. I can even see the car keys in her hand. As she swipes at nothing with her fist, they leave a trail of gold behind them in the air.

For a moment I wonder if she's under attack by tiny insects that I can't quite see, a swarm of invisible bees, but then I see him, stepping out from the shadow of the house. A boy, I think at first because he's wearing a bright orange T-shirt with a picture on it and knee length shorts. Because he looks so small and pale next to Rene's dark, boxy suit and her set greying hair. He's barely real beside the noise that keeps on coming from her square, pink, screaming mouth. But as he takes another step towards her, the rush of sound falters and falls apart and I can finally make out the words beneath it.

"Don't touch me, don't you touch me," Rene's saying, again and again. And then, breathlessly: "You can't be here. You're not allowed."

And now I can see that of course he's a man. He isn't even very young. There's a new thin spot in his mousy hair and his clothes today are odd, but nevertheless it's dawning on me who he is, this man who isn't supposed to come to the house, who isn't supposed to come within a two-mile radius of Rene. He's Rene's husband, Uncle Pete.

And immediately I wonder if he'll hit her, because I know that's what he does, or at least, it's what he used to do. It's the reason she's got a court order against him, the reason why she left him all those years ago and ran away to us. It's one of the reasons anyway, one version of events. But seeing them together now, it's a struggle to picture how a fight between them could even start. All I can think is that it would be a quiet thing, his fist in her face. Her shouting mouth, all that noise and drama, would be silenced right away. There wouldn't even be a soft thud before there would be nothing. And amidst the silence and the sunshine, the blood on Rene's face would shine; a cheerful party balloon red... But even as I try to picture it, I don't believe it could actually happen. The idea of Rene bleeding is almost laughable; it's so utterly unreal.

And suddenly I realise that the shouting has stopped. I don't know how he managed it, but somehow, Uncle Pete has crept in close and he's actually clinging to Rene now, his arms crossed tight behind her back. And though she's not actively returning his hug, she isn't stopping him either. She's just standing there with her hands over her face, solid and immovable, like a dark, boxy bollard, while he hangs off her in his orange top, once more a naughty child. I cannot believe what I am seeing. This is the man who broke Rene's heart and her wrist and her sharp, slim nose - at least twice, from what I've heard. He's the man who came here one rainy night two years ago and wouldn't go away, but simply sat dripping on our front step until a police car came and took him. And we heard so many whispers and stories about this man when we were small, that we'd muddle him up with the fairytales in Diana's colourful, dog-eared book, so that somehow Uncle Peter *was* the wolf, or the troll, or even the giant. Except he was human, he was real, so much, much worse. He's the man, as we've always understood it, who made Rene the woman she is today; snappy, long-faced, and unlovable. *So what does she think she's doing, letting him hold her in his arms?*

It's worse than the shouting. More stupid, more horrible even. *What's wrong with everyone?* Disgusted, I turn away to face her room and am immediately confronted with another two square-shouldered, sharply ironed suits hanging on the back of the wardrobe door. Like ghosts of Rene, her headless siblings, these suits are identical to the charcoal one she's currently wearing, except they're lighter, one smoke coloured, one stone. For a moment I struggle with the urge to grab them and throw them from their hangers. I imagine mashing them between my grubby baseball boots and the empty, vacuumed floor. And I don't even know why I want to do this - hurt her in some stupid way - and where this sudden spurt of hate is coming from. Somehow, it's got something to do with the way this room is the only clean, neat place in our whole stinking, shabby house. The way that since she got promoted and started working longer hours, Rene's made it repeatedly clear that she isn't picking up after us lot anymore. We're old enough; she's not our slave, and isn't it about time we realised she isn't interested in us, or our excuses? And perhaps it's also about the way that Rene doesn't hug, not anyone, in any way, not ever. And that there are some things that you know about a person that aren't supposed to change...

But perhaps it's not about any of that. Perhaps that's *simply bollocks*, as Diana would declare and maybe I'm just angry because today was supposed to be *my* day, for my plan, and I'd been so determined that nothing, not Diana, or anyone, would pull me any other way. I throw myself back on to Rene's tight, neat bedclothes and deliberately wipe my blazing face, my running nose, across one puffy, snow-white pillow. *Bitches,* is what I'm thinking. Diana and Rene, the pair of them. So wrapped up in their own small lives, they don't even care. They don't care that two young girls are missing and nobody knows why.

I close my eyes and make myself breathe. In, and slowly out, until I'm practically gagging on the purple stink of Rene's stiff, conditioned sheets. I screw my eyes up even tighter and concentrate, willing back the daydream of my heroic return with the Missing Girls, turning to again see all those waiting cameras and journalists, the policewoman and her smile. I cling on to these images. They're as soothing as the old blanket that I used to drag about with me when I was small; a ragged tartan smelly thing that one day just disappeared.

I picture the Missing Girls' mothers breaking away from their skinny daughters and turning round, arms opening, to skinny me, the one who's brought them home. Together they'd rush at me, pulling at me and pawing at me, hugging me tight around my neck.

"Thank you! *Thank you* for bringing back our babies..."

And all the while, I'd keep my mouth closed and my head bowed low. I'd stand there very quietly and let them cover me in tears.

I've got to find them.

Wiping my face and blinking, I sit up and set my feet down firmly on Rene's spotless floor. On the table next to her bed there's a fat gold novel with a peasant girl on the front cover, and a hairbrush and a lipstick. Absently, I pick up the lipstick and roll it out. It's a soft pink colour, very different from Diana's stark purples and her browns and her countless bloody reds. For a moment, I think about mashing it up inside the lid or using it to draw a moustache and beard, perhaps an extra pair of comedy breasts, on that dreamy peasant girl. Instead I go over to Rene's floor length mirror and smear it briskly over my mouth. Then, without taking a final look through the thick beige curtains, I turn and march downstairs.

Outside, the world has changed again. Rene's still there

and Uncle Pete's still there, only they aren't hugging anymore, and Dad is with them too. He's standing just a couple of feet away, nursing a coffee cup and staring vaguely down at his unlaced shoes. From where I'm hovering in the open doorway, I can see he hasn't put his socks on, either. I don't know what's happened to bring him out here now and not before. Perhaps previously, like me, he'd simply watched, but now I'm wondering, despite myself, what Rene's done to shake Pete off? I haven't heard her screaming or shouting again, but maybe all it took, after all that noise, was a whisper in his ear? Or maybe, I think, she's finally hit *him*. Though I've seen Rene angry many times, I've never seen her face like this. She's fuming. She's so angry I can feel it from the step. She's staring right at Uncle Pete as if she can burn him to nothing with those eyes, and for a moment I can almost believe that invisible flames will actually come licking off Rene, engulfing Uncle Pete until all that's left of him is a puddle of melted shoe rubber in the middle of our drive.

Beyond them all, the thick green trees seem to have gathered in closer. Dad's staring across at Rene too now. I hold my breath, like the trees, as he takes a step closer, stops, and then sets his cup down on the ground. He moves soundlessly over to Pete, raising one hand as if considering placing it, gently, on the other man's shoulder.

"I think you'd better go now." Dad says and Pete nods and swings around before Dad's hand can touch him. He walks out of our drive as the branches overhead start whispering, and then he's out, on to the street. He doesn't glance back. I watch him go, straining my neck to see if he's got a car out there, parked up against the curb, a long white car, perhaps? With a woman at the wheel? But the road is empty and suddenly he's gone. From the far side of the street, a lawnmower jerks, and then purrs, into life.

"Rene?" Dad calls, but she's already turned away. She's pressed up against her car door, and I can see from the way her shoulders have risen how angry she still is. The car keys are trembling, jangling softly, in her hand.

But then she turns her head and looks right at me, right through me, a horrible stark emptiness in her eyes. Her anger's so solid, so hungry and ferocious that, suddenly, I'm shaking too, unable to turn away. Something inside me leaps up as though scalded. *You can't get to me, Rene* I vow. *I will not let you get inside my head.* But her gaze is eating away at me. I struggle; over and over, I tell myself that she's not important, that this does not matter. But finally, it's the Missing Girls' mothers who save me. It's the thought of the way they'll gaze at me, the way they'll reach for me, when I bring their daughters home.

Their eyes, I think, like stars.

Six

When I reach the car park overlooking West Beach, it's still too early. The ice-cream van is here, but its hatch is down and I can't see anybody through the windscreen. There's no one else about either, no other cars, no customers. I hover among the small battered bushes at the edge of the car park, my heart still banging from the climb. I can't seem to get my feet moving again. Beyond the rocks and heather and scrappy little shrubs, I'm aware of the beach below me, and the pure dizzy blue of the sea beyond. From up here, the rush and retreat of the tide sounds as soft as breathing. Every now and then it's lost altogether beneath a burst of screeching gulls.

Down on the beach, the deckchairs are still stacked up together in a flat, canvas parcel and, despite the heat, there are only two people out this early. One's an old man stooped over his metal detector, the other a woman, walking a slow line along the dark sand at the edge of the water. Her dog splashes back and forth, running loops in the breaking waves. These strangers hadn't seemed worth bothering with as I pounded along the cliff path, (my head was still bursting with Rene and the desire to escape, my mind fumbling to remain focused on the image of two skinny, running girls). Although I'd intended to retrace all their last known movements, there hadn't seemed much point in going all the way down those steep sandy steps just to climb back up. I thought I'd go straight to the ice-cream seller in the hope that, since that early interview, he might have remembered something new.

But now I'm wondering if I was wrong. What if the dog woman had been there the day the Missing Girls vanished? Perhaps she saw them and spoke to them, or they to her; one of the girls bending down to run her slim, freckled hands through the dog's wet fur? Or what if, even as I'm waiting here, the old man's metal detector is bleeping? Suppose he's reaching down, right now, clawing past the pale, powdery top sand to unearth a cheap gold chain, bearing a locket or a heart or a name in curly script. *Tara* or *Stacey*, it might say. Or maybe he's found a purse belonging to one of their mothers, still bulging with notes and credit cards. A pocket straining with unspent change? Perhaps I should go back...

I realise that I'm rubbing at my cut again, that I'm rocking on my heels with the rhythmic sighing of the sea. I hold myself still. It would be all too easy to waste the morning running around in circles, and already the tops of my arms and the back of my neck feel like they're reddening, tightening, about to burn. Already it's too hot. But I'm here now. I should wait. The car park gravel stretches away from me, almost luminous beneath the cloudless sky. I'd never realised it was white before. It's as white as the soft, deep heath grass in my dream. I take a single step on to it and then pause, scuffing my baseball boot back and forth. I think it'll make a scraping sound, a rattle - all those little gritty stones grinding together underneath - but I don't hear anything, except the sea, the birds. The ground puffs up and I watch the dust creep over my boot, higher and higher until it's speckling the black canvas like television static. Later on, I think, I'll be trailing white footprints down our hall and up the stairs. I picture Rene coming after me on her knees, sweeping up the evidence with her dustpan and brush; those familiar sharp swipes that leave most of the dirt behind. *But I'm not thinking about Rene*, I remind myself. I'm not thinking about all the layers of mess, all the confusion back at home.

I close my eyes, once more conjuring up the Missing Girls' familiar freckled faces, the neat brush strokes gleaming in their hair. I've got a job to do, I remind myself. I've got a plan. When I open my eyes again, the ice-cream van shimmers and for a moment looks like something that's just landed, some battered alien space craft, dropped as it is, in the middle of that empty gravel, in all that white. Beside the hatch, a homemade Donald Duck is staring at me with one badly painted eye, disconcertingly larger than the other. MIND THAT CHILD is printed in black letters across his puffed up chest. *A spaceship from Planet Duck*, I think and try to smile, but part of me just wants to turn and walk away.

What if the ice-cream man's not coming? What if it's the girl instead? The girl with the pale plate face and fat fingers who has served me countless times before, handing out warm cans of Coke that have been sitting on the side too long. Before I saw him on the news, I'd never seen the ice-cream man before. I wonder now if he's married to the plate-faced girl, though with the age difference and those big round heads it seems more likely he's her father.

And suddenly, there he is, strolling out from around the back of the van and coming to a stop right next to that bulging-eyed Donald. They're shoulder-to-shoulder, neck and neck. THAT CHILD the sign reads now. The whole time I've been standing here, I realise, he's been here too, smoking a cigarette around the other side of the van. He sucks on it now, a tiny stub mostly hidden by his fingers. He lets out a ring of smoke. *Not so good as Diana's*, I think. Not so round or perfect. The ice-cream man is shorter than he looked on the news, but just as red.

He raises his head and looks right at me. Immediately, I turn away. I glance back over my shoulder at the great, grey clumps of heather at the edge of the car park, at the skinny bushes and stunted trees. There's a slight breeze running through the wrinkled leaves. They lift in sections, a Mexican wave, and goose bumps rise along my arms, despite the heat.

What is it that I think I'm doing here? I try to remember how it is, precisely, that I'm meant to find the Missing Girls? I look back and the man's still staring. I feel the heat coming in closer and closer, until even the air inside my mouth tastes thick and scorched. He keeps on looking and then opens his lips and shows his teeth; a grin? I can just make out a small black space where a tooth is missing from the front. I know I'm blushing. I'm sure of it. I'm turning as red as he is. I'm burning up, as though there's something infectious in his gaze. He flicks his butt onto the dusty ground, spits after it, and then strides over to the driver's door, flings it open and leans inside. As soon as his back is turned, I feel released, but for some stupid, moron reason, my eyes have started burning too. They're suddenly wet as though with tears. I wipe them quickly on my arm and make myself walk over, slowly, before I can persuade myself to turn and run.

Like Uncle Pete, the ice-cream man is wearing a T-shirt and shorts. Little boy clothes. His shorts are cream coloured. They stick to him in stripes around his thighs. As I get up close, I see the hair on his calves is dense, straight and grey.

"Two minutes, love," he says, without turning round, "running a bit late this morning."

Peering past his round cotton shoulder, I watch as he struggles to lift a box from the floor of the van. It seems to be wedged beneath the driver's seat and when he finally works it free, he staggers backwards, grunting, and then mutters something that I don't quite catch. There's an aftershave smell coming off him, a heavy earthy odour that's probably supposed to represent forests or dark Eastern spices, but to me just smells brown. He turns, swinging around with the box in front of him so I have to take a quick step backwards not to be hit. He looks me over with eyes that are narrow between puffy, papery lids. They're such a pale hazel colour that in the sunlight they're almost yellow, like a cats'. When he speaks, he's no longer sounding friendly:

"Two minutes, I said, darlin'. I've got to get this lot unpacked first. Now if you don't mind?" He waits for me to move, but I just go on standing there, too close beside him, like an idiot, having no idea what I'm supposed to say.

"But I don't want an ice-cream," I blurt at last and even to my own ears, I sound about six years old, and possibly unbalanced.

"Oh, yes?" the man says. "What is it then, exactly, that you're after?"

"I need your help," Immediately I realise this is wrong. What I need is information, not help. Too late, I understand that I should have thought this through. I should have planned out properly what to say, but instead I've just gone rushing in, like a fool, like I always do, and now, in truth, I've no longer got the foggiest what it is that I want exactly. My mind, for the moment, has gone as white, as blank, as the gravel beneath my feet. And the blush is back too, like a pair of fat red hands, clamped flat around my cheeks. I try to concentrate. I blunder on, regardless.

"I saw you on the news," I say, "talking about the girls. My Missing Girls."

"Your missing girls, eh?" the man says. "Know 'em then, do you?" When he speaks, I catch a purplish glimmer of his tongue through the gap between his teeth.

"Yes," I say, "they're my friends." I don't know why I'm lying. Nor what I'm saying, or doing here at all, for that matter.

The man shifts the box up towards his chin, his creased red neck.

"You should have told your friends to be more careful," he says.

I look quickly away from him, from his yellow eyes, and almost jump at the sight of my own footprints trailing off behind me. Like footprints on the moon. I've got to calm down. I've got to focus.

"I just wanted to ask some questions," I hear myself plead.

"Alright," he says, "seeing as I'm running late anyway, seeing as they were friends of yours, and all. Hop in."

"What?"

"Go on, get in the van. Then we can talk. You can ask me your questions, whatever you like." He's already climbing into the driver's seat, settling the big brown box awkwardly across his lap. He reaches over to the passenger door and swings it open.

"Ok. I'm coming." But it takes me another moment of staring at my dusty boots before I can make them shuffle over to the other side of the van. Before I'm even half way into the seat, he tells me to shut the door.

"You'll let all my cold air out," he says, and I do it, though it doesn't seem to make much sense. It's even hotter inside the cab than out, and the air feels thicker, dense with the smells of vanilla and tobacco, an undercurrent of vinegar, and that aftershave that's everywhere suddenly, sticking to my damp palms and my sweaty face.

"So, you know 'em, then?" he says, as if it's me that's needing questioning.

I nod and try to sit up straighter in my seat, as if I know what I'm doing here, as if I'm responsible, clear-headed. But immediately I jump forward, I can't help it; the metal on the loose seat belt that's caught beneath me burns straight through Diana's flimsy top, like an iron in my back. I inch forward, one hand clamped on to the cluttered dashboard. Beside me, the ice-cream man shakes gently as he laughs.

"So," he continues, when he's finished laughing, "was you on holiday with 'em too, then?"

"Yes," I reply without meeting his eyes. His face is way too big in here. Too close and red and shiny, like a balloon about to pop. I glance around the cab instead, taking in the dirty windows, the dirty floor. There's a collection of kid's things on the dashboard. Forgotten things, lost things. A yellow plastic hair bobble, a yo-yo, a baby's little, faceless bear. There's a homemade friendship band hanging from the rear-view mirror, turning in strands of pink, black, and electric blue. Dangling beside it is a troll with bright green hair.

I stare down further and there's his leg, lolling just a few centimetres from my own bony little knees. His heavy thigh squashes out in a single solid lump from beneath the box, and I don't think I've ever seen leg hair like it before, not on anyone, not so long and silky and straight-looking. It's like he's combed it. The bottom of the cardboard box is darker than the rest and I wonder if it's leaking on to his lap right now, and whether he'd even be able to feel it through all that hair. On the lid of the box, there's writing. MINI MILK x 250 it says in bold black 'mind that child' type print and there's a picture of a grinning cow, one of its horns bent backwards beneath his fat red thumb.

"It's a funny thing," the man says, "they talked about all them little ones, the brothers and sisters and that, on the news, but they never mentioned you. I don't think no one's said anything about a third young girl..."

I realise I'm still hanging on to the dashboard and snatch my hand away. Between the toys, the collection of lost things, there's a small shiny patch on the black plastic where my fingers were. I cross my arms tightly, wedging my spongy hands deep inside my armpits. I think they're shaking again, like Rene's hands. *Get a grip*, I tell myself. *Turn this thing round.*

"Well," I say, trying for a cool Diana style of voice. "They gave *you* quite a lot of coverage on the news." I glance up at him, at his stubbly chin, his yellow eyes. He's nodding, smiling, staring through the windscreen. Probably reliving his fifteen seconds of local fame. There are tiny tufts of shorter, rougher looking hair coming from his nose. "So you were here," I say, "the day they vanished?"

The big red head snaps around, looming down at me.

"Listen, love," he says, and shifts in his seat, tipping the lolly box nearly on to its side against the steering wheel as he turns his whole body towards me. His great hairy knee slides closer until it's skimming mine. It fills me with a strange, crackling sensation, like when you lick the end of a battery, or how the skin tightens on the back of your neck when the thunder first rolls in at the beginning of a storm. I can't move back away from him any further. My shoulder's already pressed up tight against the door.

"I'll tell you what I told them," he's saying. "Maybe they was up here that day and maybe they wasn't. Mad busy we were, all day. How am I supposed to keep track of all you little girls, wanting your Zooms and your raspberry ripples and all your diet drinks, with never the right change. Never a please nor a thank you neither, not these days. It's enough just keeping up." He's breathing faster, leaning closer and I'm boiling, dissolving, underneath that slick, gold gaze.

"And later?" I say. "After the news thing, I mean. Thinking about it all later, you haven't remembered anything? Anything since?"

He sighs. A hot sigh that pours tobacco and toothpaste straight into my face.

"Jesus, I didn't see nothing! Jesus! You little girls are all the same. Wanting this and wanting that. Won't take no... And people are surprised when they go missing, when bad things happen. But it don't stop 'em coming, does it? Don't stop 'em wearin' them incy little tops and them incy little skirts. Nothing on 'em, but string and suntan oil."

I've started to feel sick. Really sick, like I might actually puke any minute all over my baseball boots and the cab's gritty floor - or all over him maybe, over his hairy thighs and his cardboard box, over all those fresh little Mini Milk's turning to mush inside their wrappers. I turn away quickly, into a new wave of dizziness. *This isn't right*, I'm thinking. I glimpse my face, my mouth, in the wing mirror. Lips that are not mine. They look bloated, stupid, still shining with Rene's watery, rose lipstick. I want to rub it off, make my mouth clean, but suddenly I'm so scared I've forgotten how to move.

Because it's not just his knee that's touching my leg now, but his hand too. His knuckles have slid down the box to graze my knee. They're paler than the rest of him, the same sickly pink as Rene's lipstick. Gobstoppers that have been sucked then spat out, and lined up in a row. They're sticky like that too. *He could just drive off*, I think. *He could drive us both away*. I lean forward, craning my neck to scan the car park, trying at the same time to wriggle out from under his hand and away from the pressure of his thigh. But there isn't any room ~

His fat red thumb rolls softly back and forth over my skin, like plasticine, and outside, there's still no one, there's nothing. Just all that empty white.

"Well, thank you for your help," I say. "I think I'd better go. I'm late. They're expecting me... My friends... They're waiting." My fingers squeak over the door handle, but I can't make it turn. I can't get a proper hold. My hands are too wet, too weak and clumsy. Far too young and fumbling, they simply slip away.

"What?" he says. "What did you say?" and I realise I've been whispering.

"I have to go now," I almost shout, and he presses even closer so that his aftershave is killing me. Suffocating me, sharper than ever. I get a flash of the industrial cleaner Rene sometimes splashes down the toilet to cover up the germs. He leans across my chest, stretching his hand out for my door, pinning Diana's tie-dyed vest taut across my ribs. I'm suddenly conscious of my nipples, my little nothing-breasts. *This is it*, I think. I don't know what *this* is, but I'm convinced it's about to happen. It's *happening*, even. I don't know what to do. Through the hazy windscreen the blue sky hangs down ahead of us, like something from an advert, not like anything that's real.

"You want to be more careful," he says, his elbow pressing into my lap. "Didn't your mum ever tell you about strange men's cars?" With a soft click, he twists the handle and sits up smoothly, touching nothing but the box. The door swings open and I practically fall out of the van, onto the gravel. I skid, regain my footing, and then skid again. My shadow's all over the place, scattered here and there among the stones.

"Maybe you'll think twice next time," the ice-cream man shouts after me, and then something else, but I don't hear it and I don't look back. I'm already running, running and running, tearing my way through the sea's slow breath and the bird's raw cries, over the white ground that's rising up around my boots, that's chasing me in puffs of smoke.

Seven

I don't stop running until I'm home. The ground rolls and jars beneath my feet like broken bottles, but I don't look down. I stare straight ahead all the way. The sea flashes past, but I don't turn my head to glance back down on West Beach and when I reach the arcades and a gang of boys start shouting, I keep going without once breaking my stride.

The boys are from my class I think, but I can't be sure. They're just a blur of pink faces and roaring mouths that vanish in a blink. One of them throws a can after me. It hits my calf, but I hardly feel it. Not like I can feel the ice-cream man's hand, as though it's still stuck to my thigh like a piece of warm, damp ham, which, however fast I run, I can't shake off. The can clatters away behind me, ringing flat and metallic as it bounces into the road.

"It's gone," I hear myself panting. "It's gone, gone, gone." And it's only now that I realise I've been talking to myself in whispers all the way, and pulling faces too. Stretching my ridiculously lipsticked lips back into a square, my eyes narrowing and then stretching as though I'm willing them to pop. I'm wearing my shame, my stupidity, right here, for everyone to see. It's my real face, the one I manage to keep hidden behind test results and being in the 'achievers' group - writing a seasonal poem for the Governor's Newsletter. I am stupid, that's the truth. I might have taken some GCSEs early, I might understand irregular French verbs and the periodic table, but I know nothing about men. Or boys, or even women and other girls. I've only ever pretended to understand other people. Anyone who gets to know me properly finds that out pretty fast. And anyone who could see me now... All brains, no sense, that's what Rene says. Diana simply rolls her eyes. And I wonder what the policewoman from school would say if she'd seen me climbing so thoughtlessly into that cab, whether she'd even bother saying anything at all. Perhaps she'd merely shake her head. Or sigh, maybe, like Dad.

Didn't my mother ever tell me about strange men's cars?

And now I'm thinking *Mother? What mother?* And what do I do - despite my terror and my shame, the feel still of *his hand* against my thigh - but burst out laughing? I'm laughing like a loon, gasping for breath as I weave between the Saturday morning shoppers on the High Street; the old men dressed in overcoats despite the heat, the girls with low-slung jeans and fake-tanned stomachs, the tourist families that are everywhere, continually in the way with their coolbags and their cameras and their stupid ringing voices. I dodge and dive to avoid a blue-rinsed woman with a sunburnt nose, screaming at the grandkids - the grandkids, sticky-skinned and bulgy-eyed, screaming just as loudly back. I leave them all behind, tutting and turning after me, no different from the spinning, clacking postcard racks I barge into as I run. Nothing can stop me, not even the sight of the estate agents where Rene works. The little houses in the window scatter and then stream away behind me like a tiny, tumbling dolly's town. Even the MISSING posters can't slow me down or wipe the manic grin off of my face. I'm soaring. I gasp for breath as I duck beneath the heavy hanging baskets that drip down between the shops. The red, purple and garish pink blossoms blur together like letters into words, an incomprehensible graffiti bleeding past. As I run, their fruity perfume comes and goes in waves, accompanied by the manic buzzing of bees. I'm still laughing, gasping, as I leave them and the rest of the High Street far behind, as I thunder up the hill towards our house.

The people fall away behind me. The colours fade as the bright shop fronts and swinging pavement signs give way to garden walls and sheer-shorn hedges, distant windows flat with sky. The world grows muffled. I watch my baseball boots pound the road, but I can hardly hear my footsteps. I watch as the ground billows up around my feet again, and I can't stop thinking of the ice-cream van behind me. I can't shake off his hand. By the time I reach our driveway, everything's sticky, not just my legs, my thigh, my tie-dyed back, but my hands too, my hair and face. And it's not just sweat there either. My cheeks are covered with snot and tears. I slow down. I wipe my stupid nose against my stupid knuckles. I press a palm across my stupid mouth, but my stupid laugh's already gone. The muscles in my legs feel waterlogged and weak, there's wet papier-mâché in my calves. I no longer trust them to hold me up.

The world's gone even quieter. I see the gulls, the rippling trees, but I've lost the noisy rush of leaves and feathers. The birds say nothing as they circle overhead. I jog tentatively up our drive, watching the sunlight flare and soften as it moves between the branches of the trees closest to the house. The light's like shattered glass. I close my eyes against the flash of splintered rays and think about lying down, right here, on our grassy drive. I imagine giving everything up to the soft ground and the dry grass, to the gentle swaying of the trees...

But this is no place to hide, to curl up small. Anyone could see me here, walk over to me, touch me. From behind my stupid hands, there comes a shallow gasp, a croaking sob. They're only small noises, but I feel them rising, sharp as stones inside my throat. What I need, straightaway, is to be home.

But what I find, inside the house, is a whole new universe altogether.

They're in the hall. There's no way of getting past them without being seen. Dad and Rene are standing, stiff as pillars on opposite walls, blocking the doors to the kitchen and the living room. Diana's beyond them, at the foot of the stairs. And everyone's shouting, even Dad. Especially Dad.

"You can't just throw away your future," he's yelling at Diana, "You don't know what you're talking about. You're just a child yourself."

Diana's backing away from him, stumbling up another step, and all the while, Rene is babbling something generally supportive of Dad's argument, something about personal responsibility, stupidity.

I can't even hear what Diana's saying in response, it's just another layer of shrieking, ragged and more painful than the rest. They haven't seen me. They haven't even noticed the front door opening, the blast of sunlight that's shrunk the shadows between the hooks and coats, but turned them blacker than before. It's like they're glued in place and their argument has made the air thinner. It's hotter than outside. I find myself struggling to remember the proper way to breathe.

I close my eyes and right away, he's there. The ice-cream man with his gappy grin, that curl of purple tongue. I open my eyes, but nobody's moved. They're still blocking the hallway. Still shouting. I turn away and glimpse a rash-red patch on my thin, white thigh where he pressed against me. I think of that grey, dense leg hair. His fat pink hand. But it's only me who's making the skin flare up. My fingers are rubbing at my leg as though they've got a life of their own; some scuttling-scratching spider creature leaving milky, then bright red streaks behind. At the foot of the stairs, Dad and Rene are closing in upon Diana. She stands her ground, raises her chin. Her beautiful jaw casts a perfect triangle of shadow. No wonder nobody's looked at me. I'm like a ghost, I think. I'm like that woman in white, with her pale yellow hair and set blue eyes, her skirt floating up behind her as she steps slowly out of her white car. *His white cab...*

"Don't you lecture me!" Diana is shouting. "How dare you lecture me when you're running round with Pete again, when your own life's so fucked up. What do you think you're doing? Are you deliberately trying to drag us all backwards? To keep us stuck here, all of us trapped?"

"Diana!" Dad shouts.

"You little bitch!" adds Rene.

There was a man, I could say. *There was a man in the car park, over at West Beach. It was my own fault; I was stupid, I didn't think.*

Behind me, the front door's still wide open and there's a small, friendly breeze licking at my back. It lifts me so I stand taller, though I'm wobbling a little, as if I might just float away. Somewhere out there, the grass is rippling and the sun is still sparkling in fragments through the trees.

With one foot on the bottom step, Rene starts to cry.

"Maybe you'll think twice next time." The ice-cream man had said, and maybe I will. Maybe I'll just stop thinking altogether. After all, it occurs to me, they're probably dead by now, my Missing Girls. They're probably long gone.

Diana's shouting the loudest now and her voice has lost its sore, raw edge. "I'm *not* a child, don't you get that? I've never been a child, your little girl."

I tune her out. They're nothing, the three of them. Cardboard cutouts swaying haphazardly back and forth. I'm no longer aware of the ice-cream man either. His hand has gone, it's slipped away, and I can't quite feel my legs beneath me. The second that I realise this, I'm down. Not even aware that I'm falling, it's so fast. I'm just lying there all of a sudden, among the dropped, forgotten coats, in a pile across the floor. The floor is covered in a thin film of dirt. There are grains of sand crushed against my chin like stubble. For a moment, Dad's here, hovering over me, but then there are brown flowers floating across my vision, blocking out his face.

"Janie?" he says, but then he's fading. The petals open slowly, gradually growing darker, finely veined and rusty edged. I'm looking down between them. It's like looking through a tunnel, a telescope, a ragged, velvet hole, and then all I see is *them*, my Missing Girls. They're no longer missing. They're no longer even girls really, but things; twin bodies in a ditch, dumped in the bushes by the side of some narrow country road. They've been thrown on top of one another, thrown away. They're still in their swimming costumes and their pale, bent legs are marked with flat dead leaves and little twigs, with long smudged streaks like rust. There are ropes around their wrists. The ropes have been there for so long that they actually seem a part of the girls themselves, like the blue and yellow bruises they wear further up their arms…

"Janie," I hear Dad calling. "Janie!" But I'm already disappearing. I'm way beyond his reach.

Eight

I'm in the back of the car. The belt is cutting into my neck and the seat is sticking to my thighs. When I wriggle my hips, trying to get comfortable, the sweaty vinyl makes a sucking sound against my skin. The sound reminds me of sellotape torn from parcels and of the wax Diana uses to rip the hair out of her legs. It's very loud, but no one says anything. We have to be quiet; it's one of the Rules. We're not allowed to speak and we certainly can't cry. We mustn't touch the doors either, not the handles or the stubby little child locks, and since we're not permitted to open any of the windows, the air is as thick as butter. When I breathe, my mouth is full of it. Full of grease and heat and something fustier, like old brown feathers. The girl sitting in the back beside me has her head bowed and her shoulders hunched. She's wearing a beige velour vest top and matching shorts, the same as me. Her soft brown legs are bent and drawn up in front of her, her toes clinging to the seat. *Monkey fingers*, I think, though the way that she has closed herself up so tightly reminds me more of a crab. Hiding her meat inside her bones. I can't see her face and so I don't know which of the Missing Girls she is. Her hair looks much brighter, blonder, than in the posters. Perhaps she's dyed it, I think, or someone else has, though it's probably just the sun, so brilliant today, so harsh, it's blanching the colour, the life, from everything. It's inescapable, this yellow light. It pours in through the sealed windows, past the specks of grime and the remains of various flying things that smack, every now and then, against the glass. We're driving fast. The yellow sky swallows us over and over again and the way it flashes and ripples creates an illusion of water. Like we're driving through a desert, into a mirage.

The driver's head, in the seat in front of me, is no more than a black shape, even when I raise a heavy hand to shield my eyes, even when I squint. The effect reminds me of what happens when you find yourself staring straight into a bulb. How you can't get rid of it afterwards, how you can't see around it for a while. I stop looking at the driver, at the black shape. I glance back towards the girl. Her hair is dazzling. She's dazzling. But her head is still bowed and you can tell just by looking at her that something bad has happened, or is happening, or is about to happen, very soon.

Although there are only the three of us in the car, it feels like there are more. It's all the body-heat we're generating and the rapid way we're breathing. The air is damp with us. I shut my eyes, thinking of leg wax again, of my Diana. For some unknown, 'retro' reason, she uses those really old-fashioned wax strips, the kind you have to soften in a saucepan on the stove. They turn the kitchen steamy, and if

I concentrate I can smell that wax smell even now. A distinct
burnt-honey scent. She let me try one once and I couldn't
believe the stinging pain of it. It was like yanking off a
sticking plaster, only a hundred times worse. I couldn't
believe I hadn't taken off my skin along with the hair, that I
hadn't drawn out flesh and blood, tugged at the bones lying
deeper underneath. Yet when Diana uses them, she doesn't
even wince.

I open my eyes, trying to feel nothing, like Diana feels
nothing, but it's no good. I'm frightened and I want her. I
need my sister, but there's no way out of here. It's actually
growing hotter. The air inside my mouth is fat with heat now,
like a man's great pink hand curled up into a fist. And the car
is turning. My stomach slides with it. Possibly, I think, we're
slowing down. I don't know where we are or where we're
going, but I'm pretty sure we're miles and miles away from
our kitchen, from Diana with her wax strips bubbling and
turning in a pan. About as far away as you can get, I think. I
still can't see anything through the windows except this
yellow sky. There are no trees, no fields, no shops or houses.
No tarmac shimmering in hot wet waves. There's nothing
else out there, not even sea. But then, perhaps that's just an
illusion because of the way I'm sitting. The air has pushed
me so far back into my seat, it's made me squat and stunted
and barely here. I'm sticky and thick-headed. A small wax
doll.

The car is definitely slowing now. It's creeping to a stop.
And the air is even wetter. I'm wet all over. Melting. I glance
over at the space where the driver's head should be and I see
that the darkness is spreading, running. There are fingers of

ink curling and dripping towards us with the heat. I feel a touch, soft as tissue, against my thigh. I look down and there's the blonde girl's small, brown hand. She's lifting her face to me. She's looking and looking and all I can see of her now are her eyes. They're as black as the darkness in front of us, as black as wet earth. They're huge, as if everything she's feeling is spilling out of her, out through her eyes, and her fear slips into me. It slithers down towards my stomach. Heavy fear, like mud. I want to be sick. The inside of my face is burning now, and I wish I could cry. The engine tick, tick, ticks and then falls still. We're here, wherever here is. It's happening.

I don't know what to do, but the blonde girl does. Her little hand is flickering against my hip like a bird - brown feathers - and then there's a click, a release, and I realise that the seatbelt has sprung loose. She grabs me. Starts hauling me across the seat and I'm crying, babbling, despite the Rules. My tears taste foul. They're brackish water. More dirt. The blonde girl's much stronger than me, and taller than I thought. Somehow her door is hanging open and she's out, pulling me after her. I haven't got a chance. There's a wrenching ache in my shoulder and a sharper pain at my wrist where her nails are digging in to me, and then I'm falling. Into the yellow sky, into nothingness.

But I shut my eyes and when I open them the sky has broken. It's changing colour, and the fractured pieces are becoming other things, solid things - a car tyre, stones, a gravel drive. There are tiny white pebbles interrupted by bright green weeds. And there is the imposing, grey wall of a house too, and too many towering trees. Millions of leaves shuddering overhead, starry with light.

"Run!" the blonde girl screams. At the same time there's a metallic crump ~ the driver's door, I realise, slamming open.

We run.

We run towards the house, the blonde girl - this bigger, stronger, faster girl - ahead of me, but holding on to me, yanking me after her so that I'm almost flying, hardly breathing. My bare feet scuff the jagged stones, but I scarcely feel them. There's a rushing in my head, a wave crashing, breaking, but never broken, going on and on and on. And then we're at the door to the house. The blonde girl gets there first and she's pressed against it, pushing at it, fighting with it while I stand beside her, panting. And I'm gazing at her shoulder blade, that golden wing, because I'm too afraid to look anywhere else. There's the scrape and spray of footsteps just behind us and I'm too afraid to turn around.

But then the door is opening and she's bending over me, with one hand on the back of my neck. She's pushing me inside.

"Remember," she says, her breath in pieces, her words in pieces. "It's just a game. You count."

And then I'm in. I'm in a cool grey place, soft with shadows, a clay smell coming from the walls. She's stepping back outside. She's shutting the door on me, making everything safe, but before it's quite closed, before the latch clicks, I hear her gasp. I stand beside the door, but I can't bring myself to close it. I look out through the crack she's left. The narrow gap. I see yellow light, and then I see her blonde hair spread out across the gravel. A shadow, that darkness, is moving on top of her, all over her, like a feeding animal.

And then I don't want to see anymore, and so I don't. I'm going. Drifting away. I'm somewhere near the ceiling. I'm looking down upon myself and I'm so little down there on the dusty floor, so scared. I want to reach out and touch myself, but I can't. I'm lost; I'm gone.

Nine

When I come round, I'm lying on my bed with just a single sheet on top of me. It's one of Rene's; un-creased, pristine. I have a vague memory of her folding it over me like a clean white page in a brand new drawing pad, and for a moment, feeling almost tearful, I was so grateful, so relieved. As she smoothed the cotton across my chest, there was a sudden, fleeting sense of freedom, like nothing mattered. I was being packaged up, filed away. But while the sheet above me might be perfect, my bottom sheet has grown damp and curdled and my mattress smells like armpits. It's because I'm sweating so much; apparently I've got a temperature of a hundred and four. I have a hazy recollection of Rene glancing at the thermometer and then staring down at me as if I'd willed the mercury to rise. Her lips were stretched as taut as her bed-sheets as she flicked it viciously up and then back down.

The doctor's coming. I don't know when. Someone took my watch away and so I have no idea what time it is. All I know is that, although I've been out of it for a while, the day's still bright outside. Rene drew the curtains, but the sun's leaking through anyway. It's dripping over the sill and down the walls, forming bleach-like puddles on the floor. My throat feels dry and sore, as if it's been stuffed with thick, folded cardboard and when I sit up in my sweaty nest, Rene's sheet feels almost sore against my skin. I'm still wearing Diana's tie-dyed vest, but that's all, and I'm very conscious of my ugly rag-doll body. As I reach down for the glass and water jug, which Rene set on the floor beside the bed, I'm careful not to look at myself. I don't want to see Diana's vest glued in sticky bunches to my individual ribs. I certainly don't want to catch sight of my skinny, burning thighs. The jug is ridiculously heavy. I can hardly hold it. My wrists feel floppy as though my stitching's coming loose, and my hands are shaking. When I do finally manage to lift it to the glass, it's empty. I could call out, but I don't have the energy so I huddle back down under Rene's sheet instead. I'm tired again, but that's ok since I'm probably quite sick. I'm allowed to drift. I close my eyes and right away I'm slowly sinking, the room a warm dark bath.

Later, when I wake, there's sawdust in my saliva and a pounding in my head. A small but relentless hammering as if something inside is desperate to get out. Any sense of comforting befuddlement has gone. The twisted sheets are back. The light is back. The room is all sharp angles and shards of sun. The pictures have returned to me in glaring Technicolor; the car, the run, the blonde girl sprawled across the ground.

There's someone here. I catch them in the flutter of my opening eyes. A black shape bending over me, close enough for me to catch the heat of their skin and their tobacco-yellow breath. I keep my eyelids shut, but I can feel this presence, this dark fleshy weight, just beyond them, and it's moving closer.

"Janie! You little drama queen!"

I sit bolt upright in my bed. The shadow falls away like Rene's sheet, which slithers, in one motion, onto the floor. It's only Diana, sitting on my mattress, her big brown eyes all over me. She can't have a clue about the pictures in my head. Nevertheless I'm suddenly, unstoppably, flushed with shame.

"Actually fainting! I'm impressed," She reaches out to lay her palm across my forehead. "I hear you're feverish as well. I wonder if you're contagious."

Against my skin, her touch feels as cool and smooth as china. Straight away my mind starts emptying. The pictures are fading and my eyes are closing again, as if that's what her fingers have told them to do. When she begins to draw her hand away, I reach up and press it back in place.

"Poor little Janie," she murmurs.

And this is how it was when I was really little, when she always looked after me and took care of me when I was sick. I get a flash of Diana at ten, her yellow plaits swinging as she dropped a pile of books and pens on to my covers. She understood how important it was to keep me busy, to prevent me feeling sorry for myself. She'd stop me thinking. And then I'm remembering how one reeling, windy, winter night, she stayed up with me till dawn, holding back my hair as I threw up into Rene's best glass bowl. Throughout chicken pox and diarrhoea and all those bouts of flu and tonsillitis, she was there. All I wanted, all I needed then, to make me better, was my sister. It must be months, I think - no, years - since I've been sick. It doesn't matter, I realise. She's what I'm needing still.

"Diana," I hear myself saying, "I think I'm coming unhinged."

I say it like this because it's what Rene used to wail at us when we were young, when we would drive her quite deliberately to distraction - hiding her car keys, putting stones in her shoes - once even slipping a flat dead frog into her knickers drawer. We never had any mercy or sympathy for Rene, and I loved it when she said *"unhinged"*. Setting up the trick, I'd imagine her face hanging open, her brain rocking loose. It meant we'd won. And so I think if I say it like this now, it might make Diana laugh, or smile at least. Perhaps we could smile at me together. At the pictures in my head and my desperation to find those Missing Girls. Perhaps even at the ice-cream man with his creeping, fat, pink hand... *Ha Ha*, Diana might say, *how silly.* Then she'd give me a simple, one sentence explanation that would make everything all right.

"What? Are you delirious?" And there isn't a hint of humour or remembering on her face.

"It's just. I can't stop thinking about, wondering about, those Missing Girls..."

I hear her sigh. She takes her hand away from my forehead. Her eyes are rolling.

"Janie," she says, "What are you like? I thought you were

supposed to be the brainy one." She shakes her head. "Listen to me. There's nothing new about this. About any of this. Every year, every single summer, it's the same. Children go missing. There's a huge fuss and it's all very sad and then everyone forgets it ever happened. You haven't been getting into a state over this, have you? This isn't what the fainting and the silences and the acting weird is all about?"

"No." I'm staring at the turquoise pendant quivering from a grubby lace around her neck.

"Good," she says. "Because it's pointless. Random. There are nutters out there and there's not much anyone can do. The only difference with these girls is that they were here when it happened, but they could have been anywhere. Do you hear me, Janie? Their killer or kidnapper, or whatever, he'll be long gone by now." She glances over her shoulder, towards the window, taking in the closed curtains and the sunlight, pooled across the floor. "Janie," she says, "do you understand?"

But I can't answer, not right away. I'm gazing at the window too, thinking about what's out there... The ice-cream van parked amidst the gravel. All that pale dust. And now my head feels as though it's being squeezed, wrapped in tight, white bandages. Strips of Rene's sheet. I'm too firmly bound up, tucked in, but despite the muffling effect, his hand is back. A slab of raw meat, warm as reality against my thigh.

"But what if," I ask, "what if whoever took them was someone local?"

"Forget it." She stands up and wanders away from me, over to the window. She flicks the curtains apart, just a little, and peers out through the glaring crack. "This place just isn't big enough," she says into the glass. "Don't you think if there was some paedophile living round here then we'd have heard something by now? The police would have records or something, or there'd be others, other kids, coming out of the woodwork with dirty little stories they need to tell."

I stare across the room at her raven hair spilling down her back. In the parts between her curls I can see twist and threads of gold, where her yellow roots are just beginning to grow through. On her left shoulder blade, peering out from beneath her vest strap, is her flower tattoo. It's supposed to be an orchid, but from where I'm lying, it doesn't look like a flower at all, but a smudge, a stain, a print, perhaps, from a child's grubby hand.

"But Diana, I can't seem to get those girls out of my head. I've been dreaming about them. And Diana, I went up to the car park by West Beach. I retraced their last known steps…"

I wait for a moment with my mouth still open. I'm waiting for her to turn around and face me. And I'm waiting to find out what I'm going to tell her when she does, but my sister doesn't turn. Instead she grabs the edges of the curtains and yanks them wide apart. The sunlight crashes into the dusky room like an iceberg, bright and devastating.

"I said forget it," she snaps. She's vanished, becoming a silhouette, a dark featureless shape against the flash of day. "Get over it. It's not your problem. It's got nothing to do with you, with any of us. And besides, we're all 'unhinged', Janie. I would have thought you understood that by now."

As she talks, Diana lowers her shadow-puppet arms in what seems a deliberately exaggerated gesture. Her elbows bend and her hands move lower still, clutching not her hips, but the slight slope of her stomach. She turns sideways to make it clearer against the light.

"And some of us," she says, in a voice as smooth and cold as the side of Rene's best glass bowl. "Some of us have real things to worry about. Genuine problems, you know?"

I close my eyes against the glare, that gleaming voice. Did she ever have blonde plaits? I wonder. Did she ever really stroke my hair back from my face? Did she ever hold that bowl? I don't want to hear her going on about a baby, not again. Not now. I don't even want to look at her. I reach for Rene's sheet and drag it all the way up, over my head, like I'm a ghost, like the kid I so obviously still am. In my crisp white cave I curl up tight and wait for my sister to get fed up and disappear.

It's almost dark when the doctor arrives. He comes after his surgery has closed. He isn't supposed to make house calls, not these days, but though he hasn't been here for a while, he's one of my father's oldest friends. He's known us all, in fact, forever. He doesn't knock before pushing my bedroom door wide open.

"Evening Janie," he calls. "Can I come in?" His creamy face floats high among the shadows on the landing.

"One minute." As he pulls the door to again, I scramble over to the drawers searching for pyjama bottoms, knickers - anything clean to cover up my bottom half. The drawers are filled with a tangle of sweaters and tights, nothing appropriate. In the end, in a panic, I settle for a pair of old PE shorts, which are too small for me now and have a mud stain on the front. I'm just diving back on to my mattress when the doctor gives up waiting and walks straight in. He's quite a large man, with a solid barrel stomach, but after flicking on the main light switch, he picks his way daintily across the room, attempting (quite impossibly) to avoid stepping on the piles of clothes and discarded tissues, the bangles and forgotten magazines.

"Sorry about the mess," I say.

He looks right at me, smiles; a twinkle in his eye. "You girls," he says, "you're all the same."

I remember then that he has a daughter of his own, a grown-up daughter, and that there was some town gossip, some scandal, surrounding her. She ran away, to London, I think, and got involved in drugs maybe, or was it petty crime? Possibly both. I can't remember if she's in prison now or not. It's another one of those things I half overheard that I'm not supposed to ask about. That I'm not supposed to know.

As the doctor bends to haul his bag on to the end of my bed, the little shiny bald patch on the top of his head strikes me as pitiful, tragic even. I wonder if it was after his daughter left that he started losing his thick, fair hair? He's tried to hide the patch by dragging a few of the remaining strands over it, but they're far too wispy now; clearly not up to the job. Briefly, I'm filled with the ridiculous desire to reach out and cover up that pale exposed patch of secret scalp with my bony little hand. Still smiling, he glances over and I blush, locking my fingers firmly together in my lap.

"So you fainted?" he says. "And you've got quite a temperature, I hear. Anything else that I should know?"

I open my mouth, but before I can answer, he's sliding a thermometer in, expertly jamming it beneath my dry poised tongue. While he's waiting for a reading, he glances at his watch and then takes a stethoscope out of his bag and hangs it loosely around his neck.

"There's a couple of viruses going around at the moment," he says. "A bit nasty, but nothing serious. Nothing to worry about, you've probably picked up one of those. Rotten luck though, eh? Getting sick just as your holidays begin."

I nod because that's what I'm expected to do. Also with the thermometer in my mouth, I can't correct him, I can't tell him that actually it almost feels like a relief.

"Let's get a bit of air in here," he says, taking more of his well-intentioned, tentative steps over to the window. As soon as he yanks it open, the summer rushes in. You can hear the goodnight twittering and chattering of the smaller birds and a wood pigeon's deeper coo. There are the shrill squawks of children arguing, and then a parent barking in a self-important London voice. I picture them, tourists in cool linen, with their gnat bites and their sunburn, on their way back from a restaurant in town. I smell our neighbours' newly cut grass, and the heavier stink of our own compost heap, like a giant mushroom that's been baking, blackening, in the sun. The doctor glances at his watch again and then comes back to me, knocking the thermometer against my teeth as he slides it from my mouth. He holds it up, like Rene, to the light.

"A hundred and two. Well, I think that's come down a bit, hasn't it?"

I nod again as if the thermometer is still beneath my tongue.

"Now let's have a listen to that chest."

In my bed, I sit up straighter as he comes to stand behind me. I feel his hands on my hips, my back. He's sliding up my top. My heart starts banging, I can't help it, and I know that he'll hear it. I try hard not to think about the ice-cream van, but to concentrate on the doctor instead. This friend of my father. This man I've known for years. He doesn't smell of aftershave, but slightly leathery. From his bag, I think, or perhaps his shoes. As he leans in closer, I catch a soap smell too, it's a practical bluish scent; it's how a doctor's supposed to smell...

I wonder if, when they bring the Missing Girls' bodies in, he'll be the one asked to examine them, whether he'll have to write the death certificates, or if the police have their own special people to do all that, experts from outside? If it is left up to our doctor, I think how difficult it's bound to be for him, with his own daughter disappeared somewhere. Will he think he sees a similarity between his own lost child and the bodies the police have given him, the ones that they'll leave lying on some slab? Two slabs.

The end of the stethoscope is freezing as it creeps and presses slowly across my back. Stop it, I tell myself. They are not dead. My Missing Girls.

He takes his hands away, and the stethoscope, and lets my vest fall back into place, but the doctor isn't finished with me yet. He comes around to stand in front of me. He cups his hands beneath my chin, and then around my throat. He doesn't look at me as he does this, but at something, or more probably nothing, on the ceiling. He presses very gently and then he makes me raise my arms.

"Not like that," he says. "Higher."

In the air, my hands are trembling as if I'm in a film, expecting to be shot. He reaches out to me and runs his fingers slowly down from my left elbow to my shoulder. Still staring into space, his hand goes lower, prodding a slow circle around my armpit. I don't like it. I'm sweating, sweating on to his fingers. My mouth is even drier than before and it's hard, almost impossible, to keep the ice-cream man shut out.

He moves on to feel the other arm, the other armpit, his fingers pressing around the narrow hollow of almost hairless skin like he's wiping a rag around a dirty bowl, cleaning out an ashtray maybe. I could ask him what he's doing, what this is for, but I don't. I'm not sure I even can. I think how, in the ice-cream van, I was whispering at first and then shouting as if I no longer owned my voice. His hands aren't like other doctors' hands, I think, they're way too warm, and suddenly - like I really am back there, in that car park over West Beach - I think I might be sick. I squeeze my eyes shut tight and immediately seem to feel his eyes, rolling across my chest, like stones. Don't touch me I think, please, not there. Not anywhere. I can't move. There's not enough room behind me to wriggle back, away from him.

"I'd like to take some blood, Janie. Run a test or two. Is that ok?"

Cautiously I open my eyes. I stare. The doctor's at the end of my bed, pulling a ladder of sterile-packed syringes from his bag. He's nowhere near me. His hands aren't anywhere near me, and they haven't been for a minute, maybe more. What have I been thinking? He's a doctor. He's dad's friend.

He's been examining me, that's all. I smile at him, ashamed and relieved.

"Sure, of course." I glance over at the needle, pointing up towards the light. "Do what you like."

Ten

It's late when I wake. The room's coal-black. My throat hurts and there's something wrong with my tongue, and my hands too; they feel massive, swollen, sickeningly thick. The rest of my body feels fragile in comparison, like damp paper about to tear and fall apart. I wait for my eyes to adjust, to scrape away at the shadows, the great matt curtains of floating dark. It takes a little while to convince myself that I'm actually awake.

And then I remember that something woke me. I prop myself up on one elbow, squint out across the black.

"Diana," I hiss. "Diana, is that you?"

There's no reply. The darkness shifts. I'm about to give up, to bury myself back down when I hear it, a muttering, a whispering, voices from the landing beyond my bedroom door. It's Rene I hear first. Even hushed, her voice still has that Brillopad edge.

"I don't need your analysis, David."

At first I can't catch my father's reply, it's just a murmur, but then his voice deepens, as it grows more urgent. He probably thinks he's being much quieter than he is.

"Please, Rene," he's saying, "I didn't mean to intrude and I know he's had help, had therapy. I know people can change, but, it's just... how can you be sure? When you're close to someone, it's hard to see..."

They're talking about Uncle Pete. Despite my resolution to keep out of Rene's dramas, I'm interested. I sit up straighter, clutching a handful of cotton as a wave of dizziness descends, the shadows turning and seizing like part of some machine.

"How dare you?" she says. "After everything that happened with Caroline, how dare you offer me advice?"

My mother's name is Caroline. The air thickens in my throat.

"Rene..." Dad pleads. He's sounding softer, sadder. "That's exactly why... You know, I wish that... "

But his voice is sinking away from me, though I'm straining forward now, suddenly desperate. And I wonder if, on the other side of the room, Diana's listening too. Her eyes as wide and dry as mine, her body tense. I scan the misty waves for her, trying to distinguish her from the black hump that is her bed.

"Don't pretend that you know what it was like for us," says Rene.

And Dad goes on mumbling, his response muffled as if he's speaking through a towel. Rene tears right through him.

"So, all of a sudden I'm supposed to believe that you're going to look after me, is that it, David? After the way you looked after Caroline - the girls - I can rely on you, can I, to keep me safe?"

I lean towards the door, desperate to catch Dad's response, but there's nothing now, not even a murmur. I imagine them standing out there in their very own darkness, not looking at one another, not moving. Even their breathing small. Finally Rene speaks.

"I didn't think so."

There is a creak, followed by the resigned click of Rene's bedroom door. A moment later, the quiet pad-pad-padding sound of Dad's slippers as he walks away. And they're gone. That's it. The argument's over for them, but not for me. Their whispers go on circling in my head, and it's already too hot in there, too crowded. My face feels tight. Stretched and rubbery as though I've leant too long over a fire.

But they were talking about my mother. I didn't think anyone talked about my mother.

I don't want to deal with this alone. I shift around, wobbling, and swing my feet down to the carpet. The bed seems to be rocking underneath me. With a grunt, a burning surge, I stand and, on trembling legs, kick my way through the flotsam on the floor. I practically throw myself at Diana's bed.

But of course, she isn't there.

The heap of sheets and pillows sinks beneath me, her duvet slips onto the floor. The window's open as far as it will go. I lean across, to stare outside. There's no moon, just a spattering of stars, glinting gently like pennies under water. Beneath them, the tops of our trees look even blacker and deeper than the sky. I gaze out until my vision glazes and the trees bow closer, their rustling like gossip. I want my sister.

And suddenly it's huge, this wanting. It's everywhere. It's bigger than the trees, the night. *I want Diana*. I want to describe to her the things I overheard. I want to tell her about all the secret stuff inside me. I want to tell her what happened when the policewoman came to our school and about the dreams, the daydreams and the nightmares I've been having. Most of all, I want to explain, in full, about the ice-cream man and his fat pink hand. I want her to listen this time. I need to tell somebody about the fear, inside my mouth like feathers. And I think how impossible it was to talk to her this afternoon. And how I've never kept anything, not anything like this, from her before. Though hasn't she always had *her* secrets?

I put my hands over my face. My big, inflated, rubbery hands. I press my alien fingers to my eyes, my mouth, my raw throat, trying to hold everything inside. To keep things steady. But I'm already thinking how, years ago, I gave up asking about our mother. How Diana would always turn away from me, however forcefully I demanded, however pathetically I begged. And I'd accepted it because she'd always seemed to own our mother in a way I never could. After all, I wasn't much more than a baby when she left, but Diana was six; she'd already started school. She'd been old enough, certainly, to have memories, while I had nothing. I have nothing. Just emptiness, a missing space, that's all.

And it's dawning on me that there are way too many secrets in this house. That this very room is layered and suffocating with secrets. And then, I can't help it, I'm thinking about Diana's old metal box. Of the pictures inside. About how it's probably still right here, buried directly underneath me, in the thick dark beneath her bed. And before I can properly consider what I'm doing, I stretch out until I'm lying on my stomach. I push one hand, and then the whole of my right arm, down the side of the mattress. I'm pressed against the pillows, smelling Diana's skin, her white musk stink. I can't imagine what would happen if she caught me. I don't think about it. Instead I slither slowly along the bed, trailing one clammy arm between the mattress and the wall. My searching fingers skirt across fabric, discarded clothes and old night things slipped under and forgotten, but then, as if it's been waiting for me, my hand hits cool, smooth metal. My fingers jump as if it burned.

I can't believe it. It's right here. There's no real hunt, no suspense, nothing. I send my hand back down again, more cautiously this time. I feel the dust like fur, the sharp tinny corners. It's the box all right. It's too large and awkward to drag back up that way so I drop on to my knees on the bedroom floor. Hurrying now, I slide under Diana's bed, elbowing my way past balled up tights and cotton wool puffs, abandoned revision notes, and crumbs. Something crunches beneath my knee and I catch my hair on a fleecy spring, but before I know it, I'm sitting up again, cross-legged, sliding the box out after me.

At first I can hardly pick it up, I'm way too eager. I paw at it clumsily, with my big, sick, floating hands. I'm a little kid again, fumbling the pass-the-parcel present on its final thrilling layer. My breath has become short and shallow, and I know that if I reached up to touch my sweaty face, I'd find myself smiling. I can't believe that after all these years, it's been as easy as this. I lift the box, considering the padlock -

it's just a cheap, flimsy thing, it won't take much to break it open - when I notice something stuck to the box's bottom. A white thing, brighter than it should be amidst the watery dark. I reach out to snatch it off, assuming it's simply an old, squashed school sock, or a pair of forgotten knickers - just another of Diana's leftovers, her remains. But the white thing is actually wedged flat against the box's base, one edge hooked beneath a thin metal seam as if it's been tucked in there deliberately. I run my fingers over it. It's something hard and flat, wrapped in sheets of wadded tissue. I start to pull, to shred. Pieces of tissue float down around me, like snowflakes. I'll find pieces in my hair tomorrow morning. As I dig deeper into the wrapping the whole thing finally comes loose, dropping heavily towards the puddled shadow in my lap. I gasp as it falls, as it hits my knee, but lands, thankfully, flat side down. It's so cold against my bare skin that it feels wet, though of course it can't be. It hasn't been wet for a long, long time. I lift it gingerly, mindful of these hot baggy balloon hands, that aren't quite mine. I'm careful, over-cautious, of the blade.

Nevertheless it's shaking as I lift it up towards my face to look more closely. Not that I need the confirmation. I know this knife already. I know it very well. It's a keen little knife meant for fruit perhaps, or cheese. I squint, but there's not enough light in here to show me the scuffed gold circle in the smooth bone handle, or the way that the handle itself is more yellow than white. It doesn't matter. I know this is how it is, without looking. I know it all too well. I realise that, with my other hand, I'm gripping the photo box too tightly. I'm clutching it against me so that the metal's digging into my ribs and I'm shivering, freezing suddenly, where as I was burning up before. I'm aware of the open window, of a breeze curling inside, bringing with it the hiss of the trees. There's a sharp edge to the air that you can taste as well as feel. A dark glitter of sea spray on the wind, but it's not just that. *It's because I'm sick*, I tell myself. It's not because I'm scared.

I'm exhausted suddenly. My skin is aching as though it's spread too thinly; I'm all sharp jutting bones and shadow, and not much else. I'm covered in weak spots, in holes and gaps, like ladders spreading rapidly down a pair of cheap black tights. I'm more made up from all the things that I don't know, or only half know, than the things I do. So much of me is missing. So much of me is lost. But I'm not scared, I tell myself. *I'm only sick*. I'm feverish, and that is why I'm frozen. And that is why I can't open the box tonight, why I can't look at this little knife for a moment longer. A wave of nausea rolls over me. My stomach's squeezing, curdling. I can already taste the acrid flavour of vomit in my tender throat. There are hot, shocked tears springing to my eyes.

I stand shakily and go stumbling, practically falling, back across the room. I start to crawl into my own bed, but I'm still holding the box, the knife, and that's no good so I climb back out again. I crouch on the floor with my teeth chattering, my hands trembling - *look how sick I am.* I can't possibly deal with this now. I claw through the sea of junk, struggling to see past the shadows and the clouds of my own exhaustion. Eventually I dig out my school bag. The bag I won't be using again for the next six weeks. As I shake it down, making space among the pens and books and folders,

I tell myself that I'm not hiding, that I'll simply look at these things another time, I'll think about them later. When everything's better, I tell myself, when I'm strong again. When I'm well. And it's with a sense of relief, of almost vicious vindication, that I'm able to stuff the box, and the knife, way down deep inside.

Eleven

I lie in the garden, staring up into the trees. I can hear birds singing and leaves rustling. Engines passing on the road. It's another picture-book-perfect summer day, the sixth that I've spent out here. It's been almost a week since the doctor phoned with his diagnosis of Glandular Fever, and Dad dragged the battered sunlounger out of the shed. Until this morning, the garden has been my haven, though it's grown wild and full of weeds, the lawn dense with dandelions and stinging nettles. Despite these things, the air is clean out here, and everything looks fresh. Even now, I can't help noticing the dozy bees that go floating by and the way that the sun winks through the foliage, sprinkling the great floppy leaves with sharp little beads of dazzling solder. The effect is hypnotic, a slow liquid rhythm of breeze and branches and shimmering light... If it was yesterday or the day before, I'd find myself floating away with it, expanding up towards the treetops like a loaf of bread kept warm to rise, but everything's changed now. Today, as Diana would say, everything's fucked.

But for a little while, life has been simple. I've been sick. Happy, almost; lolling about, gazing after butterflies, flipping through Diana's pilfered magazines, and playing with the cat. I've hardly thought about the Missing Girls. Or the box I buried in my bag. Instead I've dozed and watched my family come and go, following their outlines through the windows of the house. I've watched Rene as she hunched over the sink or carried laundry or stacks of plates or bin bags; she always had something in her hands. I've watched Diana flitting from room to room as light as a butterfly in comparison; her hands quick and mostly empty, often running through her mass of wild black hair.

Yesterday I spied on her as she led Carl upstairs. I watched them kiss, her back pressed against our bedroom window. They merged into a single mass as he leant over her, burrowing into her, before they dropped down, as if exhausted, beyond the glass.

And every morning, I've looked out for Dad too, appreciating the way he reads the newspaper at the same time as he makes his coffee. Since he caught me watching, he's started to raise his little espresso cup to me when he is done. A small white salute before he appears on the kitchen step to shout across the birdsong, about breakfast.

And so it's become easy to lose myself in other people's rituals. To think of nothing more than Lucozade and gnat-bites and twinkling sea-green light. It hasn't really bothered me that I've been living in a dream. But now, after days of drifting and not worrying, the Missing Girls have reappeared. They've crept up on me until they're closer than they've ever been before. They're anywhere and everywhere. If I let my guard down, even for a second, they'll be here, flickering among the reflections on our kitchen window or caught with the sun between the leaves. For a moment, I'll seem to feel them standing right behind me, or I'll blink and find their silhouettes trapped in the corner of my eye. Most of all - if I turn my head just so - I'm certain that I'll catch them sitting just a few feet away, their blanket flattening our dandelions, our wild grass. And they'll look just as they did in the home video footage on this morning's Breakfast News.

I'd never seen this piece of film before. I'd never seen any picture of the girls except for the official one with the Guide uniforms. The sight of them stopped me on my way out to the garden. They pulled me back and I stood there, in the living room doorway with my mouth hanging open, watching them laughing, leaning across one another, being alive. It was a shock to see the girls like that. For a moment I thought that they'd been found. But of course they hadn't. It was just a fresh appeal, a fresh angle, which actually felt very old and sad and sour.

"We won't stop praying," said one of the Missing Girls' mothers, her voice jarring with the frivolous banality of the film.

I was dragged out of the doorway, drawn towards the screen by the rise and fall of their little freckled shoulders and their dancing hands - by the spooky way they vanished, every now and then, behind a sun flare on the lens. They were on their knees. Dressed in faded jeans and T-shirts, one lemon coloured, one hot pink, their brownish-blondish hair pulled back in gleaming ponytails. Every so often, these ponytails bobbed and bounced as they shook their heads. They raised their arms and their eyes glittered as they giggled, though they didn't make a sound. I'd thought, at first, because of the green behind them and the tartan beneath, that they were sharing a picnic. As I floated closer to the screen I realised that all the bright little pools of colour that surrounded them, that were strewn across their blanket, weren't food at all, but threads. The girls grabbed at these threads now and then. Their denim laps were littered with colour and between the moments of silent laughter and wordless speech, they were concentrated. Their heads were bowed; their fingers flew. Restlessly, obsessively, my eyes darted back and forth between their weaving hands and that rainbow of cotton. Over and over I took in all the little twists and coils of fiery red and gold, of grey and of green. The electric blue bunches and the pink, the piles of purple, the strands of black.

As I stood there, with my bare feet sunk into our faded rug and my dressing gown hanging open where the belt was lost, the ice-cream man came back to me. His van came back to me; that friendship band hanging from the rear-view mirror, turning around and around and around. I switched off the television and remained standing there for a moment, staring at the remote control and at the blank, black screen. Then I came straight out here, the way I've done every morning, but I didn't lie back on my sunlounger and watch my family rise like I normally do. Instead I pulled my dressing gown up over my head and pressed my face into the moth-eaten canvas. And I cried like I was four years old.

He's got them, I just kept thinking. *He's the one.*

By the time I'd finally pulled myself together, Dad had already left the house. After Rene and then Diana also disappeared, I thought about what I should do. I thought about ringing the anonymous hotline number that's on all the Missing posters and in the newspapers, the number that they flash up every evening on the news. But I couldn't get it out of my head that the call would be traced, that they'd track me down somehow, even if I used the old red telephone box on the way into town. I kept picturing a police car pulling up. I was certain that they'd find me, that they'd take me away and make me talk. I'd end up in court, in a witness box, trying to avoid the ice-cream man's narrow, yellow eyes. I couldn't do it. I couldn't face him. Not even for the Missing Girls, not even for their mothers. And what did that say about me? I could hardly think about it. I felt sicker than I'd felt for days, all that shame, that cowardice, rose up inside me. I had to do something.

I decided on a letter. A truly anonymous letter. I went into the empty house and pulled a sheet of paper from Dad's printer and a pen from his desk, bringing them back outside. I wrapped my dressing gown even tighter around me despite the growing heat, and rested the paper on one of Diana's magazines. For a long time I stared at it, my mind equally blank and flimsy.

'*Gifted*' *Janie* - it was ridiculous. I couldn't, for the life of me, figure out what to write. I thought about anonymous notes on TV; ransom notes, blackmail letters, ominous text messages and e-mails, and words cut out from different newspapers. I swapped the pen in my hands, deciding to use my left in order to disguise my handwriting, the way Diana used to do when she wrote her Valentine's cards. The pen drew a shaky line, a couple of dots in the corner of the page and then stopped. I had no idea how to begin.

Dear Sir or Madam?

Dear policemen (and women)?

To whoever it may concern ~ please help...

The whole thing was absurd.

Except it wasn't funny in the least. Those girls could be alive still. He could have them tied up somewhere right now. Or they could be dead already and he could be lining up the next one; he could already have her in his sights.

No salutations. I plunged straight in.

I have some information regarding the recent disappearance of Tara Matlock and Stacey Hughes...

And so the letter's done now and still I'm sitting here with it balanced on my lap. The sun's still shining and the birds are singing and I can't stop tugging my fretful fingers through my sweaty, tangled hair. I've read the letter back to myself so many times that it stopped making sense ten minutes ago. Ordinary words like 'girls' and 'urgent' float out of the paper towards me. They've started to look as if they're spelt wrong or belong to a foreign language. Perhaps, I think, it genuinely doesn't make much sense. Perhaps I've written the whole thing in code.

The swish and sway of the trees fills my ears like water. It's inescapable, interrupted only by the monotonous groaning of cars driving past and the little birds' gibbering. The odd cursing of a seagull. There's an eruption, now and then, of panicked wings. Beneath these sounds, there is another, quieter rushing, a soft clattering, as of tiny stones. It makes me think of white gravel, of swirling dust.

I picture a long white car with its back door hanging open and a woman in white standing beside it. Her eyes are so blue that they look synthetic. They're the blue of a cocktail, spiky and vibrant, shimmering through glass. Crackling with ice.

I don't know why I keep coming back to her - this ghost - not now that I know what I know about the ice-cream man, now that I've seen those friendship bands... Except, it is occurring to me still, that perhaps he doesn't work alone. Perhaps I've been experiencing some kind of psychic flashes and there actually are two of them, two paedophiles, two kidnappers. After all, don't they often work in pairs? I remember other cases; numbered police mug shots set lovingly side-by-side on the national news and covering pages and pages on the internet. They were always cold and grey looking, those couples. They always shared those same dead eyes.

But isn't the ice-cream man enough? That van, it's more than enough. It returns to me; how the cab stunk of *him*, of his aftershave and his fags and that cloying, vanilla scent. I remember the box of Mini Milks melting onto his wide hairy lap. I think of the long white freezers in the back. And I think how stupidly I went to him; the idiotic questions that I asked and how he *peered* at me while I just sat there, quite blatantly examining the contents of his van.

I stare down at the letter in my lap. *He'll know*, I think. *Even if the police don't find me, he'll know, somehow, that it was me who told...*

"Excuse me."

My body jumps. The letter, along with the magazine that I was leaning on, go flying from my lap. Horrified, I watch them land, still together, still face-up, on the grass with a gentle thud. There's a boy standing among the daisies and bright yellow dandelions, just a few feet away. He looks about sixteen or seventeen, though he's possibly a bit older. He's wearing a pair of cheesy mirror sunglasses and I can't see what the rest of his face is doing because of the enormous bunch of flowers he's carrying, which are shoved out in front of him like a shield. I don't think he's one of Diana's; he looks too clean. I have no idea who he belongs to and before I can stop myself, I'm picturing all the different kinds of lads who hang out at the car park overlooking West Beach. After all it isn't just little kids and bikers up there, there are the skaters and the odd cyclist too. And there are other awkward, neat-looking boys who somehow seem to *yearn* as much as hang about.

And I know it's mad, but I'm suddenly sure that he's one of them and that the ice-cream man has sent him, and I'm thinking how if I try to grab the letter back he'll definitely see it if he hasn't already. And then I'm wondering what he could be hiding behind those flowers. A gun, a knife, a coil of rope? He could be touching himself, even.

"Who are you?" I snap. "What do you want?"

For a moment he says nothing. A pale butterfly weaves carelessly between us on greenish moon-coloured wings.

"Sorry. I'm, um, sorry I came. Sorry to disturb..."

He sounds almost nervous, but it's impossible to tell

because I can't see his eyes. I wonder where they're looking behind those flashing lenses.

"Are you Rene Clark?" he says at last. "It's a delivery for Rene Clark."

I'm so surprised I have to stop myself from jumping again. For a minute, I'm too confused to speak. He mumbles on:

"There was no answer at the front door, so I came round the back, I hope that's ok." He's coming closer. Leaning over me, blocking the light. Carefully, he bends forwards and lays the flowers down beside me on the frayed brown canvas. "I'll need a signature, please. Rene."

"I'm not Rene," I say. It comes out much louder than I'd intended. Angry sounding. I feel so stupid. "She's my aunt."

He sighs. "Whatever."

He's certainly not nervous anymore, if, in fact, he ever was. I can't see his eyes, but I know what he's thinking now. Like the kids in my year, he's decided that I'm some kind of loon and after my panic, my sheer paranoia, how can I blame him?

My head is aching with the effort of all this. My throat is hurting again and I'm afraid that I might cry. Hurrying now, he pulls a pen and a crumpled piece of paper from the pocket of his jeans and shoves them towards me. For a moment, I think that it's a note, like the ones I find sometimes folded into the pages of my textbooks or dropped on to my desk at school. 'Nutter', they say, or 'weirdo', or something like that. When I stare at the paper and don't take it, he sighs again and then ducks down grabbing Diana's magazine, *my letter*, from the grass. Sweat breaks out all over me. I smell that yellow, school sick-room stink. *It is him*, I think. *He has been sent*!

It's only after he's unfolded his little piece of paper and pushed it at me mercilessly, repeatedly, until I'm forced to look, that I understand that I'm supposed to use these things simply for leaning on, so I can sign his florists' receipt.

Aunt Rene appears only a minute after the boy has left (I tried not to watch him stalking off, kicking at our unkempt grass, shaking his head as he gets caught in the great tangle of weeds at the side of the house, blocking off the cellar door).

"Janie," she calls, practically skipping over the kitchen step, hurrying towards me, her summer suit jacket rising behind her in a charcoal coloured cloud. "There was a young man outside. He says he brought something. For me?"

She looks as dazed as I feel, and her eyes go even wider and whiter when she clocks the size of her bouquet. She stops running in order to simply stare.

"Well. Well, I never..." Her fingers start crawling around and through each other. I know she's scared to pick the flowers up and it's quite easy now for me to lift a corner of my dressing gown and slip my letter under.

"Go on, Rene, they're for you." I make my voice go calm and soft. It's suddenly become easier to think about Rene than anything else. "It's ok," I tell her and then she sags, dropping right there, among the grass and bugs and dirt, on to her sun-bed orange knees.

"Well," she says again and I hand her the bouquet.

Taking the flowers, Rene closes her eyes. I stare at the

deep purplish shadows circling her yellow sockets and have to forcibly stop myself from picturing the skull underneath. Her jaw's hanging slack and I'm gazing straight into the familiar dark vortex of her mouth. It's her sleeping-face, her migraine-face, temporarily raw and utterly unguarded. Her breath rushes out in short, thick bursts. I don't think she can have any idea of the noise she's making. I look away and catch sight of the undergrowth parting and rippling, a long, slow breeze running through the patchier grass and taller nettles that crowd beneath the trees. There's a shadowy flicker - a crawling shoulder, a lifted hand? Fingers bound in dark brown thread? But then I see a side of bronzed black fur and I understand it's nothing, just the cat. Head down, he's hunting, slithering snakelike through the weeds. With a rustle and a soft thud, he pounces, misses. Stops to wash his paws.

Rene opens her eyes at the sounds. Her face is her own once more; lined, but careful. Her lips are thin.

"Aren't they beautiful?" she says, but she isn't looking at the flowers. She's looking hard at me.

I nod.

The cat starts prowling towards us, following something fluttering through the grass, some tiny doomed creature that I can't quite see. As I strain to look, he pauses, raising his head to sniff the air. His whiskers look very white. His eyes are glossy mirrors, full of sun. They close to smiling slits as he drops back down onto his belly in the grass.

"Janie..." Rene says. "Do you believe that people can change?"

She says this so quietly that I wonder if she meant to say

it at all. She isn't looking at me now and there's something about the way her shoulders have hunched and her feet are pressed so neatly together. She looks like a little girl, I think. She almost looks shy, like she's gathered herself in. In her pink palm, the white florist's card flashes as her fingers curl open and then snap closed. Her words sit between us, and suddenly I'm thinking about Diana; how she used to draw with me and read to me and wrap me up when I was sick; how all of that is gone. Like the Missing Girls are gone. And then I'm thinking how I used to believe I knew such a lot of things, when actually I can't figure out anything at all. Like the way a man can one day just be selling ice creams and the next he's something else?

Although I don't know whether I'm really meant to answer Rene's question, I hear the words come tearing out of me.

"Yes! Yes, of course people change. Everything's always changing, you can't get away from it. People are changing all the time."

Twelve

The next morning I tell Dad and Rene that I'm well. That what would help now is a walk, a breath of real sea air.

"About time," Rene says. "All this lazing about. Demanding things."

Dad's not so sure. He looks at me with his chin in his hand and a little whistling sound comes out of his nose.

"I'll tell you what," he says eventually. "I'll come with you. I've got a few bits to do. We could even grab something to eat, a little snack, if we get as far as town."

I smile and nod, but my heart sinks. The thick little square of my letter is squeezed into the pocket of my jeans, but I can't think of anything to say that will dissuade him.

Sighing quietly, I sit at the bottom of the stairs while he searches for his keys, shoes, and wallet. Smoky light breathes heavily against the tiny window over the door. I can't remember the last time Dad took it into his head to take me out somewhere. *I'll just have to slip away later*, I tell myself; *it'll be all right*. But when I reach down to rethread my laces my hands are shaking, just a bit. *Be still*, I warn them, *you are well*.

Rene can't be bothered to wait for Dad to finish fussing. She clips down the hall and holds the front door open for us. Since she's got the day off today, she isn't wearing one of her suits, but a pink blouse and wide cotton trousers. Caught in the sunshine on the step, she looks younger, maybe happier. Her grey hair is lit up as though it's woven through with tinsel.

"Bye," she calls, waving her fingers in our faces. "Have a nice time. Bye."

Before we've even left the step, she's swinging the front door closed. I don't pause to listen, to check whether or not she's already grappling with the chain. Outside, the empty street is glaring. We walk, almost self-consciously, past the well-maintained hedges and lawns of our neighbours' gardens, past their foxgloves and their sweet peas. Great regal bushes of vivid pinks and spilling purples, shuddering with bees. Despite his eagerness to join me, Dad is silent. He walks quickly, a step or two ahead, with his shoulders sloped and his grey head bowed. He's lost to something, but I've no idea what. I decide I haven't really got the room left in my head to wonder, and besides, the sky is so beautiful today. It's a bright, distracting blue, too enormous and brilliant to gaze at for very long. It hasn't rained, I realise, the whole time that I've been ill. All the houses on our road seem to be sleeping, and there's something about the day, this sky, that makes me realise how small everything is down here: the new builds and the cottages, even the trees. Dad and me, we're antlike too.

For a moment it's hard to believe in the Missing Girls, in the letter folded stiffly in the back pocket of my jeans, but as soon as we reach the bustling High Street, everything leaps back to life-size. I'm surrounded by the goosy gabbling of tourists and the frustrated stop-starting of their cars. The pavements are still cluttered with sunburnt legs and plastic tubs filled with buckets and spades and little windmills. The hanging baskets still jostle for space at head height, except they're no longer blooming. They're drying up, their straggling leaves have yellowed; their flowers are scrunched up paper balls. I think about the last time I was here, how I raced between the shoppers, how terrified I was, as though the ice-cream van was in hot pursuit behind me. Even now, I can't stop myself from glancing over my shoulder, from scanning the broiled, flaking faces of tourists in the crowd. I remember how helpless I felt and how I couldn't stop laughing. I remember his hand.

That friendship band.

My stomach squeezes.

"Janie," Dad calls, and I have to turn around and take a few steps back to get to him. Somehow I've ended up rushing off ahead.

"Janie," he says, resting one flat palm on the clean glass door beside him, "let's stop here."

Stella's, the ice-cream parlour, has been around for as long as I can remember. When I was little, it was full of old men and foil ashtrays and the menu was more about fried egg sandwiches than choc-nut sundaes, but a couple of years ago they had a refit. Now it's supposed to look like some

1950's American diner, like something out of Happy Days, I suppose, or Grease. There's lots of red plastic seating and big black and white squares across the floor. The walls are hidden behind giant posters of Elvis and Marilyn Monroe, and in the corner, there's an old-fashioned jukebox with real vinyl. Occasionally it works.

Stella's is packed today. There are children everywhere you look. Sticky little kids jostling at the counter and crawling under tables, racing back and forth between the booths. They all seem to have the same huge mouths and sea-wet hair. Their eyes are dark, glittering with sugar. Somehow, amidst the chaos, Dad manages to find us a narrow table in the cooler shadows at the back. He installs me as its guardian before going up to the counter to fetch our food. We're squeezed in right next to the kitchen and every now and then, the door swings open and clips the back of my seat as one of the counter staff comes whirling out, an extra tray of sundaes or smoothies wedged up against her 'fifties' style pointed, gingham breasts. Her eye make-up is melting into the kind of mask you might wear for Halloween, and each time the door behind her bangs, she releases a wave of laughter and clattering from the kitchen. There's a gust of cigarette smoke, and a blast of freezer air.

"Look what I've got for you!" Dad says, attempting to slide a tray on to our narrow table while climbing awkwardly into the chair opposite. I hear his knees crack quite distinctly when he finally sits down. As if I'm about four, he's brought me one of Stella's Specials. It's a car crash of an ice-cream; a great cut glass tub of multi-coloured scoops, stabbed through with wafers and buried beneath a powdery-looking layer of chopped nuts and sugar strands. To top it off, there's a fat, glistening curl of raspberry ripple sauce that's so bright it's almost violet. For him, there's just plain coffee, with a small yellow biscuit on the side.

"Thanks, Dad" I say, though for the moment I can't even bring myself to touch the spoon.

"Eat up! Eat up!" he urges.

There's a small pink spot, like blusher, in each of his cheeks and the wrinkles around his mouth have sunk so deep you can imagine running a fingernail along inside. His smile looks embedded. He's gone into enthusiastic father mode. It doesn't happen often and it makes me suspicious, and embarrassed. In a minute, I think, he'll start rubbing his palms together or snickering, overflowing with artificial glee.

"I'm so pleased you're feeling better," he says. "The walk wasn't too much? You looked a bit shaky outside."

"I'm fine, Dad" I say. I pick out one of the wafers. When I pinch it, it cracks and sends a puffing cloud of creamy crumbs tumbling into my lap. Dad pretends he hasn't seen.

"Good, good. I thought you were on the mend, but it's been a bit of a nasty one, eh? And last night I thought you were having some kind of relapse."

"What are you talking about? Last night?"

He picks up his biscuit and takes a tiny, snipping bite. Amidst the wrinkles, his teeth look very young and white and strong.

"Oh, it was nothing, really. Don't you remember? I told Rene you weren't actually awake. You were having a dream. Some kind of nightmare, I think. Shouting, thrashing about, that sort of thing. You soon calmed down, but I did wonder about your temperature, if perhaps the fever was coming back? But no, you're fine, and you really don't remember any of it?"

The kitchen door bangs against the back of my seat as I shake my head, but even as I'm dismissing the dream, I'm rediscovering pictures - colours - a blur of yellow, a blinding amber, a deep and murky red. I don't really recall Dad or Rene coming in, but, out of nowhere, I'm remembering fragments, bits and pieces, and then, in a rush, the whole of it; an orange, burning dream.

I was in our house. It was night and before me, the rooms were grey and empty. Until I entered them that is, until I touched them with the torch or bottled rag or whatever explosive thing it was I carried. Until I brought the furniture, so suddenly and vividly, to life.

I shift in my seat, the red plastic sticking to the backs of my arms as I remember how the whole house blazed. There was fire everywhere. The floating shadows on the stairs were torn away, the chairs and tables and piles of books, which had been no more than faded shapes a moment before, flared stark and gold and then turned black. I could see it all so clearly, every detail. I suppose it was because it was a dream that there was hardly any smoke...

I place my broken wafer down and slowly brush the crumbs out of my lap. I make myself smile, but just inside I'm quivering. The dream's inside my mind like a swarm of summer bees. Too clearly, I remember the excitement; chasing from room to room, with the wall of glowing flames surging close behind like tattered, dancing ghosts.

The guilty thrill of it comes back to me. It fills my mouth, a taste not of fumes or ash, but of smooth, clean metal, like a blade stroked across my tongue. Hastily I shovel a massive, heaped spoonful of strawberry ice-cream between my lips. It's because of the fever, I think. The flames, the madness, that's all it was. There's no need for any guilt. I remind myself that you can't help what you dream, and besides, the house was empty. Nevertheless, it takes three more pink, freezing spoonfuls before I can lift my head and meet Dad's eye.

"When we came in last night," he's saying, "me and Rene - to see what all the commotion was about - Diana wasn't there. Her bed was empty. She'd climbed out of the window, that's what Rene thought. She does that often, I suppose?"

"No, I don't think so," I say and now I have no trouble rising to Dad's gaze; my big sister's taught me well. "How would I know, anyway?" I ask. "If I was sleeping?"

Dad looks away, down at his fingers, clamped tight around the coffee cup. He sighs.

"Listen, Janie, there's been a lot happening at home, lately. A lot of changes. Its one of the reasons I wanted to talk to you today."

Still, he doesn't look up, but one of his hands slides from his cup and falls open on the table between us. I wonder if I'm meant to take it, if this is what he's offering, but it's too strange, even more un-Dad-like than his fake enthusiasm. So I don't reach for him in return. Instead I keep piling up my spoon and loading ice-cream into my mouth. My stomach's not really used to eating yet. I feel it stretch and roll. Towards the middle of the dish, there are tiny, brittle shards of real ice, buried among the chocolate scoops like broken glass. They're so cold my tongue goes numb. I can see goose bumps popping up along my arms.

"You know," Dad says, "that Rene's started seeing Pete again?"

I try not to groan, but I realise now why Dad wanted to come with me today, and why he was so brooding on the way. He has something to discuss. Haven't I got larger, more urgent, matters to think about than Auntie Rene? I shrug, though there is admittedly a tiny part of me that's interested.

"What do you mean, *seeing*?" I hear myself ask a moment later. "I know he sent her flowers. I know that she screamed at him for half an hour outside the house."

Dad hunches forward in his chair and presses a thumb into the bridge of his glasses, his shiny nose. "Well," he says. "Hmm. I don't know. I think, with the screaming, the shouting... Hmm. I think it was very hard for Rene, at first, to let Pete back in. But now that she has, I think she's happy. Things seem to be moving pretty fast; getting serious already."

"But why did she?" I ask. "Let him back in, I mean. How could she, Dad? It's so, so stupid." As soon as the words are out, my fingers jump up to my mouth. *Calm down*, I tell myself. *Think of what's important, how you need to slip away.*

Dad lifts his hand too. He holds it flat in the air between us like a traffic warden, showing me his dry palm with its cracks and calluses and whirling lines. *Stop*, he's asking me, his fingertips trembling, begging me perhaps. I notice how his lids have started to drag down over the outside corners of his eyes as though even his skin is getting tired. But I ignore his hand, his plea, and my own advice.

"It's ridiculous!" I babble through my fingers. "After she went to court and everything. After all he's done to her. What makes her think he won't start hitting her all over again? I mean, how stupid can you be?"

"Janie. It's not that simple. Despite everything, she still loves him, I think."

And still I'm leaning forward, about to protest, but the *stop* hand flashes open once again. It's very irritating. It's almost in my face.

"I know, I know," he says. "I don't really understand it either. But it's complicated. There's history. You know, Rene and Caroline had a very hard time growing up. Their mother, she was... Well, never mind."

"What do you mean, never mind?" I say.

At the mention of Caroline, my mother, I'm sitting up straighter, leaning even closer, but he's mumbling on, not hearing me as usual.

"I just wanted to prepare you, Janie, about Rene and Pete. In case things change. Change more than they've started to, I mean. And I wanted you to know how things stood, for tonight."

"Tonight?" A wave of tiredness floats through me, though tonight's a world away. There's the letter first. The police station. "What's happening tonight?"

My stomach's aching from the ridiculous amount of ice cream I've eaten and there's the start of a headache, a bright cold crack, opening just behind my eyes. Around me, the diner is growing hotter, perhaps even busier than before.

"We're having a dinner party. I've offered the olive branch; asked Pete along."

Suddenly the headache flashes white into my eyes. I want to put my head down on the table. I want to close my eyes.

"Dad." I can't help myself. "How could you? Just because Rene's going stupid, you don't have to go along with her. He broke her nose, for God's sake. Twice."

Dad leans back in his chair, the wrinkles on his forehead bunching together in a frown. His strong white teeth have disappeared. I imagine him wondering how I know these details, who told me, and what other secrets I might have overheard?

"I'm not as clueless as you think," I mutter. And again, he pretends not to hear.

"Janie, it's happening. There's nothing anyone can do. Rene and Pete are back together. He's done some sort of anger management course, and I think it would be nice if we could show some support. Your aunt has done a lot for us, you know. I think the least we can do is to be there for her this evening and be civil. She's going to a lot of trouble. I think she's probably started cooking already, while we're out from under her feet... There'll be three courses apparently. All home-made."

The lines on his face change. He makes a sheepish grin. I know what he's up to, he's trying to appease me, to bring me round. Hasn't the state of Rene's cooking always been our private little joke? But I don't return his smile. I won't give in. Instead I look beyond him to where two boys are sitting, hunched together, by the window at the front of the cafe. They're about my age, wearing carefully shredded T-shirts and dog tags at their throats. I'm about to glance away when one of them leaps to his feet and smacks his palm against the glass.

"Oh, come on, Janie," Dad's saying, dragging me reluctantly back to him with his apologetic eyes. "It won't be that bad, will it? Things are difficult right now, for all of us, but it's at times like these that we need to pull together, as a family."

"What, like we've always done?" I say, but my sarcasm sails smoothly over his head. His eyes don't even flicker.

"Yes," he answers, even nodding, and still looking at me hard.

I watch as one of the boys at the front of the ice cream parlour slopes over to the door. He heaves it open and shouts into the street. There's a wallet chain hanging from the sagging belt loops of his jeans. It swings like a pendulum as he moves, catching the full blast of sunshine from outside. For a moment, as it turns, it looks as though it really could be made of solid gold.

"And I think I've persuaded Diana to bring Carl along tonight too. There are quite a few bridges that need building. We all need to start getting along again. Especially if Diana's serious about going through with this, this pregnancy... It's important. For the baby's sake, if nothing else."

As Dad says this, the pink spots in his cheeks vanish altogether. His skin looks very grey. The word, baby sticks in his throat. I watch the way his Adam's apple struggles to rise over it, before he can carry on.

"Oh, Dad," I say, because suddenly I pity him. I'm not angry anymore. I want to lean across the table and put my arms around his neck; I want to run my fingers over the soft wrinkles in his serious, worried face.

I want to tell him the truth, that of course there isn't any baby, that it's just another of Diana's dramas, but he'd never believe me over Diana. And besides, he'll find out soon enough. I don't have time for this today.

Ignoring the way my headache's started throbbing - that odd white flickering before my eyes - I scrape the final spoonful of ice cream from my bowl. I think I'm behaving normally, but he must see something; some sympathy or something, flash across my face, because when Dad speaks again his voice is gruffer, nearly angry. I can tell he doesn't like the idea that I might actually feel sorry for *him*.

"Janie," he says, "I think we all need to start facing facts. Your sister…"

But that's when I see them. Two blonde girls, long limbed and familiar, standing in the doorway, talking to the boy. Under the direct sunlight, their hair is dazzling, so bright it's touched with white around the edges, as though with snow. The closest girl, the one who has stepped inside and is easing herself around the table towards the other boy, is wearing denim shorts and a cropped, black vest. I see that her belly button's pierced and, as she slides across the seat, the stone that she's hooked in there winks at me. All over her shoulders and running down her lean, tanned thighs, there are freckles. Hundreds of them, a spattering, like soft, brown paint.

It's them, I think, although at the same time, I know that of course it can't be. There's no way the Missing Girls would simply turn up here, and aren't their faces a little round, a little older? Isn't their hair a shade too light? If only Dad wasn't sitting opposite me, I could stand up and take a better look. Then I'd know for sure it wasn't them. But Dad's still talking, his fingers moving on his saucer, spinning his coffee cup gently around and around and around. Discreetly, I crane my neck to get a better look over his shoulder.

The second girl's still standing in the doorway. She's talking to the boy, her fingers flicking her hair away from her face in a slow, shining arc. I tell myself: *She isn't one of them.* Her lips are too thin and her heavily made up eyes are too sly and bright. Nevertheless, my heart is pounding, overtaking the drumming in my head. I have to grip the edges of the table with both hands to stop myself from jumping up, away from Dad, from calling out their names. As I stare, the boy in the doorway lifts one arm. He's holding up an ice-cream cone, offering the girl a bite. She shakes her head, swinging her blonde hair, but then I watch as her thin lips open anyway, as they close again around the soft white peak. I see the small dark flicker of her tongue.

It isn't them, but *"Tara!"* I'm thinking, *"Stacey!"*

And for a moment I wonder if what is actually happening is that I am going mad.

Everywhere, between us, little kids are running about, getting in the way, but I can see straight through them, and now, as he lifts his cup, straight through my Dad's right elbow too. Like in my dream, I can see everything so clearly: the way the girl ducks her face to wipe some ice cream from her nose, how tightly the boy's fingers are wrapped around the cone. And his hand is much larger than I'd have thought. It's ruddier too, the kind of hand, I think, that if it touched you, would stick to you like glue.

I look away quickly, knowing that what I'm seeing, what I'm thinking, isn't right. It's not quite real. And still Dad's talking, going on about Diana, the whole stupid baby sham, but I can hardly hear him for the slamming in my head. I try to concentrate on my breathing. On the letter in my pocket. *I will keep calm.* I take deep breaths, in through my nose and out, slowly, through my mouth. But all around me, the air is heavy, saturated with the scent of vanilla and chocolate. My empty bowl sits in front of me, taking up almost half the narrow table. The cut glass is clouded and in my discarded spoon, there's a small congealing milky pool. All the ice–cream, which I can't believe I've eaten, seems to return, in one go, to curdle in my throat. It's not cold now though, but burning. Over and over again, I try to swallow it back down. *Don't puke*, I think. *Don't think.* I shove the bowl away and put my face down on my open hands.

"Janie," Dad says, "are you ok?"

I try to reply, but against my palms, the headache has erupted. It's not glacier-white anymore, but a blistering red. For a moment, it surrounds me, and again I'm in last night's fiery dream. Though my mouth is filled with the warm, sweet taste of vomit, it's a wave of guilt, not nausea that makes me shudder. Because it's dawning on me that what I told myself about the dream was wrong. The house, I remember, wasn't empty. The whole time I crashed between those dark, familiar rooms, setting them ablaze, something else was happening too. There was a constant noise, a thud-thud-thudding like this angry headache, like one of Rene's migraines, coming from behind Dad's study door. The door was locked - I had locked it - and Dad and Rene, and quite probably Diana too, were banging their hands bloody on the inside, desperate to get out.

Thirteen

In the brilliant sunshine outside Stella's, Dad sits me down on the pavement, and I put my head between my knees. I stare down at the cracks in the concrete and at my ratty black baseball boots; at their grey shredded laces and the white car park dust that's still gathered there, collected in the canvas seams like cobwebs. Despite all the time I've spent lying on the sunlounger in our garden, the skin on my shins remains chalky-pale, and where it stretches over my jutting ankles it looks gauzy, almost transparent. You can imagine seeing straight through it to the sharp little bird bones clustered underneath. I stay in this shin-gazing position for several minutes, with my head bowed and my chin tucked tight into my neck, the soles of my boots pressed flat and hard against the ground. I ignore all the other shoes, the sandals and trainers that scuff past or pick their way around me, all those inconvenienced tourist feet. I pretend not to notice the thick black shadows they leave behind. I sit there, quite still, until I reckon enough time has passed to convince Dad I'm feeling better.

"Much better," I say at last, squinting up at him, with one hand cupped across my eyebrows, as if my skinny fingers could provide any kind of shield against all this light.

Dad drops into an awkward crouch in front of me, peering into my face. I concentrate on my smile, making sure it's not too wide, too toothy. I leave it hanging, despite the seriousness of Dad's expression.

"Thank God we got you out of there when we did," he mutters. "I don't think I've ever seen you looking quite so ill."

I don't mention that he's no longer looking quite the picture of health himself. There are sweat lines pressed along the creases in his forehead - chains of tiny bubbles, like air trapped under Clingfilm - and his skin's as pale as ash.

"This is all my fault, dragging you out here, buying you that ice-cream. I don't know what I was thinking." He shakes his head. "After your fever last night, it was much too soon."

"No, Dad. I'm fine." I reach out and touch his shirtsleeve. His pearly cuff button feels cool and smooth, a tiny beach pebble beneath my thumb.

A woman with a double buggy stops beside us, waiting to see what we're going to do next. Together, we're taking up half the pavement; she can't get by. I tug Dad's sleeve and we stand together. As we rise, the ice-cream parlour window is greenhouse-hot against my back. I'm aware that sitting at the table behind me - right behind me - on the other side of the glass, are a pair of teenage boys and a pair of teenage girls. The girls are blonde, with freckled arms. As I went rushing out, stumbling straight past them with Dad shuffling close behind, I felt them stare. The last thing I'd do now is turn around and look at them again. I can imagine how they'd react; their gazes touching, glinting, as they bite back whispers and piranha smiles.

Dad moves to stand beside me. He puts one hand lightly on my throbbing forehead and strokes a strand of hair out of my eyes. I stiffen and try to focus, to concentrate. I make myself think of gushing sprinklers and cool blue swimming pools - a freezer full of ice - anything so that he won't sense how hot I am, inside as well as out. The woman with the buggy pushes past and her children, twin toddlers, roll their big brown eyes all over us. Their faces are raw-looking, livid from the sun. They have matching marks around their mouths, a rash of tiny, picked-at blisters.

"Come on," Dad says. "Let's get you home."

"But Dad," I say, "don't you have things you need to do?" I'm careful to make the words drop slowly, casually, from my mouth. I can't let him know how badly I want him out of the way.

"I'm fine now," I say. "It was just a... A wave. You don't need to stay with me. I'll be all right."

"Well..." He pulls a handkerchief, a proper cotton handkerchief with curled up corners, from his trouser pocket and dabs his long, lined face. "Rene did ask me to pick up a few bits for the dinner tonight."

"I bet she did," I say and watch him smile behind the cotton.

"But it's not a problem. I'll just walk you back home first."

"Dad, I'm not a baby. I'm perfectly capable of taking

myself home."

He sighs and gazes down at his shiny brown shoes. Eventually he nods, as I knew he would. It's far too hot to be standing here arguing, beneath the weight of the midday sun.

"If you're sure?" he says to his shoes. "And you promise you'll go straight home. And you'll lie down for a while, when you get in?"

"Yes, Dad."

He nods again and is about to leave me when he swings back suddenly to press a kiss on the top of my head. For several seconds, he remains there, with his chin in my hair. He murmurs something, but I don't catch what it is. I'm careful to keep my smile even and unchanged when he finally steps back.

"Bye Dad," I say. "I'll see you later."

I watch him drift off through all the other people, past the pub and underneath the fudge shop's huge gold sign. He passes the estate agents, with its busy glass front full of rows of small bright squares. He doesn't glance at any of them and I think how, when I look at him lately, I often seem to catch him like this, walking away with his shoulders slumped, caught in his own private world, somewhere far away from the rest of us. He never used to be like this. Actually, he never used to be around much at all. He worked long hours as one of only three anaesthetists in the little hospital just outside town, but two years ago he gave it all up for a part time teaching post at the big university thirty miles inland. Now he works just two days a week during term time and spends the rest of his time, like Rene and me (but not really like Diana anymore), hanging around the house, looking useless, slightly dazed.

I watch as he meanders away, growing smaller and paler in the crowds. When he is completely out of sight, I wait for another minute before crossing the road. Once I'm over, I turn my back on the busy High Street where Dad has disappeared in one direction, while the shops trail off down the other, the road growing quieter, narrower, as it curves away, and then ascends towards our house. I slip instead up a narrow cobbled alleyway behind the fish shop and I don't look back.

As I make my way up the hill towards the police station, the day seems to grow hotter with every step. I thought it would be a relief to leave the alleyway, with its dustbins and its flies, the stink of fish-batter in the air, but walking out on to the wider street, the full force of the sun is stifling. There's no shade here, no escape. Too late, I think of things that might have helped; I should have bought a bottle of water, and I should have nicked Diana's shades. I can still feel the ice-cream, a swinging weight inside my stomach as I walk. The houses here are old and tall. I don't think that there's a B 'n' B amongst them. They're rich and private, the top two stories framed with wrought iron balconies, holding empty designer deckchairs and terracotta pots. The curly railings gleam. There's no rust here, no seagull-droppings, despite the fact that there's a whole row of gulls lined up along the metal. As I pass beneath them, the birds don't squawk or rise, or even stretch their large white wings. They just sit there, stupefied and silent, like stuffed and mounted versions of themselves. The odd car slides past, but apart from the gulls and I, there's not really anyone else about. Many of the houses have their shutters closed or their curtains drawn, but I imagine the people inside: delicate, moneyed people lying about on sofas or on milk-pale sheets in darkened rooms, their breathing regulated by the purr of soothing fans. Out here, just outside their walls and cool thick doors, it's an absolute ghost town. The air is gritty, hazy, and if I squint, I can turn the whitewashed walls and balconies into the shuttered saloons and stores of some faded Western film set. The road shimmers in the distance and I half expect to see a ball of tangle-weed go skittering by.

You'd have to be mad to be out, that's what Rene would say, but in a way, the heat helps. It helps to keep everything slow and simple in my head. At the moment, all I need to concern myself about is getting to the police station. This journey, nothing else. But as the pale cobblestones roll away beneath my feet, I can't help wondering at the way I keep letting myself get tangled up with all these other things. I think how I nearly blew it just now with Dad, worrying about Rene and that dream, allowing those two blonde girls (who, after all, weren't really anything like my Missing Girls) to confuse me so much... Too easily, I'm distracted. Too easily, I panic. My imagination gains control. And even as I'm thinking this, I'm aware of a picture, a snap shot in my head. That blue eyed woman again, with her cloud-white clothes and her clean white car. I can't help seeing her. She's always there, too near the surface. As if she's waiting. As if she's real.

I need to watch myself, I think.

A couple of months ago, during spring term, Dawn - one of the other girls from the 'achievers' group - developed obsessive-compulsive disorder. In the last few weeks before her parents took her out of school, you'd hear her whispering to herself almost continually. She'd count like a machine under her breath and when she did try to talk to you normally, she'd make high little humming sounds between the words.

I pull myself up short, coming back with a jolt, to the ghost-town street and my sweat-sludgy body. I've arrived at the police station. Actually, I've nearly walked straight past. It's another big, detached, whitewashed building, though it's even larger than the others and surrounded by a square of black tarmac and a low brick wall. Apart from the old-fashioned blue lamppost just outside and a single, badly parked police car, it doesn't look any different from a library or a museum. It has that same sense of sighing municipal quiet about it. A quiet that manages, somehow, to be even deeper, even denser, than the rest of this dozing, empty street. I'd expected some kind of action here, but there's nothing; no shuffling shame-faced criminals, no television crews. Everything feels so dead here, so muffled and deserted, that I can almost hear the heat stirring and murmuring beneath my laboured breathing. I step around the police car and a set of orange traffic cones, stacked together like a child's giant toy. The tarmac stretches out before me, glittering darkly and smelling rubbery, perhaps melting a little in the heat. I run my hands over my head and neck, trying to flatten my hair a bit and wipe some of the sweat off of my face. I reach for the letter in my back pocket. I take a deep breath as I march across the tarmac, telling myself that I can do this, that it's not only the right thing to do, it's also going to be easy. There's no one about and all I have to do is slip the letter into the police letterbox, if there is one. I'll slide it discreetly between those heavy industrial looking metal doors, if not.

But the sun is scoring into the back of my neck and the short distance to the entrance seems to be taking me forever. As I walk, my baseball boots make distracting little sucking-sticking sounds against the ground. I'm too self-conscious, way too aware suddenly, of the long dim windows lining the chalky walls ahead. It's all too quiet, too creepy. I feel my face flush, my shoulders shrinking. Anybody could be watching me from in there. And, quite probably, there are cameras. Ridiculously, I wish I'd worn a hat or other clothes. I could've done something different with my hair, at the very least. But it's too late for any of that now. I'm here, standing inches from the great, metal security doors. I dare not look at the letter I'm clutching, crumpling, in one twisting, nervous hand. I'm sweating all over it. I imagine the ink running beneath my slippery fingers, my message reduced to nothing. A meaningless blur. For a moment, I don't even care. Perhaps I could just drop it where I stand and then swing back around and run? (After all, I'm delivering it, aren't I? Can't just that be enough?)

I close my eyes and rub the sweat through my hair again. Slowly, deliberately, I re-run that home video footage in my head. I picture those friendship bands. Then the ice-cream man. His sticky, almost swollen-looking hands. *Do this properly*, I tell myself. *For God's sake, concentrate. Remember: he's the one.* I open my eyes. There is a small reinforced window embedded near the top of each door and, panting raggedly, I pull myself up to stand on tiptoe so that I can peer inside. I drop back down on to my heels immediately.

They're here, my Missing Girls.

My heart is banging stupidly. There is a moment when I can hardly see, when all that I can hear is the black-red pounding of my pulse. *Stupid, stupid.* I remind myself to breathe, before I stretch up again to press my face against the warm, wired glass. They've been blown up to life-size, if not a bit larger, and mounted on the wall directly opposite me, above a row of plastic chairs. The word MISSING, blazing over them, is huge. It's just the picture again, of course. The one with the guide uniforms. The freckles. Yet I can't take my eyes off it, though I can't quite focus on it either. The shatterproof security glass gives everything a brownish tinge and divides the bare little waiting room into squares. It's like looking through graph paper. Perhaps it's the glass that has made the girls look so unreal? When I turn my head slightly, they grow immediately blurry, their edges double. It's a bit like when you catch your face (slightly contorted, watery, monstrous) in a train window at night.

And suddenly none of this feels real. I'm suspicious. *It's the poster*, I think. *It's too big.* It looks like something faked. Like a movie poster, almost. How can these girls be missing? Aren't they too fresh and fit and young for anything truly bad to have happened to them? Isn't their hair too brushed? Aren't their teeth too clean?

As I gawp at them, it crosses my mind that perhaps they aren't actually missing after all. Perhaps the whole thing's one big scam. Some strange, sick joke. In reality, they're sitting somewhere cool and safe and clean, laughing at their own flickering faces on a television screen.

Laughing, perhaps, at people like me?

I think of the letter, of the words I wrote, in a baby's scrawl, holding the pen crooked in my awkward left hand:

'I have some information regarding the recent disappearance of Tara Matlock and Stacey Hughes...'

"Are you alright there, Love?"

I swing around fast, and there's a policeman standing right behind me. I don't know how it is that I didn't hear his big black shoes approach. He's a proper 'beat bobby'; his buttons gleam. I look in panic from his buttons to his smooth, enquiring face, and then down again, to his neck, bulging out of his collar like a toddler's rubber swimming ring. His flesh is shiny and pinched-looking.

I open my mouth to tell him.

Nothing. Nothing comes out.

Involuntarily, my eyelids flutter and he wavers before me, this big, jolly, rosy-cheeked, glossy-skinned policeman. I feel dizzy at the sight of him. As I rock from foot to foot, shifting my weight, I'm dumbly aware of the way my thighs are sticking to one another as though with blue-tack. The policeman clears his throat and takes a step forward. He's very big, I think. He's very here. I feel myself blush, an extra layer of heat rising up over my face. My cheeks are crawling.

"Sweetheart?" he says.

The hot black tarmac rolls out behind him, full of pinhead sparkles. The cones and wall and blue police lamppost look very far away. Along the grand houses on the far side of the road, the gulls are still lined up across the balconies. They're still motionless, still stuffed-looking, except I can easily imagine how they're watching me now; waiting, like the policeman, for my response. Their beady eyes, like the tarmac, twinkle softly.

I ball the letter smaller in my fist. It's just a tiny wet thing now. It could be anything; a dirty tissue, some gig or Jesus flyer. I glance down at my trailing laces.

"I'm lost," I mutter. "I was looking for the beach."

I feel the policeman's gaze follow my own, skipping down my body, to my jeans and then down further, to my ratty looking shoes.

"Tourist, are you?" he asks.

I nod, pleased for once, in a small vague way, that I don't have a local accent, that I'm different from almost everyone at school.

"All right," he says.

He puts a hand on my shoulder and guides me away from the doors, away from the MISSING poster and back out onto the pavement. Through the stiff dark cotton of his jacket, I'm aware of the packed bulk of his body, the layers of fat and muscle, a male strength boxed tightly inside. He uses his whole hand to point in the direction I've just come from and then, in a soft, careful voice like the voice of our Special Needs teacher at school, he tells me to make a sharp turn on to the High Street. I stare up at him and nod a lot as though he's helping.

"All right?" he says when he's finished his explaining.

"Yes, thanks. That's great. That's fine."

I start to turn, to walk away, but he catches my arm and for a second I feel it again, that dense, heaped strength he keeps inside. For several seconds, he stares directly into my face, but then he smiles and I smile back, although inside my stomach is lifting. Squeezing.

"Well, you're a sensible kid," he says at last, releasing my arm. "You did the right thing coming here when you got lost. But you know you shouldn't really be wandering about by yourself, not right now. Tell your mother."

He glances up at the blue sky for a minute, blinks and then shakes his head.

"I don't know if you've heard," he says, "but recently, we've had two young girls go missing. From West Beach. So you take care."

Retracing my steps beneath those seagull-lined railings, I glance back over my shoulder. The policeman's already vanished inside his police station and I imagine how much bigger he'd seem behind those double doors, in that little brown tinged room. I picture the giant Missing Girls poster. Their massive eyes watch me through the heavy, closing doors.

What have I done? I wonder. *Not done?*

Staring ahead, I try to walk quickly away from their printed gaze, through the heat. But the girls are with me anyway of course, inside me. And they're not as bright and clean as they are in the MISSING poster. They're just ordinary. Ordinary girls sitting on a blanket in someone's garden, surrounded by coloured cotton, weaving a pattern, a gift, from scraps and threads. Or they're in their swimming costumes, I think, racing up the steps from West Beach, giggling and jostling, falling against one another as they climb. Or they're somewhere else entirely. Somewhere damp and cold with boarded windows or bent black trees. They're lying huddled together on old, stained sheets, or perhaps on a different kind of bed - one of mud and roots. Smashed glass? Dead leaves... They're paler than they were, their bones are pushing through their skin. Their mouths are open, but they aren't moving anymore, or perhaps they are, but only just.

I stop. Look up. The gulls are still there, in their stony rows. Now and again, the odd bird preens and stretches, unpeeling a white triangle of wing. But mostly they do nothing but gaze down at me with their piercing, otherworldly eyes. I open the letter. My handwriting is still clear. Readable, more or less. I turn, heading back the way I came. There's still no sign of the policeman. Nevertheless, I hurry, though I'm already breathless. By the time I reach the empty police car, parked at an angle on the tarmac, my hands are shaking. The letter's shaking as I lift up the windscreen wiper and leave it tucked like a parking ticket, just behind. I back away, wiping my hands on my thighs, feeling the dampness through my jeans. I can feel the gulls behind me too. I can hear the rustle of feathers as first one, and then two, and then perhaps half a dozen spread their wings and take flight. It happens fast. I stare up and all of them are airborne, circling the street, cawing and cawing as they dive and rise and find their way. Finally, they scatter into the sky. Cool white pebbles in a clean blue pool.

And underneath them, way below them, I start to run.

Fourteen

Between the white houses with the black balconies, I run.

With the sensation that I'm being tracked and hunted, that I'm about to be caught at any moment - humiliated, exposed somehow - I run.

For several seconds, I'm steeped in shadow as the gulls pass over me and in their wake, the air seems to press into me, but I don't stop. I can't stop. I push on through the heat, gazing at the cobbles reeling out beneath my dusty, flying boots. I think of the police station receding into the distance, at my back. That poster disappearing.

I'm running so fast, downhill, that it feels like falling. Over and over, I actually glimpse myself falling, a spectre flailing in a dozen darkened windows. But I don't ever hit the ground. My feet, they hardly touch it. And my mind is racing with the rest of me. I'm thinking about my mother again (*'your muh-thur'* my feet beat against the bumpy ground).

I can't help wondering, when she vanished, all those

years ago, did anyone put a MISSING poster up for her? Did anyone make enquiries even? Perhaps it wasn't necessary. Perhaps, like me, she left a note. I've no idea. It's all confused, more confused than ever.

And amidst it all, there's the other doubt that keeps resurfacing, the worry, still, that I might have misinterpreted the ice-cream man's actions in his van. The concern that remains, despite that friendship band and all the earnest conviction in my letter, that I might have got him wrong? *What are you doing?* My feet pound and my pulse throbs. *What have you done?*

I reach a small twist in the road just before the slope drops even steeper and I glance up, blinking, without breaking my stride. I can see the sea, just, beyond the rooftops. As I keep going, trying to hold my head high - attempting, impossibly, to clear my thoughts - it comes at me in fits and starts, in silver flashes; foil tatters between the satellite dishes and chimney pots. Eyes glinting in the trees. My packed head shimmers with it and my mouth is filled with salt, but as I get closer, descending, the sea vanishes altogether. The road narrows and the roofs close in. The walls gliding past are speckled with seagull-droppings now and the odd senseless scribble of graffiti. As I dive back down the alleyway beside the chip shop, I'm very aware of the High Street, and of West Beach just beyond. You can smell these places before you see them. A smell of rotting fish and dripping doughnuts, a rush of tourists on the wind.

And as soon as I hit the High Street I want to turn back, I want to hide. I'm repelled by all the shoppers and all the shop fronts, by the thousands of brightly coloured pieces of plastic crap for sale. I want to get away, far away, from this road. These people. I want to keep on running all the way home, but I know I can't. Not yet. There's one more place I have to go first. Although I'm pretty sure that it won't do me any good, there is one person I need to see.

So I swerve in the opposite direction to my house. I zip between parked cars and crawling cars. I duck around all the slow, burnt people squinting despite their shades and caps and sun-hats, huddling together in groups beneath striped awnings, as if cowering beneath the sun. I dodge them all. I head directly for the car park, his ice-cream van. I don't stop. I try not to think. My heart is banging in my chest, my gut, my throat. I tune out all the other noises. I simply run. Past the arcades, the rocks, the steps curving down to West Beach - which I won't look at. Not today. I narrow my eyes instead. I concentrate on a square of blanched blue sky ahead.

And then I'm back there, before I'm ready. Before I've prepared in any way. I'm teetering at the edge of the car park, surrounded by the familiar stones and cracks and heather. A butterfly swirls past, like torn paper.

I don't look directly at the ice-cream van, not right away. I bend over with my hands gripping my damp denim knees. I need a moment to catch my breath, to quiet the rushing in my head and the drumming of my heart. My throat is parched. I'm aching and there is sweat clinging to my lashes that you might mistake for tears. But after a while, though my heart's still jumping, the world around me slows, bumping gradually to a halt as if it's all an illusion, as if it was the ground that was moving, and not me.

As I straighten up, I take in all the people, there's a crowd shuffling about up here today. The van sits in the midst of them, stark and white, like something grown up from the gravel. As I stare, the milling people smudge together, merging into a blur of brown skin, pink skin, and more pallid white. Their bikinis and Speedos are reduced to triangles, like kites, of coloured cotton. Although some of the holidaymakers are standing separately, most of them are gathered into a straggly line, snaking from the other side of the van. Baking patiently as they queue up for their drinks, cones, and crisps.

But they're not all tourists up here today. There are some local people too (you can tell because they're less lively, less shiny, and because they wear more clothes). They're kids mostly, teenagers. Several feet away from me some older girls are sitting in a semi-circle in the long, sharp-looking grass at the edge of the car park. Closer to the van, a group of young men are standing about, wearing leather jackets and faded hoodies, despite the heat. Light bounces from the bottle that they're passing back and forth. Every now and then, as they lift it to the sky in celebration or explanation, or to their thirsty, grinning lips, this light flares up and flashes. More quietly, their cigarettes burn gold. All along the railings, they've filled the parking spaces with their motorbikes. A rack of hulking machines; the metal blazing in the sun. Apart from the ice-cream van, there are only two other cars parked here today, one's a slate coloured people carrier, the other's small and blue.

No white cars. Well, that's something, I tell myself. A small relief.

I rub my sticky eyes.

The ice-cream van is parked at a different angle to the last time I was here. Its bonnet is facing me today, a tropically patterned sunshade filling the windscreen with garish jungle leaves, blurred parrots. I can't see the ice-cream man from here, or his hatch even, the place where his endless, hungry queue begins.

Cautiously, I shuffle along the white gravel, though I'm careful to keep to the very edge of the car park, to keep my distance. My strong running legs don't feel so certain anymore and I can smell a sweet, grainy sweat coming from my armpits. My feet perhaps, my groin.

For a second time I find myself wondering what I think I'm doing here, what I'm expecting to see, to hear? What evidence am I seeking? Perhaps some kind of screwed up reassurance that I was right to leave that letter?

Certainly, I think, *I can't speak to him.* The thought of approaching the ice-cream man again fills me with panic, and though I'm boiling, I've started sweating ice.

My vision swims as I blunder onwards. Tiny stones cascade ahead of me in a soft white shower, but I find myself glancing over my shoulder, studying the shadows in the heather and the thin, dry grass. I'm turning back to stare at rocks in case they've suddenly stopped being rocks and started being bodies. I blink away the sticky vision of a damp, grey foot, and tufts that might be thistles, or brownish-blondish hair. I try to get a grip, attempting to focus only on the cleanest, palest pebbles. I concentrate on their cool smoothness, their very whiteness... I think of bones.

Ahead of me, the car park shimmers. *But look at all the*

people here! What could happen? Surely I'm safe today... I finally round the van to face the noisiest end of the ice-cream queue, the place where children are jumping up and down and screeching out their orders, obscuring my view of the serving hatch (with its shadow just inside).

And Donald Duck's still here, looking me over with that artless saucer eye. And then, staring at him, staring past him, I can't help it, quite suddenly I laugh. It's the ice-cream man; *he isn't here.* It's the plate-faced girl instead, doling out handfuls of twinkling lollies, and cans of Coke, Sprite, and Fanta. I step closer, with one hand over my mouth to stop the giggles, to watch her winding ice-cream into cornets, jabbing in flakes and then turning around abruptly to dig amongst her freezers. Her customers are demanding, relentless. Her flat, round cheeks are so brightly red that they look enflamed and I watch as she lifts the hem of her man-sized T-shirt to wipe her hands and then her face. Despite the grubbiness of her work, she has decorated her hair at the front with swinging beads and tiny plaits. Scraps of rainbow colour. I feel like I could kiss her, I'm so relieved. Instead I keep walking, deciding to complete the circumference of the car park before beginning the steady, humid walk back home.

And that's when I see him. That's when I realise, he isn't serving from the side of the van, because he's hanging out the back.

And he's not alone. There's a girl with him. A teenage girl.

I've stopped walking without realising it. While everyone else, all around me, continues about their normal business -

buying and eating, shrieking and drinking - I stand very still among the dust and pebbles, with my hair falling lankly into my face, and I just stare.

He's sitting between the van's open double back doors. Unmistakable with that flushed red head of his, those heavy arms. But it's the girl he's with that I can't tear my eyes from. It's the young girl, laughing up at him, wriggling her shoulders, who turns me cold. She has long brown legs; perfect Barbie doll legs, pouring out of a baby-blue mini skirt with a soft, white fringe. Her top is tiny, blood red, all skin and strings. It's some kind of halter neck; not the sort of top that I would ever wear.

I blink. *Remember to breathe.* Her hair looks dark, but perhaps that's just a trick of the light, because she's caught in shadow as she leans towards his van?

Tara? I wonder. *Stacey?*

Whoever she is, I will her, with all my might: *don't climb into that van.*

But she isn't listening to me, there's no connection. I watch, aghast, as she bends towards him, bowing her head so that it almost touches his chest. His huge fleshy hand is reaching out towards her in turn, hovering over her shoulder, her slender neck before just lightly brushing, and then lifting, a strip of pitch black hair. But then she's slithering away from him; she's standing back. A bluish ring of smoke rises and breaks above their heads and I realise that she was lighting her cigarette from him and that was all. I see it clearly, hanging from her mouth as she turns away laughing. And as she turns towards me. *I know that smile.*

For several moments, the whole world turns black. It falls

in on me, cold and dark and secret, the way the beach hides a coldness, a darkness, just beneath the top layer of powdery sand. But gradually the blackness breaks and scatters. It comes apart, erupting with specks of glittering white, a constellation of car park dust. My eyes sting with it, but, as my vision clears, I can't drag them away. I can't not look.

Because it isn't Tara or Stacey joking, perhaps flirting even, with the ice-cream man at the back of his van. It's Diana.

Fifteen

"Janie. Janie. Wake up."

Her white blouse is burning into the shadows by my bedroom door. For a moment, it's the only thing I can see. I lift my head up very slowly and rub my eyes. It's all right; it's only Rene.

"Dinner's almost ready, Pete will be here any minute. God knows what time your sister and Carl will show up. If they turn up at all, that is."

Gradually the rest of the room starts taking shape - the wardrobe, the drawers, Diana's bed - everything sinks slowly into its correct, comfortable place. The room's dim, the air like syrup. Over at the window, the curtain hems are rippling with a breeze so soft and light that I imagine how it would feel against my skin. Rene walks quickly, heavily, over to the bed. She leans in close. There are tiny beads of perspiration covering her nose, they're tinted a pale toffee colour by her foundation. She smells like her make-up too, with bright clashing undertones of icing sugar and garlic.

I'm very small, very naked, beneath the sheet.

"Make sure you wash your face," she says. "Wear something nice."

And then she stands again, and is gone. For a long time, I lie unmoving beneath the clammy covers, taking long, thick breaths. From below, there's the familiar crash of Aunt Rene in the kitchen, and piano music rises, muffled through the floor. It's one of Dad's CDs, something polite and vaguely familiar, some light-classical compilation. The birds in our garden are louder, whistling and chirruping, and even screeching every now and then, as if someone out there's getting angry. There's the drone of traffic too and underneath that, like an echo, there's the sea.

And despite everything, I'm as calm as the waves. Against the warm mattress my waking, naked body feels strong, like I've borrowed someone else's. I squirm my shoulders higher up the pillow and stretch. Despite what Rene said, I'm in no hurry. Where the top sheet brushes over me, I tingle. I let my hands slide slowly down my sides. It's a surprise; this sense of peace, of well being, because when I climbed under the covers, my head was pounding. I was angry, close to tears. I was furious with my sister. *What was she doing?* And I knew it wasn't right that I was back here, at home, tucked safely in my bed, while she was out there still. Out there, with that man. I should have confronted them at the car park. I should have marched right over, dragged her away. At the very least, I could have waited where I was; I could have watched over her. At the very least, I should have seen her safe. But I didn't do any of these things. I was too shocked, too bewildered. I was too inadequate. Too me.

All the way home I kept telling myself that Diana would be all right. That she knew what she was doing. But I couldn't outrun my growing anger, and by the time I got back here, I was raging. Mostly with myself. I was worse than useless, I was pathetic. What was wrong with me? How could I have fled my own sister? Abandoned her? Everything, everything about me was wrong. And I gave up all over again, pulling the pillow tight across my face, closing my eyes... But it's the sleep that's somehow saved me. It was such a heavy, forgiving sleep, like a velvet wall surrounding me. I didn't dream of anything at all, and now, though nothing's changed, and I'm still feeling tired, I also feel good. Ridiculously good. My stomach's settled. The headache's long gone.

After all, I left my letter. I was frightened up at the police station, but I did it, didn't I? (And can't I feel proud - just a tiny bit pleased with myself - for that?)

With a sense of hope, of satisfaction, I think how the police must have found it by now. I picture them passing my note quickly back and forth, exchanging frowns as they make the short drive down to West Beach. I imagine a whole gang of burly uniforms searching the ice-cream van, delving into freezers and ripping open boxes. I see hands in plastic gloves carefully unhooking that friendship band from the mirror, bagging it and labelling it, 'Evidence. Item # 1'. They could be arresting him right now.

And though it's true that I shouldn't have left my sister, it's also true that, of course, she will be safe. After all, she isn't a little girl. She isn't some innocent Guide-type with soft brown freckles and a wobbly smile. She's tough. She's confident. She's always been a grown-up. If anyone can protect herself, it's my Diana. And thinking this, (though perhaps it's an effect of the Glandular Fever still, or the heat, or the simple fact of that dreamless sleep), I feel suddenly light-headed, as well as calm. For a moment, I feel carefree, almost light-boned as if I might just sail away. And I'm actually smiling. Genuinely smiling, and I wonder if this is how it feels to be drunk, this dumbly happy, weightless feeling. Is this how Diana feels when she's sitting by the light of a fire down in one of West Beach's little caves? For a few seconds I picture her, laughing with her friends, dancing maybe. Her eyes would be bigger than ever, but light and shining, filled momentarily with this airy sensation, this sense of floating, of freedom. The possibility, maybe, of escape.

I stretch again, for once enjoying the length in my arms and my skinny string thighs, and I think how, if I didn't know that Rene was bound to come back up to look for me, I wouldn't go anywhere. I'd just go on lying here, drifting, nuzzling into my mattress and listening to birdsong. Before I get up, I allow my hands to rest for a moment, one on my hip, the other lying across my little flattened breasts. I think how my skin's like a stranger's too. It's smooth and cotton-soft. I press down gently, picturing the blood moving steadily, cleverly, inside. Behind the curtains, a wood pigeon calls, low, loud and close.

Then suddenly, as if I truly am someone else, I know exactly what it is I want to do. As if I'm someone strong and impulsive, (someone like Diana), I'm full of resolve as I sit up on my bed, as I fold back the sheet and swing my feet down to the floor. I cross the room to where my school bag is lying in a heap behind the open door. I push the door to and, still light-headed, but determined, I crouch over the bag and tug at the zip. I reach for the metal box of photographs I've stashed inside.

I'm going to see my mother, it's that simple.

I hold the box very lightly between my palms. It's cool against my lap and more solid, somehow more real, than my bony fingers or my lanky thighs. I'm aware that I'm naked, but it doesn't bother me right now. In fact, in a funny way, it makes me braver still. I press a thumb against the padlock. It shouldn't be difficult to break. I leave the box where it is for the moment and wander around the room, picking things up and setting them down. What I need is something hard and sharp, like a stone. Something to smash the lock open cleanly and quickly, without much noise. I drop back down to rummage on the floor. I'm sitting in a stripe of daylight that's crept in between the curtains. It rests wide, warm hands against my back. Gently, it fingers the long, curved wire of my spine. Digging through the clothes and magazines, all the lipstick-printed tissues, I find the carved, wooden corner of Diana's jewellery case. I don't stop to think, to worry. I feel as careless, as selfish, as the cat, as I prowl naked around my room. I don't believe anyone will catch me, not unless I decide that what I want is to be caught. I open the case and start trawling among the tangle of beads and bracelets, scratching my palms on the sharp, glittering hooks of what seems like a hundred mismatched earrings. I pick out a weighty silver crucifix, wondering if this will do. I imagine bringing it down hard, bullet-fast, against the lock.

But then, there, underneath it, among the greenish dust and crumbs, I find a key. It's a tiny, flimsy looking thing, like the key to a doll's house. The yellow metal glints cheaply against the case's torn silk lining.

Behind the curtains, the birds continue their music.

And I'm not floating anymore, but moving through mud. Nevertheless, I'm still determined. I wade back over to the bag. The key's so light I can hardly feel it in my fingers. It seems magical.

Of course it fits the padlock. Straight away, it turns.

Downstairs, the doorbell rings.

"Janie!" Rene barks. "Janie, I need you down here right now."

And like that, the spell is broken. Rene will be up for me any minute and I'm sitting, scrawny and naked, on my messed-up bedroom floor. My ribs are jumping with my breath and the shadows between them are clear and ugly. My body's all my own once more. Panting, I ram the box, with the key still in the lock, back into my school bag and when it doesn't want to fit, I handle it roughly, forcing it deep down among the papers and the textbooks and all the dried-up, lidless pens.

"Janie!" Rene shouts again, and I jump up, looking about frantically for something clean to wear.

When I finally get downstairs, Rene comes flapping out into the hall to meet me. She looks like a giant seagull in her pale blouse and a long grey skirt, her head peck-peck-pecking towards me. She's rearranged her hair in a way I've never seen before. It's pinned up in a complicated arrangement of clips, perhaps attempting sophistication, except that something has obviously gone wrong. The hair behind her ears is puffing out in a frizzy silvery ruff, and it's not just her foundation that's melting now. There are brown spider legs of mascara creeping on to the skin around her eyes and a smudge of something white and powdery, caught dead in the centre of her livid left cheek. On the bottom step, she catches me, clamping a hand on each of my shoulders while she looks me, slowly, up and then back down. She sighs. I'm wearing a dress - a clean dress - I'd thought that's what she wanted. I see now that it isn't. Not this dress anyway. It's Diana's', a black thing with short crocheted sleeves and a hem of lace around the bottom. On Diana, it looks classy or trashy, depending on her mood. On me, I realise, it's just not right. It's supposed to be short, but it dangles to my knees and the neckline gapes where it should be filled with proper, grown-up breasts. I see myself through Rene's beady eyes: a scrappy little rag-doll thing, dressed in scraps and rags.

I wonder if I should tell Rene about the very un-Rene-like smudge across her face - about the general way she seems to be coming undone - but when she smiles, she does nothing to hide the effort behind it. Her skin wrinkles stiffly as if there's a secret system of tiny, buried hooks operating her mouth. So I don't say anything at all.

As she leads me towards the living room's closed door, the sounds of Dad's voice and his CD merge into a drone. Moving down the hall, there's a moment when we pass the kitchen that's like climbing inside a boiling metal pipe and I can't help noticing the way the air has coloured here too, thickening into a brownish haze. There's quite a smell as well, like burning wool. *Mmm*, I think, *dinner*.

In the living room, Dad and Pete are sitting opposite each other in the high-backed leather armchairs like contestants in a quiz show. Though Dad's the only one talking - something detailed and rambling about a medical examining board - they're both nodding as they knock back tumblers of whisky. On the coffee table between them, the bottle gleams, half-full. It's the posh stuff too; the bottle Dad usually keeps in his study upstairs. The piano music changes into something more rousing, with horns. Still hanging on to her tight, resistant little smile, Rene steps past me, and goes over to the stereo. She turns it down.

"Well, Janie, aren't you going to say hello?"

Pete turns his head and looks at me. He smiles. I don't think it's a fake smile. He's wearing a sensible pair of wire-rimmed glasses that I've never seen before. He looks very different to the man in the orange T-shirt and shorts, the man who made Rene scream outside our house. Today, in his glasses, and his ironed, mint-coloured shirt, he's old, though behind those clean, square lenses, there's a light. A hope? Or perhaps just some kind of whisky-desperation, shining in his clear, blue eyes. The cat is sitting, purring, on his knee.

"Look at you," he says softly. "Come over here and say hello."

I glance at Dad, who's still nodding, staring at something, or perhaps nothing, on Pete's shoe. I go over to their chairs.

"Hello Uncle Pete."

He snatches at my wrist to pull me in closer. He lifts his cheek for me to kiss.

There's a small, spiky clump of hair on his jaw that he's

missed when shaving. He smells like Dad - like Dad's whisky - and this close, even with the glasses in the way, his eyes are shockingly blue. But he looks happy, I think, or like he wants to be happy anyway. I find myself remembering when he came to the house two years ago, how different he was then, sitting on the step with his head in his hands, the rain streaming like silver necklaces through his fingers. And I remember how quietly he went away when the police finally came, as if he'd been waiting for them all along. The gesture, the melodrama of it, feels familiar. It seems like something Diana has done, or something I might even do one day, and for a second or two I almost feel sorry for him. Or on his side. Or something. But then I see the way his heavy fingers are drawing circles in the cat's dense fur. I see the size and strength of his big red knuckles and I make myself remember who he is. Who he really is. I straighten up and turn away.

"Well," says Rene, striding over to us. "I think we might as well start dinner, seeing as Diana doesn't seem to be gracing us with her presence tonight. Shall we go through?" But when she reaches Pete's chair, she stops, looms over him. Carefully she lets one hand fall, to touch his neck. "Pete," she says, "can I borrow you in the kitchen for a moment? I could do with a hand opening the wine."

Dad and I trail obediently away from them. When I push open the door to the dining room, it's a shock. Everywhere, there are pale, fatheaded roses dipped in candlelight. Flames are gently puttering from several brand new candlesticks spaced evenly about the room. They make the shadows into something pretty and fill the waiting wine glasses with tiny pools of light. The table is draped in a delicately embroidered blue cloth that I've never seen before and all the cutlery is gleaming. Dad and I stand in the doorway, staring.

"What has she done?" one of us whispers.

The smell of roses is heady, fruity; so powerful it even manages to hide the scent of singed things from the kitchen. It's the sort of smell that makes you want to lie down quietly on the floor. Dad rests his hand, like a cap, upon my head.

"Hadn't we better find our seats?"

In his other hand, he's carrying the whisky bottle. He holds it before him, like a trophy, as he slides around the table. The napkins, I see, have been folded, origami-style, to look like birds. When Dad sits down, he puts the whisky bottle straight on top of his, squashing it flat.

I'm just tucking my knees under the table when Aunt Rene and Pete return. They arrive like a series of floats in the August carnival. First comes the tray, with it's basket of bread and glinting dishes, held aloft, with Rene just behind. Next there's Pete, an open bottle of wine - one red, one white - in each fist and behind him, a small group of eager zigzagging flies. *Tourists,* I think, *from the kitchen.*

"To start," Rene declares, "salmon and mushroom-walnut mousse!"

Pete sets the wine down in the centre of the table and then reaches across to move two of the candlesticks so that Rene can set her tray down on the sideboard. As he swings them out of the way, the flames rise and lean and jump, scattering handfuls of hot white wax into the scented air. I watch Rene watching the wax drops too, her eyes following them all the way down to the dining room carpet. Her smile tightens again, but she doesn't go running off for kitchen towels or a damp sponge. Instead she turns and starts shuffling the plates together. She doesn't say a single word. Grinning at the tablecloth, Pete awkwardly sits down.

I stare at the mousse when she places it before me. It's the shape of a tennis ball, cut in half, and in the candlelight it's difficult to tell what colour it is. It's sort of pink and sort of grey. Sort of mottled-looking too. What it reminds me of, with its pattern like bruises and its tiny darker threads, is an old woman's waterlogged ankle. Experimentally, I press my knife across the top. The whole thing quivers violently, but refuses to part. I drop my knife as quietly as I can and reach for the breadbasket instead.

It's then that the front door bangs open. There's what sounds like a small scuffle in the hall, and Diana laughs. I should be relieved - she's back with us, she's safe - but the sight of her at the car park over West Beach seems far removed from me right now. Like I might have dreamt it, made it up. I glance from Dad to Rene to Uncle Pete. Apart from me, nobody's registering the front door opening. Nobody's looking at anything except their personal mounds of wobbling mousse. But then Diana bursts into the dining room, seeming to drag in with her all the humidity from outside, as well as the kitchen's heat and smoke, and you can't help looking. Or worrying. I can feel the tension, a gritted-teeth fury from across the table. I don't need to look over to know that Rene's already wishing that my sister hadn't come.

Diana sways slightly, one strap from her strappy red top

peeling down her smooth, brown shoulder. Her lipstick's red too, a thick, cheery poster-paint scarlet. Her mouth looks enormous, but she isn't smiling. After a moment, Carl appears in the doorway just behind her. He looks too tall and dopey, a bit embarrassed. The scent of roses shrivels before the smell of them; their sweet hand-rolled cigarettes and their cider.

"Hi Diana," I say, since no one else does.

Her eyes find me. It only takes a second or two for her to focus, not as long as I'd have thought.

"You're wearing my dress," she says thickly and then leans forward across the table, the flickering candlelight dabbing her perfect cleavage with spots like butter. She pours herself a glass of red wine, downs it, and then pours another.

"Well!" she says. "Isn't this cosy?"

Dad picks up the whisky bottle and fills his own glass to the top.

The wine has left two little marks, like cuts, at the corners of my sister's brilliant red mouth. As she keeps drinking, bending over her glass, almost into it, like a cat lapping milk, her dark hair falls in ragged springs before her face. Behind the hair, her eyes glitter out at us. Chunks of smashed, black glass.

I don't think I've ever seen her looking more dangerous, or more beautiful. And it isn't just me - Carl, Dad, even Uncle Pete - they cannot take their eyes off her. Only Rene looks unimpressed. Determinedly, she clutches two extra plates of her laboriously prepared, alien mousse.

"Sit down," she says. "Right now."

And they do, Diana and Carl. They drop into the nearest chairs immediately. Pete, who happens to be seated next to Diana, squares his shoulders and leans towards her. Something cracks very softly in his back.

"Hello Diana," he says. "It's been a long time."

She twists her neck and stares at him, but she refuses to see him, or to hear him. Her glossy red smile's still there, but her eyes have grown harder and more intense. I know those eyes. And I can guess that inside his toothpaste coloured shirt, Pete's probably already started sweating; beginning to squirm. Very slowly, Diana turns away from him. Of course, she won't reply. And I wonder how I ever could have worried that my big sister might be vulnerable in any way, in danger even? As she looms over the plates, her eyes flash silver and her half-open mouth glints as though it's full of tiny hidden knives. In the candlelight, she's menacing, impenetrable, perfectly contained, even as her wineglass sways, scattering the tablecloth with fat, dark, bloodlike drops. My head reels as I watch them fall and I'm wondering all over again, what was she doing at the car park? Can it really be possible that she knows the ice-cream man? That they are friends? I remember how she leant towards him, how she bowed her head and laughed.

She laughed.

And then it occurs to me, like it did before; *don't they often work in pairs, in couples?* The thought only comes at me for a second, it flickers by snake-fast before it's gone, but nonetheless I'm shocked that I could even think it at all. *I'm still sick,* I tell myself. *I must be.* Heat rises from my neck, creeps up my face. I'm sickening, even to myself.

I bend over my starter, frightened suddenly that I might unwittingly catch Diana's eye. There's a row of grapes on cocktail sticks arranged around the far side of my plate. They look like skewered eyeballs. I try to pick one up without wincing, but there's no way that I can do it.

"What's this?" Diana says, raising her knife. "Some kind of fish thing?"

"It's salmon and mushroom-walnut mousse," Pete says. He's not giving up.

"I can't eat it," Diana says, pushing at her plate. "I'm pregnant, remember? No pate, no soft eggs, no supermarket salad."

If that were true, I think, *then no alcohol either*, and I'm sure everyone is thinking the exact same thing, but not one of us is about to say it out loud. Not even Rene.

"Dad," Diana says, "did you tell Uncle Pete that I've got myself pregnant?"

She keeps her tone light, Canderel-sweet, and it raises the hairs on the back of my neck. Dad freezes, a hunk of bread trembling before his opening mouth. He's gazing at Diana with such desperation I can hardly look at him. He looks too frail suddenly, too sad. Carl places one of his large clumsy paws over my sister's wrist. I don't know if he's trying to support her or restrain her. It doesn't matter. She shakes him off; he isn't there.

"Yes, a baby," says Diana. She's almost singing. "A lovely, bouncing - what's the word? Bonny, yes. A bonny little baby. I wonder what it'll be, a boy or a girl? What do you think, Peter? *Uncle Pete*?"

She turns deliberately towards him. He isn't smiling

anymore. His face has gone very still and very blank.

"Oh, but I forgot!" Diana trills. "You don't like children, do you, Uncle Pete?"

I snatch a glance at Rene and her eyes have deepened. They're the same as my sister's now. Hostile, and simmering beneath a dark unbreakable seal.

"Diana," she says slowly, "that is enough."

"But I haven't even started yet" my sister murmurs.

"What?" I say. "What's going on?"

No one looks at me.

"Diana," Rene says. "I think you'd better go."

Behind his bread, Dad's nodding.

"This is my house," Diana replies. "If anyone's leaving, it should be him."

And with that, she pushes Pete's shoulder. It's a hard push, I see the muscle rise above her elbow, but he doesn't move. He sits there like a rock, solid and expressionless, scraped bare.

"*Diana,*" Rene growls.

Beside my sister, Carl shovels more mousse into his mouth. He's the only one of us eating. His lips move around and around like a machine, but he's not fooling anyone. He's looking scared.

Diana and Rene glare at one another across the wine bottles. The candles sputter light, and then shade, over their faces. Rene rolls her bread knife back and forth against her plate and my ears pop as though the air pressure's changing. As though, if the candle flames should stretch high enough, the room might actually explode... I feel the blood rushing to my head, thumping and thickening, squeezing up inside my skull. Desperately, I wish I were upstairs. I wish I were folded safely back inside my bed. Drifting in the empty quiet of my room.

"Stop," I say, but no one's listening.

Diana leans forward, her hair almost falling into the flames.

"You're so stupid, Rene, so thick, can't you see that? Anyone can see that. How can you invite him here after all he's done to you? How can you be seeing him again?"

"I want you out of this house," Rene hisses, "right now!"

"Don't you get it?" Diana asks, picking up her glass, splashing wine across her own brown wrist. "You just don't get it do you? I'm only trying to protect you here. I'm the only one in this whole fucked up family who actually cares."

Rene laughs. It's a low breathy sound. "Why, Diana?" she asks. "Why do you care? After all, what are you - what have you ever been - to me?"

Diana's face falls apart. In the soft, skittering light, it seems to actually melt. It's like we're back in that cave again, just after she first told me that she was pregnant, and I know that the very worst thing's about to happen; that my sister's going to cry.

I don't want to see it. I won't see it.

Let the rest of them scream and shout and send their chairs wheeling as they rise, I sink away from all of them. I lay my head down gently on the pretty blue cloth. I put my hands over my ears. While Rene raises both her hands and Diana rushes past, I don't move a muscle. I simply rest there, unthinking, unfeeling, eyeball-to-eyeball with a fat, green grape.

"I'm gone," I tell it in a whisper. "Already, I'm not here."

Sixteen

It's dark in the garden, but as warm as day. The little black dress, Diana's dress, is sticking to my armpits and the small of my back. As I walk out through the long grass, I'm pleased I didn't bother wearing shoes. The grass bends softly, soothingly, beneath the soles of my feet. It doesn't break, but springs back gently, stroking my calves and catching in the line of lace that runs around the bottom of my skirt. The air is damper than it's been for a very long time as though the bushes and trees are panting wetly. They've gathered in around me, whisper-close.

The sunlounger's still there, a low, long block like a parcel - a present meant just for me - pushed up against the tree trunks. I walk over and lie down. The shadows and rustling sounds don't bother me tonight. Tonight the garden feels like a refuge. It's very peaceful, very mine. Directly above me, the branches make a dense, dark roof, but if I stare straight ahead, back towards the house, I can see the sky. The sky is black, but not a true black, not like the silhouette of our roof and chimneys. There aren't any stars out, but every now and then, there's a flicker of distant lightening. I can't hear any thunder yet, but the weather's bound to break, I think. It has to. I can smell it in the air, the promise of rain, that metal smell beneath the flowers. I watch the sky. With each soft flash, it turns to silver and shimmers gently closer. When our kitchen light bursts on, branding the grass nearest the house with squares of gold, I have to stop myself from jumping. As far as I can see, it's the only light on in the house. Diana, Carl, Rene, Pete - all of them - they've gone. Diana, of course, was the first to leave - sobbing and slamming doors. Carl went after her, shuffling apologetically away with his head down, muttering a stream of slurry thank yous for Rene's inedible salmon mousse. With the pair of them out of there, perhaps we could have managed to carry on, but Uncle Pete was having none of it.

"I'm sorry, Rene," he said, "but I can't do this. Not now. I'm going to the pub."

With her long chin trembling, Rene stared into the candles for a while and then decided to go with him. And I couldn't decide which was worse - Pete and Rene sitting consolingly, cosily, in a pub together, or Rene ripping tissues from the box and wailing, in her room upstairs, alone?

So then only Dad and I remained. I left him sitting at the dining table, with his hands wrapped around the whisky bottle. So many people had already flown away that he didn't even glance up when I left the room to come out here. It doesn't matter. It's a relief to have escaped. On my own, on my ratty, comfortable sunlounger, I lie very still, listening to the leaves and the waves. You can hear the sea very clearly, there's no traffic on the road tonight. I gaze up into the light that comes and goes across the sky and wait for the rain. I imagine how it will sound when it finally arrives; the gentle tap-tapping.

When I was young, very young - three, or maybe four - I had a transparent, smeary rain cover on my pushchair. The sound of the rain falling on the leaves would be like that, I think, and suddenly I can remember it so clearly; the sharp clicking noise of the cover being clipped hastily into place, the raindrops bursting and drumming just inches from my face, shattering into diamonds all around me. I'd push my nose towards the splashes through the plastic and stick out my tongue, trying to lick them, to taste them, like a kitten. With a toddler's logic, I didn't think anybody could see what I was doing through that boxy streaky case, but beyond the plastic and the raindrops, Diana would roll her eyes at me. While I was dry and cosy, she was always soaking, her gold hair a darkened bronze, sticking flatly to her face. She'd step back from clipping on the cover and disappear to take the handles and away we'd race, with the silver rain and shining paving stones flying by on either side. I remember Diana swearing as she ran. Neither one of us would have understood how silly the words must have sounded in her high-pitched little-kid voice. She must have been letting off steam because my nursery teacher had told her off. She was always telling Diana off because she wasn't supposed to collect me on her own, (she saw straight through Diana's claims that Dad or Rene were waiting in the car or on the High Street or just out of sight, outside), and because I was so often collected late. But I didn't care. I loved the sound of my sister's curses. They were like a song, streaming through the streaming world.

It's startling how brilliantly this memory is coming back to me, through the darkness and the heat. Through all these years. For a moment I feel it deeply, that sense, almost of invisibility, behind my rain cover, and the knowledge that I was safe.

But where's Diana now?

I picture her outside, perhaps on the beach somewhere, standing barefoot on the grey sand or climbing over the rocks to reach her cave. She'll get soaked tonight, I think. She still won't wear a coat, or a hood. She'd never carry an umbrella. I think about the way she crumpled at Rene's words and I wonder if Carl will have stayed there with her, to look after her. I hope so, I really hope so. And then I'm wondering about the Missing Girls too. Their open, freckled faces flit and vanish with the lightning, across the soft black sky. I hope they've got each other still. I hope they're not alone. *Where are you?* I wonder. I think it over and over so that it becomes almost a prayer. But I'm not even sure who I'm missing anymore; who it is I'm calling back.

When I return to the house, Dad's in the kitchen, standing at the sink. He turns and smiles at me and I squint back. After being outside, everything inside is too stark. Too brightly gold. The bin is full of unidentifiable food, brown things and orange things, some of it still steaming. Rene's abandoned dinner. The flies crawl away down the bin's sides or circle in the air a foot or so above its stuffed, plastic mouth. Even they are being careful not to creep too close.

"Well," I say, "I thought that went well." And Dad, humpbacked over a mountain of dirty pots and plates, starts quietly to laugh.

I pick up a tea towel and go and stand beside him. I wait for his shoulders to stop shaking. He uses the back of his wrist to dab at his eyes and then he washes, while I dry. The night presses in against the window and neither of us says anything for several minutes. But then, after most of the cutlery is clean and all the serving spoons are put away, I can't help it, I have to ask:

"Dad, what did Diana mean when she said about Uncle Pete not liking children?"

Dad stares down at the soupy dishwater between his fingers.

"Oh, Janie, I really don't think you want to know."

"But I do. I do."

He looks at me sideways, a spatter of washing up suds clinging to his chin like a tiny cobweb. His eyes are very pink, perhaps from the whisky.

"Do you?"

"I'm not a kid anymore, Dad."

He lifts a heavy ceramic mixing bowl from the side, submerges it in the sink and then raises it again to empty it. A stream of dirty water gushes out in front of him, longer and deeper than any sigh.

"You already know your Aunt came to us because she was having problems with Pete? Because Pete was... violent."

I nod, even though Dad isn't looking at me.

"Well, when he hit her - attacked her - that last time, it was worse than before. He put her in hospital. Actually, he'd put her in hospital on several occasions, but this time things were different. Rene was pregnant. She miscarried at eighteen weeks. Do you know what miscarry means?"

"Dad," I say, "of course I do." But I only say it very gently.

He picks up the mixing bowl again and peers inside and I wait for him to say something else, something more. I need to be certain. After a minute or so, I clear my throat.

"Are you sure that Diana didn't mean anything else by it, Dad? Are you sure that's all?"

He glances at me briefly - those sideways eyes again.

"Janie," he murmurs. "Isn't that enough?" His dishcloth goes swishing around the bowl, making slapping noises, little squeaks. "Everything was very sad back then. Rene was devastated. Desperate... I think that's why she was so keen to come here, to help us out." Dad pauses, plucks the dishcloth out by one swollen dripping corner. When it's free he clears his throat. "You were so tiny when your mother went, and God knows I needed the help... I think Rene thought she could make everything all right. She'd really wanted that baby, you see... We both hoped it might work out, somehow, for everyone..."

He shakes his head as he finally passes me the bowl. I struggle to wrap the tea towel around it, to hold it with both hands. I can't help thinking about what Rene said to Diana at the dinner table. *"What have you ever been to me?"* I think about the dark way that she'll look at us sometimes. And then I'm wondering how deep it goes, Rene's disappointment.

"It didn't work out though, did it?"

Dad's cloth moves in circles around a small, clean cup.

"No," he says. "No, it didn't."

And now every word from him is like a sigh.

I listen to the slosh of the water and the hum of the fridge as Dad passes me his plates and pots and pans. Mostly they're shining, but every now and then I have to pass him something back, a dripping plastic jug or a casserole dish, that's streaked with sauce or has burnt black scales caught beneath a rim. The cloth in my hands grows sodden so that after a while I'm not really drying anything, just smearing the wet spots around, but, just like Dad, I keep on going.

"Partly, I blame myself," he murmurs.

I don't look up at him, but at the smeary wine glass in my hands.

I know it isn't his fault, and that it's not completely Rene's fault either. I remember how, when I was little, the other kids would often mistake Rene for my mother. I was always quick to put them right.

"She's not my mum," I'd say. "My mother isn't here right now." And when they asked me where she was, I'd make up stories. My mother was away, working. She was an actress in Hollywood or doing secret research for the government. She was a spy. She was in prison. She was a magician's assistant in Las Vegas; she wore feathers and a bikini and disappeared behind a screen...

Never, not even in my more grey and homely daydreams, never once did I pretend that Rene was my Mum. Diana would probably have killed me if I had, though it wasn't just Diana's fault. If I'm honest, we were united against Aunt Rene from the start.

And I feel like I should perhaps say something about this to Dad, make some confession, but I can't. It's all too vague. I feel too shaky. In the black windowpane, Dad's reflected in streaks and patches. There's a shiny spot on the end of his nose and another on his teeth, where his mouth is open as he works. The white of his reflected shirt collar looks too white, while the shadows in his cheeks and at his throat are as deep as holes. In the glass he's nothing but a ghost, and beside him I'm the same. The night on the other side of the window is so thick and black it's swallowing us both. And I can't see anything beyond our reflections, not the trees, or the grass. My sunlounger has long since ceased to exist... I think how Dad wouldn't have been able to see me as I lay outside, while he paused before the sink. And I think how anyone could be out there, right now; how they could be staring straight back in. But I'm not going to start spooking myself again. Not now. I close my eyes, but I can still see us, me and Dad, our hazy outlines, our faces made of streaks and shining patches.

"Dad, what made Mum go?"

As the words fall out of me, I feel less real than ever. I can't believe I've said them, so easily, after all this time. I keep my eyes closed. I'm hardly breathing and after a minute or so, I hear the clink of the plug chain and then the thirsty gulping sounds of water disappearing down the drain. When

I open my eyes, the sink is empty and Dad is frowning down at his red, water-wrinkled palms. They have nothing left to wash.

"She did it for you. I think. I expect that's what she told herself, anyway. That it was the right thing to do. She never thought that she was good enough, strong enough, for you kids. She didn't believe that she could keep you safe."

As he speaks, Dad doesn't move, but he changes, growing even older. Even thinner. Pink blotches have appeared beneath his eyes and on the side of his mouth, and down his chin. Everything about him looks raw and tender. I turn away from his reality to his ghost face in the window. He feels me watching him.

"Janie..." he says before I can ask him what he means. "Please, Janie. I think that really is enough questions for tonight. More than enough."

I nod and what there is of my reflection barely flutters. I stare into the darkness and realise that the lightning's stopped, and that I haven't seen it flicker the whole time I've been inside. The storm, I think, isn't coming, after all.

It's much, much later, when Diana makes it home. I've been in bed for hours and for a moment, when she wakes me, I think it's morning. It takes me a little while to realise that my eyes are actually open and that it's still night, some deep, dark pre-dawn hour when the birds are asleep. The window is open wide and at first, Diana's just a shape, a surprisingly quiet shape, rising up against it. She doesn't seem to walk towards me, but just keeps growing larger and larger until suddenly she's everywhere. I think that I might be imagining things again, that I might be dreaming, but then she's on my bed, crawling up beside me. I breathe her in. Her face hangs over mine and her hair falls between us, brushing my blinking eyes, my mouth. I realise that it's damp - my sister's hair - and that she smells, very strongly, of the sea.

"Diana," I whisper, "what have you been doing?"

She doesn't reply, but leans closer. It's too dark to see her features, but as her wet head lolls against my cheek, her salt and seaweed smell envelops me. For a moment, it's overwhelming, but then she sinks down further, the sheets whispering against her breasts, her hips and legs. Finally she's lying with her face against my collarbone, the top of her head filling the space beneath my chin. I draw back the covers and pull her closer still.

"Janie," she murmurs into my throat, "what am I going to do?"

I feel each word break open, warm and soft against my skin. I wrap my arms around her. Her vest is clammy, wrinkled, and lined with grit, but her back between the straps is cool and smooth. I think of her tattoo, that little blurry orchid, lost against the dark.

"I don't know if I can do this, Janie, but... But I'd never do what she did to us. I won't let that happen. Never. Never."

There are tears with her words now, but she's drunk, I tell myself. That's all. It's just her rambling, her melodrama. Salt water, I think, everywhere.

"It's ok." I tell her. "It's all ok."

I move my hands up and run my fingers through her snarled, wet hair. I think about being little again. Not the pushchair this time, but how it was when I had a nightmare, how she'd do this for me. How she'd hold me tight and stroke me still.

There are little flinty pebbles caught in my sister's hair. They feel like tiny teeth beneath my fingertips and there are several sticky clumps of drying sand. I won't ask her again what she's been doing. I don't want to know.

"It's ok," I say instead. "We've got each other."

And already, her tears have slowed. Her breathing's quieter, steadier, and I feel better too. She's warm beside me. She's back beside me. I hold my sister tight, feeling the way she loosens and empties in my arms as she drifts away from me and into sleep. I close my eyes and burrow closer and I tell myself that we're safe, that everything is peaceful and right between us, after all.

Except. In the darkness.

The darkness ripples, dividing into layers, into gauzy shapes that might be faces. Pictures that, at first, I can't quite see. There are so many secrets that could be hiding here. There's Diana in her red top, laughing with the ice-cream man. And there's Uncle Pete and there's our mother, and there's the box that I have stolen, that's waiting in my bag.

And there's the knife too. I can't forget about the knife.

I squeeze my eyes shut tighter, willing sleep to roll back over me, into me, to sweep away such thoughts. I seize my sister's shoulders and grip her thighs between my knees. As I curl up, doing my best to fit my body around hers, I'm determined to keep things simple (Diana's with me, I need her. That is all). But now I've remembered it, that sharp little knife won't stop turning over in my mind. And though I'm doing my absolute best to get comfortable - to snuggle up like we used to, to lose myself in my sister's flesh - her small, round belly is pressing awkwardly between us. Like something separate. A barrier. A stranger's warm red hand.

Seventeen

"Let's play 'Terrorists'" Diana whispers.

She's leaning over me, and the way that her eyes are glittering, so darkly, makes me think of Space; of shimmering stars and distant planets. There's a deep velvet blackness that goes on and on and on, like there's an entire secret Universe inside her... But it makes her laugh, the way I'm gazing back at her. It makes her grab my shoulders and swoop down closer. She shakes me a little and the paintbrush tips of her thick blonde plaits whisk against my face. They're tickling my cheeks, my nose, and before I know it, I'm giggling as well.

I can't help it; she's irresistible. Contagious. And I'm lying flat on my back, underneath her on the bed.

It's a Sunday afternoon. Rain is drumming on the windowpanes with impatient schoolteacher fingers. It's drip-drip-dripping from the cracks in the guttering and gushing from the pipes. We often seem to play 'Terrorists' on days like this, when it's not just the house that feels closed in and dank and strangely empty, it's the whole world. The sky hovers, grey-faced and teary, filling every window with a mournful, murky light. It's the kind of day when all my books and comics have been read a hundred times and all my toys are uninspiring. My felt-tip pens have all dried up and my dolls are lying in a heap, their plastic limbs poking out at frenzied angles. They're empty eyed and dead-looking, every one of them the same.

In the hallway, Dad's study door is firmly closed and downstairs, in the kitchen, Rene is bristling, like the kitten. If I were to wander in there (bored, so bored), she'd reel away from me, ready to bite and scratch before I opened my mouth to ask for anything, before I looked at anything, even.

"Paws off!" she'd hiss, clawing an open bag of bread, a pint of milk, the biscuit jar, out of my reach. She'd drive me back into the doorway, where she'd watch as I went fleeing back upstairs. Back to my abandoned pyre of dusty dolls, to my stacks of re-read books. It's the kind of day that seems so endless that you might just die of boredom.

If you didn't have a sister, that is. A sister like Diana.

"Come on," she says. "Come with me." And we go creeping along the hallway; we tiptoe down the stairs.

If Rene's still in the kitchen, we have to wait (huddled together, our faces pushed between the banisters) for her to leave before we can slip out through the back door and around the side of the house. It's an unwritten rule: 'Terrorists' can only be played among the shadows and the secrets of the cellar. And, as soon as we get the chance, we dart outside. Through veils of misty rain, the garden's touched with silver and there's a powerful smell of rich, rotting earth. We run with our heads down, the backs of our necks lashed with icy water, our bare legs whipped by the long, wet grass. Almost instantly, we're soaked. We never wear coats for the dash and sometimes not even shoes. The moment 'Terrorists' is decided, normal rules, normal worries, don't apply. And besides, the raw ravaging freshness of the air, our hunched shoulders and our shivering - the exhilaration of escape - it's all a part of it. Like the ghost house creak of the little side door is a part of it, and our silence on the cellar stairs.

Aware of the grown-ups moving from room to room, just overhead, we're silent as we descend. And careful too. You have to be. For some weird reason, the light cord is located at the bottom of the steps, and once the little wooden door's whine-banged shut again behind us, it's pitch-black on the stairs. We fumble our way down slowly with our feet feeling for the step directly below, and our hands creeping and pressing along the soft, damp walls. Our groping fingers will often come away coated in brickwork crumbs and sometimes I'll forget myself. I'll pause to wipe this spongy grit on my cotton skirt or jumper and then cry out, panicking when my hands flail against nothing in the blackness, unable, momentarily, to relocate the wall. And each time, Diana will turn on me, hushing me as she steadies me, reminding me urgently that I mustn't make a sound. It's not that we've been told specifically that we're not allowed to play down in the cellar, it's something instinctive that we just know.

There are spider's webs down there and a funny churchy

smell, which is a mixture of sallow books and dusty stone, and something else - something more cloying, and more nauseating - something dead? In the past, we've found dead beetles piled up in the corners, and once, a tiny stiffened mouse. But mostly the cellar is simply filled with old and broken things. There are moth-eaten mounds of forgotten fabric, stained rugs and faded curtains, ancient crusty discarded clothes. There's a whole workshop's worth of busted furniture; backless chairs and splintered drawers. A furred up fridge without a door. A rusted, hinge-less garden gate. Generally, there are a great many sharp things and dirty things down here, and further mysterious objects packed away in boxes and bin-bags sealed with yellowed tape and grimy string. There are many things down here that are *unsuitable for children*, which is one of the reasons why we love it.

At first we love it, anyway.

The way I think I love the game 'Terrorists' before it actually begins.

At the start, although it's terrifying, it's also thrilling. At the bottom of the steps Diana tugs on the grubby light cord, and suddenly, starkly exposed beneath the fluorescent strip, we're no longer worried about being heard upstairs. We giggle wildly, recklessly; we're so scared. They're hard and breathless, these giggles. I feel them breaking open high up in my chest. Tough little bubbles, bursting. It's almost painful. The bluish, alien light flickers like lightning as it comes on and we blink, startled by the icy glare, by the shadows leaping up in every corner. In the flicker, all the crooked, broken things are bunched into shapes like hunched old women; witches, or hanging dead men; crawling bodies. I'm careful not to look at anything too closely. Not even at Diana whose eyes are gleaming now, full of white, and very shiny, like a horse's eyes, a horse about to kick or run. And her teeth are china teeth. Her thick lips, bared around them, almost blue. But it's just the fluorescent beam that makes her look this way, her skin milk-white and rubbery. Like fish skin, dead skin, while the shadows beneath her eyes and in the hollows of her throat have grown deeper and more mauve looking. It's not her fault. It's a mortuary light, an interrogation room light.

Or so Diana's told me.

For she's the only one of us allowed to stay up late and watch the cop shows, the detective shows, the Real Life Crime shows from America (though even she's too young for most of them, but she wheedles and she pouts until Dad, like always, caves in). She probably got the whole idea for the game 'Terrorists' from these programmes, along with others; a highly costumed World War II romance and stories, nightly, on the news.

'Terrorists'.

Recently there has been a long-running news story about two British men held captive somewhere impossible to imagine in the stormy Middle East. They've been held, 'MISSING', for months. Though privately, I don't believe them to be truly missing. After all, their captors have released photographs, proving their existence, and to me 'missing' means complete obliteration. To me, 'missing' means becoming nothing, being nowhere. Being utterly, seamlessly gone. Although, in these photographs, the men do look as though they're disappearing in a way. Over the weeks they've grown smaller. Thinner. They're actively fading behind their handcuffs and their beards and their prominent new bones. They've started to look alike, and a bit like Jesus too. They have those same distant, painted, Disney eyes. I wonder if Diana and I are supposed to look like that when we play 'Terrorists'? I don't think so. I think we remain exactly what we are. Two frightened little girls.

But Diana holds my right wrist lightly, casually, as we pick our way around the bags and boxes towards Dad's abandoned wardrobe propped up against a peeling wall. It's only when we reach it, (this heavy scuffed wooden thing, standing lopsided where one stubby foot is missing), that she starts looking serious, her face breath-close to mine.

"Ready?" she asks and I nod. We both nod. Everything's serious now. There will be no more giggling. Diana reaches over and pulls apart the double doors.

"They're coming," she says. "Hide."

I crawl inside. It's awkward. Difficult, at first, to get comfortable on the tilted boards. But I'm only little and so it doesn't take long until I've found a way to fit. After all, I'm mostly bone. I fold up easily, *"like a deckchair"* Diana says. I rest my small hard chin on my pointed knees.

Diana nods again.

"Can you hear them?" she whispers and her eyes aren't white anymore. They're black pebbles, prize marbles made from the coolest, inkiest glass.

"I'll hold them off," she promises. "Keep very quiet and if they come for you, pretend that you're already dead."

And I'm opening my mouth, about to protest, not liking

this bit, never liking this part where I pretend that I'm a corpse. Because it makes me remember that curled up mouse body. How husk-like it seemed, how truly empty, with its gummy fur drawn back around it's gums. I can't forget those black gums. Those milky eyes.

And I'm scared as well because what if I'm too good at pretending. Too good at imagining my eyes glazing over, my limbs turning brittle, my skin stretched taut and cold? What if my mask-face stays this way? Could I actually make it happen? Could I somehow will myself gone? But Diana's already shutting the doors and I'm not saying anything, like I never say anything, even as I feel that maybe I secretly hate this game, even though it's barely begun. But it's too late now, the doors are closing. They're clicking closed. And I'm alone in here, with the stink of sawdust and a thicker, sweeter mouldy smell like the fur on rotting fruit. At school, we've read 'The Lion, the Witch and the Wardrobe', but there's no Narnia in here. There's no secret exit and no magic. No glimpse of clean white snow.

The way this wardrobe's in our cellar, and how the cellar's under our house always reminds me of another story, an anonymous story; the one that begins 'In a dark, dark wood...' It makes me think of boxes within boxes, of Russian dolls. That's how deeply I feel buried. How walled in I am, inside.

The only light is coming from the fine bluish lines running around the doors. That unreal light. Untrustworthy as lightning. And while I'm alone and mostly in the dark, Diana's out there in the cellar, with her captors.

"Please don't," I hear her say, and her voice is a broken

crawling-fluttering thing already. A butterfly with shredded wings.

"Please, anything but that. I'm begging you."

Her words send shivers through me and I tell myself what a good actress she is, even as my hands hover in the shadows, ready to close over my ears.

"Please god," she's crying. *"No!"*

And already I'm burying my face in my knees. I'm covering my ears and closing my eyes. I don't want to think about what's happening out there. I don't want to picture it. I mustn't picture it.

Diana's all right, I tell myself. And aren't I doing this, putting up with all this, for her? Because I love her and she wants this. She needs this somehow, and besides, even if I wanted to shout, or to burst out through the wardrobe doors and run, I couldn't. I'm not allowed to come out until she says so - it's the Rules - and so I do what I always do. I screw my eyes shut even tighter and against the darkness in my head, I start to count.

'Terrorists'.

It's just a game, our game. A beloved-hated game where I'm imprisoned, and Diana's tortured. It isn't real, though she has her little knife out there and sometimes, afterwards, she'll show me what they did to her, those invisible terrorists. She'll show me the careful cuts, the nicks and scratches. Bright red wounds like tiny mouths. They're always in hidden places or secret places, like on her ankles where her socks will cover them or on her ribs, her hips, her thighs. Where neither Dad nor Rene would ever see.

It's our game and she knows how to play it. She might fight and protest. She might cry even, but she won't talk. Not ever. She'll never tell them where I am. She knows how important it is not to betray me just as I understand that I must stay where I am. That there are Rules.

And sometimes, when I'm in the wardrobe, when I'm losing count repeatedly because I can't help - can't stop - listening to Diana's fractured breathing, my mind will suddenly clear and I'll sort of understand. I'll understand that this is Diana's way. The only way to keep us safe.

Eighteen

All of a sudden, as if pushed, I'm wide-awake. For several seconds, I'm blinking without seeing. And I don't understand why it's so hard to sit up straight, or why I can't quite feel my legs. And then I remember Diana. Her musky sea scent is all over me. She's all over me. And snoring. My vision clears, although at first all that I can see is my sister's thick black hair, and a shoulder, turning rosy in the early morning light. She's lying on top of me, her face still pressed against my chest, my throat. I'm numb beneath her. The house phone is ringing down the hall. I realise that this is what woke me. I listen to it for a moment, to its persistent double peals, waiting vaguely for someone else to answer it or for it to simply stop. And then I'm gazing past Diana's hair to the wan pink light filling the window, to the thin, fleshy clouds strung out beyond the trees, and I'm wondering what time it is exactly. I struggle to heave Diana's deadweight head away from my chest, to wriggle my legs out from beneath her knees. Amidst the usual scraps and clothing, my watch is lying on the floor. 5.15am. Why would anyone be ringing us this early? It can only be bad news, I think. Some emergency. Or Laura, I think, Laura at last, confused about the time difference from the States.

I half roll, half fall, out of my bed and away from Diana. My feet are coming heavily back to life, the toes crackling with pins and needles and I go staggering across the room, through our layers of junk, like a B-movie zombie. The sound of the telephone is getting to me, sliding back and forth between my ears. At the doorway I think that I hear something else. I think Diana's said something (*"Janie, hide"*); called my name perhaps? I turn back, but she's still lying there, comatose, though she's stretched out now, uncoiling like some kind of sea creature, filling my space. She must have been talking in her sleep. Muttering, as she does sometimes, especially on the nights she's been out drinking. But with the dawn light washing over her, colouring her smooth face a delicate coral and glimmering through her hair, she doesn't look wasted in any way. She just looks clean and soft and pretty. Like a much, much younger child. For a moment, I think about returning to her, about tucking her in more thoroughly or climbing in again beside her. But behind me, the telephone is still ringing. And the noise is nagging at me, pulling at me, making me worry all over again that's something's wrong, so I have to go, though my head's befuddled and my body's stiff and tired. In my bed, in her pool of blossomy light, Diana doesn't stir.

I stumble along the dusky landing, past Rene's room, the bathroom and then Dad's bedroom, to his little study at the end. All the doors are firmly closed. Nevertheless, I wonder how it is that the phone has woken me and no one else. The amount of whisky that Dad knocked back last night might explain his absence, but what about Rene? She's always been a pretty light sleeper, and an early riser too. And, now that Diana's grown older and unreliable, she's the one who seems to deal with most of our domestic emergencies, in her resigned and put-upon Rene-way. But perhaps, it occurs to me, Rene isn't home.

I lurch through the study door. It's almost as dim inside as on the landing. There's only the one small window, furred with dust, and through the deep blushing shadows, the whole room - all of Dad's books and piles of papers, his PC, the desk, even the walls - all of it seems to be quivering with the telephone's shrill rings. I reach out clumsily to make it stop and send the receiver flying. It whacks the desk and I catch it as it goes swinging back up, into the air. There is a moment in the shocked silence when I stare warily at the receiver (gazing stupidly at the rash of small black holes), before I put it to my ear. But, as soon as I do, I know that I was right to worry. I know that something's happened, or that something's very wrong.

On the other end of the line, there isn't much, but it's enough. A frail crackling, but behind it, the rasp of laboured breathing.

"H-hello?" My voice is small. I try harder, forcing myself not to whisper, "Hello?"

I'm suddenly aware of the little bones in my spine, all pressing together, and a stiffness spreading through my shoulders. Reflected in Dad's monitor, my face looks like a kid's drawing, like some kind of pinhead with dots for eyes and an uneven, oversized mouth. I've been scribbled out in crumbling charcoal and pale pink chalk; I've been smudged by grubby fingers. And through my face, with the phone beside it, I picture Rene on the other end, the receiver wavering in one hand, while she fumbles for her tissues with the other. In the middle of her face I see a stain, a small explosion, where he's smashed her bony nose. It's horrible this image, but somehow it seems safer than picturing other things. Other people on the line.

For a short while, I just stand there listening to the rasping and the crackling. I keep hoping that whoever has called will hang up; that they'll simply disappear. When they don't, I eventually dredge up the courage to speak again.

"I'm sorry. I can't really hear you. I'm going now. Goodbye."

And I'm just about to hang up when the breathing grows louder, more rapid.

"You." The word hisses out with the exhaled air. In the monitor, I watch my eyes grow wider. It isn't Rene on the line.

"Uncle Pete, is that you?"

"Uncle Pe-ete" he mimics, his voice high-pitched and gasping. "I don't know. Is that me?"

He's definitely been drinking. I sit down heavily in Dad's chair. Beneath the alcohol, there's another layer to his tone. I can't tell whether it's malice or a simple, sodden humour. Perhaps it's some kind of game? I turn away from the monitor, avoiding my eyes. I don't know what to think. I realise that I don't truly know this man at all.

"Do you want Rene?" I ask. "Um, I mean unless… Are

you looking for Rene?"

"No, I don't want Rene," he says thickly. "I've had your Aunt Rene with me all evening. It's you I'd like to speak to. Actually."

His tone is light, mocking, but nonetheless my stomach squeezes. I feel sick, empty, awkward, and embarrassed, and I'm not sure why. I wind the curly phone cord around my left arm, drawing it tight, but I can't seem to shift the receiver away from my face, my burning ear. On the other end, he breathes.

"Me?" I hear myself murmur. "What for?"

"There's no need to sound so worried," he laughs. "Don't tell me you're scared. I just wanted a little chat, that's all. I thought maybe we could finish our conversation. The one you started over dinner."

"What? I don't under..."

"You don't understand? Is that it? Course you don't. Cause you're only a little innocent thing, aren't you?" He laughs again, his laughter deeper now and leathery. "You seem to forget, I know you. I've known you since you were a tiny thing, climbing up into my lap. Going bouncing on my knee. You remember, don't you?"

"Hmmm," I say, though this is news to me. Apart from Pete being escorted away by police, I don't have many memories of him. I remember having an awareness of him, (or perhaps just someone like him), shouting in another room one Christmas time; his shadow in the hall? But then there's so much I don't remember from when I was small. It makes me careful, noncommittal.

"Hmmm," I say into his breathing and I nod, stupidly, as

if he can see me. I'm even wearing the safe, polite smile I generally reserve for teachers and other people's mothers, while I secretly plan my escape.

"Come on," he says. "You must remember... Not so innocent now though, are you?"

"What?" I say.

"Miss High and Mighty at the dinner table, judging me. You seem to forget that I know things. Things about you. About all your family. Your little secrets."

He pauses as if to let his words sink in, perhaps to give me a moment to feel my heart banging. To taste the vomit rising in the back of my throat. I look around helplessly at the piles of books and stacks of paper, my gaze sliding over blocks of text I can't take in. Everything's covered in grey gauze, pinpricks of static. I shake my head and the static moves with me.

"Uncle Pete, you've been drinking. You don't know what you're talking about. You should get some sleep." I even try out a laugh of my own, but it isn't working. My voice is trembling. My hands are trembling.

I remember how Pete didn't move when Diana pushed him, how solid and closed up he was. Even his face was like a fist. And I remember how, earlier, his eyes had flashed at me intensely, for a single moment. A flame-like flicker that perhaps, I think now, revealed the secret Pete, our old fairytale villain, the troll, the wolf skulking inside. The man we heard about when we were little, the one who hit our Aunt Rene, the one who drank. The man on the phone to me, mocking me, right now.

"Don't you talk to me about drinking," he's saying. "I

know what you and your mates get up to. I've seen you over at West Beach, hanging around that car park. I know what you're into."

I don't feel sick anymore. I'm ice-cold. I stare down at my arm, with the phone cord taut around it. It's rubbing against the long brown scab that I've already opened once, maybe twice, before. I don't feel anything. I'm no longer sure if I'm actually awake.

"The car park?" I whisper, "What do you mean?"

Pete laughs. "Come off it," he says. "Everyone knows he does more up there than sell ice-creams."

At the window the wash of pink has drained away to be replaced by an almost greenish glaring grey. As the day outside brightens, it seems to have grown darker in here. This room, the whole house, a cave. I think of the other people asleep around me, their layers of breathing, the swirling shadows. From within the walls, comes the secret rush and click of pipes. Beyond the glass, a wood pigeon calls as if there's nothing wrong.

"What are you talking about?" My voice is a flat thing, the words like wood in my mouth. "I don't know what you're talking about."

"Listen to you, Little Miss Innocent, Miss Butter-Wouldn't-Melt. You might have your dad fooled - your Aunt even - but I know what you're like. What you're like inside. You're just the same as her y'know. You're not right. Not right in the head. You're dirty, full of lies."

As he talks, my heartbeat, or perhaps it's my pulse, seems to grow louder, faster. It's thumping in my temple where it's pushed against the phone. My bloodstream's jumping with it. It's throbbing in my arm, my left arm, where the scab is bulging now, straining, between those little loops of wire.

"What are you talking about? I don't understand."

He cuts across me, no longer slurring; his voice as smooth as glass.

"Course you don't, Diana. But you better watch yourself, girl. I'm just telling you that. Consider it a friendly warning. After all, you don't want to end up like your mother, do you?

And then I'm laughing, unless I'm crying, and the receiver is slipping and almost falling, slippery as a fish in my trembling hands.

"But I'm not Diana" I'm saying, though I'm grappling with the telephone. I can't even see what I'm doing, the shadows are rolling in softly all around me and my vision is swimming with tears, with sleep, with silvery shapes. In the monitor, I'm fading. The whole room is fading. Only the window and my fingernails stand out. My nails look white, startlingly bright, crushed together on the phone.

And I'll never know if he heard me or not. By the time I've got the receiver the right way up and my giggles, my gasping, vaguely back in my control, there's only the dial tone at the other end. Pete's gone and I'm sitting alone in Dad's study, not long after dawn. I'm gazing at my hands, at the phone wire, into nothing. Nevertheless, I tell him again. More urgently, more desperately, this time.

"I'm not Diana! I'm not like her. I'm nobody, just me."

Nineteen

They've found my Missing Girls.

After that early morning 'conversation' with Uncle Pete, I slept late and so I don't find out about it until the lunchtime news.

I'm wandering into the living room, only just dressed, my head still heavy, (weighted with Pete's words), when I see the newscaster's grimly made-up face. When I hear her words.

"Human remains discovered on the heath..."

I stop where I am, with my breakfast bowl in one hand and my mouth half-full of cornflakes. Right away, my mind's clearing, Pete's fading. There isn't an ounce of sleep left in me.

The heath. It's all I can think about - *the heath* - as if the place is more important than what they've found there. On the screen, the heath isn't white, but yellow. Shot from above, it looks much smaller than it is, and almost square. There's a tent in the middle of it and people everywhere, standing about in solemn groups. A team of sleek black police dogs are lined up in a row.

Dad, sitting in his corner of the sofa, doesn't even bother glancing up. He's hiding behind his newspaper and takes no notice of the television, or of me. I feel ghostlike drifting past him, as if I'm still in bed, still dreaming. All the air and nagging worry has been knocked out of me. For several seconds I'm bloodless, empty; everything that's living in me has been sucked into that screen. Cereal bowl still in hand, I stand, swaying, over the ancient, dusty set. But then, before I know what I'm doing, I'm sinking before it. I'm on my knees. Just inches from my face, the people are drifting across the heath now, like little black bees. I reach out to touch them and feel the screen buzz against my palm. Behind me, Dad's newspaper sighs as he turns a page. Inside, my head is buzzing too. The heath vanishes, replaced by a man's face, the camera close. I take in the middle-aged skin - like folded fabric. The deep brown earnest eyes.

"Detective Jackson..." a new voice introduces him.

"Yesterday evening," he explains, "we were contacted by a local woman, who was out walking her dog when she found what she believed to be suspicious bones."

Before he can go on any further, the detective's interrupted by a tide of questions from what seems like hundreds of reporters, surging towards him off screen. He raises one hand. There's a ragged tissue in it, his small white flag.

"We've been working on the site throughout the night, and we can confirm that the remains are indeed human. I'm afraid that's all the information I can give you at the present time."

The voices return and he lets them clamour for a moment, using the tissue to dab delicately at his forehead and his eyes. One voice rises; it's a female voice, shriller and more ruthless than the rest.

"In your opinion, would you connect these findings with the recent disappearance of Tara Matlock and Stacey Hughes?"

The detective sighs.

"At this stage, we can't rule out any possibility. However, until we receive further forensic information, we must, understandably, remain cautious. That's all I can tell you right now."

The questions rush at him again, along with a strobe-like barrage of violet flashes, but the detective shrinks as the camera pans away. He's standing up, turning one narrow shoulder towards my fingers, still pressed against the screen.

"That's all," he's saying wearily. "That is all."

In my other hand, the cereal bowl has grown heavy and ice-cold. There's a thin thread of milk running between the freezing china and the floor. As I right it, I glance at Dad. I can't actually see him behind his newspaper, just his shoes. But the Missing Girls are there. The familiar picture is folded towards me, pinned down beneath Dad's thumb. It's unnerving seeing them there, as if they've come creeping up behind me, as if we're continuing to spy on one another and nothing's changed. We're all still trapped in this together. The television's buzz is growing louder. I snatch my hand away. The detective is gone and a woman fills the screen instead. She's wearing a thin black headband in her frizzy reddish hair and too much make up. A cloudless sky rises up behind her like a painting and there's a fat, brown dog bounding in circles around her feet. Tongue lolling, ears flapping, he weaves in figure of eights between her knees. The dog's eyes, like hers, are twinkling. Excited.

They're the ones, I think, *the ones who found them*.

But I can't hear what the woman's saying because of this crackling, this buzzing, in my head. I back away from the television, knocking my calf against the coffee table. I'm stumbling past Dad - I've nearly reached the doorway - when the picture changes once again.

It's another long shot that comes swooping in, scanning a crowd of jostling camera people, sound people, journalists and photographers. It takes me a moment to realise we're somewhere else now, that we're looking out over the dark tarmac of the police station car park. Between yesterday and today, it's become a different place. In the midst of the throng, walled in by uniforms, are two small women. It takes me a moment to understand who these women are, but when I do, I feel it in my stomach. The sun is glaring, but they're huddled together inside thick overcoats as though it's the middle of winter. The camera zooms right in, trying to find their faces, but I can't see much. Their hair, a flash of sunglasses, a blurry oval of pale grey skin. Inside my head, the static roars and without thinking, I raise both hands to block my ears. The cereal bowl, forgotten, falls to the carpet. There's a dazzling splash as it lands, and Dad jumps up, exclaiming, pages flying, seeing me at last. But I don't pause to apologise. I don't stop to clean it up. Already I'm swinging around, into the hall. I'm hurtling towards the front door and I don't look back.

By the time I reach the heath, I've slowed to a breathless, stretching stride. It's too hot to jog even, the hottest day so far. The air is thick but at least the buzzing in my head has dulled. It's settled into more of a low whine now, the sound of a lone mosquito in a darkened room. Outside my head too, there are more insects, real flies. They're everywhere you look; tiny, silent, falling things layered across the gaping sky and grassy mounds. Covering everything like a film of dirt. As I walk, I pick them from my skin with sweaty fingers.

I'm already on the heath, my legs whistling through grass so dry it's almost straw, when a sense of déjà vu bowls into me with such force I have to stop. I stand very still, panting with my mouth mostly closed to stop the little flies from spinning in. I tell myself that the feeling's stupid. Ridiculous. Of course I've been here before. Countless times. And there was that dream I had too - the grass around me... It's not white; I know it isn't. I saw it on the news, a patch of yellow, but the sun's so bright up here, sucking the colour out of everything... The grass around me isn't white, but almost. Like stiff, peroxide hair.

I shake my head. The flies part and come together again, forming geometric patterns, dancing and colliding in kaleidoscopic shapes. I wish I had a bottle of water. My teeth feel gritted as though with grass seeds, and there's a sweetish, earthy smell all around. I rub a hand over my nose and mouth and gaze into the distance, beyond the flies, to the things I've seen already on the news. There's the tent, with some kind of a tunnel attached; its white plastic sheeting drooping in the heat. There are the milling people, (more perhaps than on the television earlier), and there are other things they didn't show us. There's a squat red digger, its cab empty except for shadows. A little pile of dry grey earth is still caught between its teeth. There's a truck; a long, silver thing, with equipment trailing from its open doors. There's a stack of metal boxes, cameras, tripods, and what seems like miles of cables, slithering through the grass like thick black snakes. A little way off, there are two quiet, unlit ambulances. *One each*, I think.

Perhaps I'm feeling so unreal because I've just seen this scene, in part, on a screen. It's as though I'm walking onto a set with a role to play, as though I'm following directions. I look about quickly, scanning the talking, shifting bodies for a blonde woman in a long pale skirt, or the Missing Girls' mothers, or for the Missing Girls themselves, even. I can't help myself. In the end, I have to push my body forward, telling myself all the while that I'm nothing. I'm no one. That there is nobody here who is waiting just for me.

You can't get too close. There are barriers up, traffic cones and flimsy metal rods bent clumsily into the ground. There are straggly lines of yellow police tape, rippling on the hazy air as though on water. The barriers for the television crew are sturdier than the police's; tall corrugated dividers that wall off a large section of heath between the police tent and their truck. I think about what the detective said about how they've been working here all night. Surely there can't be much left to film by now? There'll be hardly anything to see. Nevertheless, I keep on walking, straight towards the front. There's quite a crowd of onlookers lined up along the police tape. They're tourists mostly, dressed in T-shirts and safari shorts, all come up here to gawp and gloat. Some have even brought their children along, pretty little kids in flip-flops and sunhats. There's a pair of boys with coloured sun block drawn in war paint stripes across their noses. I find myself staring at all their stuff; beach bags and buckets, picnic hampers even. What, I wonder, can all this mean to them - these tourists? A detour on the way to or from the beach? Is it just something else to do between the arcades and their genuine 'ye olde', overpriced cream teas? *Sickos*, I think, *freaks*, and I hold myself apart, standing just a few feet back where I'm nevertheless still able to get a fairly decent view.

Directly overhead, half a dozen gulls wheel tirelessly, drawing circle after circle across the deep blue sky.

"Mummy," a small voice whines, "what's happening?"

"Nothing," answers the woman who is standing just in front of me. She's waving a magazine slowly back and forth, through the flies, the sticky air. "Nothing's happening as far as I can see." She leans against the man on her right. "You heard anything new, Love?"

The man is big, and grey haired. He's wearing a cream coloured, open shirt. As he shrugs the woman away, his bare red belly pokes between the flapping cotton like a second, larger face. He's holding a transistor radio like a compress to his shoulder.

"Hush," he says. "I'm listening."

I'm listening too, but all I can hear from his radio is a hissing sound, that crackling again, that buzz, but softer. From further down the audience line there's mumbling too and then the laboured bleeping of someone pressing out a text message. Beyond the police tape, a woman with a ponytail is rolling up a long grey cable as though it's a giant ball of wool. A police dog watches her from the entrance to the tent tunnel. He's the only dog left as far as I can see, a stunning creature; boot polish black, lean and muscled. A Hell Hound from mythology. Between his black gums and sharp yellow teeth, his tongue hangs, pale against his dense, dark fur. Just glancing at that glistening coat makes me feel hotter still, about to boil. Flies float around the animal's square, flat head, but he doesn't snap at them. He doesn't move, and his eyes are so dull they hardly look real. Like plastic eyes, I think, sewn on to something stuffed.

A dog with a bone.

It startles me, this thought, that after everything, after all the media speculation and the house-to-house enquiries, that this is what it's come down to. The simple logic of a children's picture book. *A Dog*, I think, *A Bone*.

I don't believe that any of this is truly happening. I can't believe they're dead.

I wipe my palm across my face again and it comes back sweaty, dotted with flies. I long, suddenly, for somewhere quiet where I might sit down, or a glimpse of the sea perhaps, an indrawn breath of clean salt air. Not that it smells bad here exactly. It's not like you'd imagine, there's no rotten meat smell coming from the plastic sheeting. No hint of damp decay. There's a waft of something limey every now and then, but that's all. It's a powdery, chemical scent; green sherbet sticking with the flies against my skin. *All these flies.*

"It isn't them," says the man with the radio.

I jump and stare, just as all along the row of gawpers, others are turning towards this man, and staring. Did we hear him right? I'm not sure... I'm hoping... But before he can explain, something else starts happening. There's movement from the tent. The police dog doesn't stir as a man emerges, ducking through the white entrance. He's all dressed in white too. More white plastic - there's even a mask - but he's carrying something dark, what looks like a bin bag. It could almost be something as innocent as his dry cleaning, the way he's holding it, folded and balanced on his arms. All around me, the people are fish eyed and eel necked, straining at the police tape to get a better look. I'm swimming forward with them. We're all in this together now. We're desperate to see.

"Is it a spaceman?" one of the war paint children asks and several of the adults clustered near him start to laugh. They do it quietly, but they do it nonetheless.

A policeman rushes over to stand before us. He's young, jacketless, his sleeves rolled up. He stands with his feet apart, his hands on his hips in order to block as much of our view as he can.

"Could you stand back please, ladies and gents?" he asks. His face is flushed.

Nobody moves or seems to hear him, except perhaps to glare.

"Please?" he says.

It's like a fancy dress party. Behind the policeman, the spaceman is striding away from us with his dark plastic-wrapped prize. Behind him, the tent flap closes.

What's in that tent?

I picture yellow grass, white grass, the ground opening up

beneath my feet. I think of spades in the dirt and more parcels, stacked in piles, in pieces. I imagine hot plastic-tasting air that's almost impossible to breathe.

They just found bones at first. I can't think of them except as bones in a museum. Dinosaur bones, clean and labelled and lined up in a row. But *'human remains'*, they said on TV. Didn't that imply other things, as well as bones? They must have found something more, but what? Hair? Clothing?

What else? I wonder. *What remains?*

The buzzing-crackling in my head is back, a soft popping and a gentle smouldering. When I touch my forehead, my fingers burn and my eyes are watering. I don't touch my eyes though, not even to wipe the slow, warm tears away. I don't want to touch my eyes I realise, because I don't want to feel them in my head. I don't want to think about eyeballs in sockets. Bones beneath skin. I don't want to think about how loose, how precarious, it all is; as though we're held together with nothing more than lolly sticks and bits of string. *How easily*, I think, *it comes apart.*

Through the crackle and the flies, I realise that the policeman and the fat man are talking. I shake my head, trying to hear.

"It isn't them, is it, mate?" the fat man says. "That's what they reckon on the news."

The policeman opens his mouth. He shakes his head or almost shakes it, a crease appearing between his eyebrows. He's either worried or annoyed. The fat man stands a little straighter and even from the back of his head, from the roll of his thick red neck, I can tell he's feeling proud of himself. He's feeling pleased.

"The grave's too old. That's what they reckon."

The fat man's voice has grown louder and clearer with every word. We're all looking at him, all of us in the crowd, waiting for his inside information. He's loving the attention. "And there's only the one body," he says, "not two."

Everyone's talking now. They're leaning towards him, asking questions. I don't move. I want to ask my own questions, I'm fluttering with questions, but I can't move. I can't speak. My head feels shaky on my neck, and my arms are weak. I'm full of air. My stomach's like a little balloon, rising up inside me. *Things are coming loose...*

The policeman runs his fingers through his mouse-brown hair.

"People," he says. "People, please." But no one's pushing at his tape now.

"It isn't them," someone's saying. And the muttering moves up and down the row, like a breeze through grass: "Not them, he said. Not them."

Already they're stepping away, these tourists. They're drifting off. I hear the snap and hiss of a can opening. I blink back flies.

Even the fat man, having told his story, once, twice, and then again ("Old bones, they're saying. Been down there years"), is buttoning up his shirt and bending down, clasping at the handle of his picnic basket. He's pulling away. The woman and the whining child a girl, I see now, sucking on a turquoise ice-pole trail after him. He walks right by me, so close we almost touch. His face is waxy, but young looking; he's much younger than I'd thought. As he passes me, I catch his smell, a heady, sweaty scent. I hear his trainers squeak.

He pauses just a step or two beyond me to push his radio into the pocket of his baggy, beige shorts. I let him do this. I let him hike at his waistband and move on, calling over his shoulder to the woman and child: "Hurry up, girls. Come along."

I watch the grass part around him and then snap back behind his soft pink knees. I almost let him go. But then I'm moving, the grass rustling and breaking around me too. Before I can stop myself, I have my hand on his shoulder and there's the shock of his flesh through cotton. In a flash, I take in his bulk, his heat. His head swerves around to me. His eyes are wide and staring. His features jump and open, and then hastily, carefully, grow smooth. He thinks I'm crazy. I hear the woman with him gasp. But I don't care. I can't care because Pete's final words on the telephone have caught up with me, they're whistling through my head: *'you don't want to end up like your mother'*

"Please," I'm begging, "you've got to help me." And I can't help it; I've started shaking, crying too. My hands are trembling even as they tug forcefully at his pale damp shirtsleeve, even as they slide around his arm. "Please tell me, if it's not the Missing Girls they've found, then whose body is it? Tell me! Whose?"

But he's ducking away from me and though his face retains that set expression of concentrated calm, his eyes are bulging. And that's when I become aware of other eyes, of all the other people, watching too. As he stumbles back (shaking his head, jowls wobbling), I can feel them watching, their gaze a brand on the back of my small neck. Sweating, trembling, I try to pull myself together. I tell myself that it's like school, that's all; *don't give them the satisfaction of looking back*. But standing alone on the pale, bleached grass, I feel too sick, too weak. And I'm turning around before I can stop myself, wiping my snotty nose clumsily on the back of my hand, trying to push the sticky hair, the little flies, out of my eyes. It feels as if the whole crowd of stragglers are looking at me. At me. As if I'm as much of a spectacle as a body, as a glimpse of what remains. A mad girl, a dead girl. Perhaps it's all the same. Helplessly, I try to return their glare the way Diana would; head held high, not caring. But my cheeks are blazing and my vision smears, though I'm blinking and blinking, as if I can cancel out a tourist face each time.

But then there, in the midst of them, I see him.

He blends in so easily among the sunburnt women with sagging arms and the men in shades and caps that at first, I think I'm mistaken. That I'm seeing things again. But he's wearing that same bright T-shirt and those same tight shorts. And there's a stubby little cigarette burning in his hand. My mouth goes dry as I watch him. As he takes a puff and one of his straggly smoke rings drifts carelessly towards the sky.

And then I'm no longer worrying about anyone else. I don't care about the eyes still crawling over me, or about the fat man walking briskly away, with his family at his heels. I don't even care about the body that they found. All I can think is that if the police found my letter - as surely they must have - it hasn't made any difference, not to their case and certainly not to the ice-cream man. And just as I'm thinking this - still frantically wiping at my nose, rubbing my mouth and blinking like some lunatic - he looks up. He squints through the flies. He sees me and he grins.

That creepy gap-toothed smile.

My stomach turns over, my shaky little body understanding before my mind does.

It wouldn't be hard for him to guess who might have left that letter for the police.

He looks at me; *he knows.*

Twenty

Back at home, Rene and Diana are fighting again. As I whirl into our hallway, panting, and slam the front door closed, their screeching voices fly at me like scratching fingers. I put my hands over my ears. After the way that the ice-cream man looked at me - after the run back through the heat, and the whining in my brain - I can't bear anymore. *Please,* I think, *not now.*

As the argument builds, I turn my face into the mound of fabric suspended from the coat hooks in the hall, burrowing my way through layers of winter wool and stiff denim, until my forehead touches the wall behind. I close my eyes and stay like that, right there, for perhaps a minute, breathing in the musty knitted scent, feeling the claylike plaster cool against my brow. But even with half a dozen empty arms trailing around my back, I can't block out their fighting. There's no stopping them. And I can even make out the words now. It's Diana's voice, I think, though they're both so high-pitched, it's hard to tell.

"How dare you? How dare you?"

It's hopeless trying to escape them. They're everywhere, my family.

I pull away from the coats and shuffle through the shadows and accusations, heading for the stairs. The doors to both the living and the dining room are closed. I can't tell which door my sister and my aunt are shut behind. Now that I'm closer their voices are so intense, it's like the walls themselves are squealing:

"You can't do it on your own. You're stupid to think you can. Stupid and selfish!"

"*I'm* stupid? *I'm* selfish? You're the one who's fucking selfish!"

I picture them, Rene and Diana, grown giant sized - like some kind of Alice in Wonderland nightmare - one in the living room, one in the dining room. Their necks are cricked, their shoulders bent; their massive heads are crushed against the ceiling. Their shrieking mouths are door sized; more doors opening on to more dark and screaming rooms.

"You don't know anything about raising a child, about children."

Shut up, I think. *Shut. Up.*

I wonder where Dad's hiding. There's a slice of sunlight coming from the kitchen at the end of the hall, but I don't think anyone's in there. Dust is pouring through the gleam and the way it falls is gentle, almost apologetic, but after only a few seconds, it turns my thoughts to glittering ash and golden sparks. To the dream I had of the house ablaze.

"How can you say that? How can you even think that?" Rene's roaring, "After all I've done for you!"

Shaking my head, I reach for the banister and I'm just about to set a foot on the bottom step, when something else catches my eye. There's a spot of blood on the worn, brown wood. The spot's dark, the colour of berry juice, but right away I know it's blood. What else would it be? Especially today.

I could almost laugh.

All around me, the argument continues, shaking the house like a snow globe, sending the dust spiralling. *How easily*, I think, *we come apart.*

There's not just the one blood spot, but many, travelling up the stairs like counters on a board game. I follow the trail.

"You're not fit. Look at the state of you! And I know what I found. I'm not as stupid as you think!"

"Yes you are, you're more fucking stupid. Did you really think I'd trust you?"

"But you can't even trust yourself, can you? And I've spent years…"

On the fifth step, I find a feather and a perfect crimson paw print. Of course, the cat's brought a bird in. That's all.

"Just listen to me. You're no mother.*"*

I pick up the feather. It's surprisingly long and clean. A pale, pale grey, so delicate and light I hardly feel it on my palm. I run my fingertips along its perfect, curving edges, and then I stroke it slowly, carefully, over my cheeks, my lips, my eyelids. But I glance back down at the bloodstains and I let the feather sail away, giving it up to the ragged sobbing from below, to those words like nails, like claws. Like little flashing, cutting blades.

I find the body in the bathroom, curled and white, wedged

into the cobwebby corner between the toilet and the cupboard under the sink. The cat himself is nowhere to be seen. I push the door closed and the relief is enormous, overwhelming, a bit like magic. The latch clicks and the voices disappear. Almost, anyway. As long as I don't actually listen out for them, I can pretend that Rene and Diana are no longer in the house. I crouch over the bird, but I don't touch it, not at first. It's a seagull, not a large seagull at all, but a seagull nonetheless. I wonder how the cat managed to pin it down, to hold it still, to catch it in the first place. Despite the bloodspots all down the stairs, the bird doesn't look hurt or even ruffled. It's only when I take a deep breath and actually manage to pick it up, that I see the red where its neck is hanging open. Its legs are poking almost comically straight up into the air. And the eyes, when you look closely... They hardly look like eyes at all. They've narrowed and sunk into its head like sewing; tiny knotty bundles of thick, black thread. And though the body's still warm, it's unmistakably stiff. Unmistakably heavy. I need both hands to hold it. I hold it carefully, thinking of the fat man on the heath, how his arm felt beneath my scrabbling fingers, how he looked at me before he turned and strode away...

I set the seagull back down to reach inside the cupboard, toppling a stack of tampon boxes as I dig out a new toilet roll. I wrap the tissue carefully over and around the body, starting with the tail feathers, leaving the head and neck - those small stitched eyes, that gaping wound - until last. It takes almost a whole roll. It isn't much of a shroud, but I do my best, winding the tissue back on itself, tighter and closer.

I don't leave gaps. When I'm done, I drop it into the bathroom bin.

"Stay there," I tell it, "hide."

It doesn't really look like much among all the old cotton buds and gummed-up razors. A fat folded wad of tissue and that's all... Despite all the time I took, I find myself wondering whether I might have wrapped it more neatly. Perhaps I could have bound it tighter too. I imagine little red flowers starting to appear, spreading out through the layers of tissue. This picture, of the blood seeping through, almost overwhelms me. I hang over the bin, feeling utterly helpless at the thought.

I force myself to stop gazing at the body, to step back. I need to wash my hands, and that's when I realise that the door is open. That Diana's standing in the doorway, staring.

I try not to jump, but I can't help it. She's been waiting there, watching, *for how long?*

Twenty-One

"Diana…"

Her eyes slide from my face to my hands, paused beside the taps. My palms are marked, I see now, as though with berry juice, and they're trembling too. Diana's gaze moves on, to the tightly bundled package I've dropped into the bin. She sways slightly, and with her colour gone and all that dyed, snarled hair, she looks like a battered china doll that's been propped up and forced to stand.

"Diana, are you ok?"

Heavily, she rushes at me. She's almost falling. I'm knocked against the sink; the sharp corner of the cupboard digs into my stomach, my knuckles smack against the taps.

"Diana!"

I bury my head in my arms. I think she's going to hit me, kick me, bite me. It's been years since we last fought, but it comes back to me, vividly, easily, as though I've been secretly expecting it for all this time. In a flash, I remember how she'd hold me down, her knees on my thighs, her nails in my wrists, her long gold hair all over me. *"You cow,"* she'd say. *"You pig. You dirt."* And as she'd bend in closer it was like being trapped inside a tunnel, the walls banging and echoing, hectic with our racing hearts.

But I'm wrong. She doesn't want to hurt me now. I'm shoved aside as she throws herself on to the lino, scrabbling towards the toilet and slamming back the seat, her shoulders rolling as she gags into the bowl.

"Oh, Diana, my Diana..." There's a rush of vomit, a quaking sob. I sink beside her, onto my knees. "Poor Diana." I say, "You poor thing."

Her back arches. For a moment she's as rigid as a rock and then she heaves again, her fingers bone-white and slipping on the edges of the bowl. I put one arm around her hard, hot back and, with my other hand, I try to scrape the coils of stiff black hair from her eyes and mouth. The skin behind her ears is clammy and burning.

"I'm sick," she whispers and it should be funny, the way it seems to have only just occurred to her what's happening, except that her voice is so little and so frail. It's not Diana's voice at all. *It's the Glandular Fever*, I think. *She's caught it from me. It's all my fault.* But I can't worry about that right now because she's started crying too, gulping for air, for words, between each retch.

"That bitch," she splutters. "That broken bitch."

She rocks back and forth and I struggle to hold on to her. Her shoulder slips damply through my hand, but we're caught together, encased by her tears and the stink of her sweet, rich vomit. As she reels, the tears are flying everywhere, like shattered glass. Her heat flows over me in waves and I catch her anger too.

This is Rene's fault, I think, *not mine. Everything, all of it, is Rene.*

"What did she do to you?" I'm asking. "What did she say?"

Diana shakes her head. Moans. Releases another stream of vomit, another wave of tears. There's a glistening string of snot caught between her nose and her top lip, but *she's still beautiful,* I think. *She's still Diana. My Diana.*

I realise I'm sweating, right there beside her. And I'm crying with her too. I reach for her hand, trying to catch hold of her wrist, her thumb, but she wriggles away from me. Her fingers move, as if of their own accord, to clutch at her belly. I look away from them quickly, breathing in her hair.

"Rene wants the baby," Diana says. Her voice is calmer, slower. She's almost smiling, but I feel her shoulders stiffen, as that hand upon her belly becomes a fist. "Can you believe it? As if she hasn't taken enough from us already. Dried up old bitch." She leans away from the toilet and yells this again towards the bathroom door. "Dried up old bitch! You hearing me?" She slumps back again, against me. "She'll never be satisfied," she murmurs. "She'll bleed us dry..."

I steal a glance at her face, that perfect profile. Her cheek is soft and pummelled-looking from all the crying, her skin between the tear tracks is as pale as clay. I look around, past the toilet bowl and tiles, checking the doorway to make sure Rene isn't there. She's not. As far as I can tell, there's nothing on the landing, no one coming up the stairs. The cupboard beneath the sink's still open, tampon boxes spilt across the floor.

"The baby?" I say.

"The baby, yes, the baby. My baby. She's nuts, that's what she is. She's screwed up, crazy. The craziest thing in this whole screwed up house. She's going to leave us, she reckons. She's going to move in with Uncle Pete and she's going to take my baby with her. This is actually what's going on in her screwed up head." She turns to me, her smile glaring now, all teeth. "Can you believe it? Can you even imagine?"

"No," I say. "Not really."

But what I'm actually thinking is that it isn't my Glandular Fever making my sister sick. And it isn't Rene shouting either. What I'm considering properly for the very first time, is that she is pregnant. My sister's pregnant, and as she leans past me, spitting bitterly, I can no longer feel the movement of her back against my hand. I can't feel anything. Everything inside me has gone very quiet, very cold.

Diana…

My mouth moves - I think it moves - but that's all. There isn't any sound.

But Diana's ranting again, making enough noise for the pair of us. I listen from a distance, but none of it makes sense.

"She started off pretending she was helping. *'A better life'*, she said. That's what she'd give it. *'With Pete?'* I said, that wife beater, that baby killer? With her? How mad does she think I am? *'A second chance',* she said, because she can't have children of her own. Because there's something wrong with her, apparently; she's too, I don't know, broken, or something. She's probably too old anyway." Diana leans past me, snatches a handful of tissue from the toilet roll, presses it to her mouth, then her forehead. "She's got it all worked out. They'll move away. To London or something. Buy a little flat with her savings. Somewhere far away from the sea and all of us. She's got money, she told me. Plenty saved up - and what have I got? Nothing, she reckons, nothing good... And they'll all live happily ever after; mad, sick Rene and wife-beater Pete. And my baby. Can you imagine?"

I shake my head, again and again. No, I can't see it. *No, no, no*, I can't envision it. But then suddenly, I can. As though a light's been switched on, the curtains swiped back, I'm seeing it that clearly. Not Rene and Pete sitting cosily in armchairs by the fire, but I can see the baby. A real, live baby with white-blonde hair and pudding cheeks, like the pictures of Diana in her pram. I have to let go of my sister to put my hands to the sides of my head - it won't stop shaking - and still, she's talking, on and on.

"She reckons Pete's reformed. He's different now. She actually thinks that whatever happens with them, however things turn out, the baby would be better off with them, with her, with anyone, than with me. She says I won't be able to do it. She says I've got a drinking problem, and she found my stash. So I've got 'issues', apparently. She says I'm a kid and I'm stupid and selfish and I don't have the first clue about what it takes to be a Mum. And, Janie..." she stops, catching her breath, a hard, glittering sheen of tears before her eyes. "Janie, I'm so scared she might be right."

She collapses on to me so I have to put my arms around

her. She's so heavy that for a moment, I think I'll drop her or that I'll have to push her off. But then I'm remembering the way she laughed as she whisked my buggy through the rain and how she'd always sit with me when I was sick, and how warm she is in bed.

"You can do it, Diana, of course you can. You can do anything."

"But how?" she moans. "How?"

Her face is in my stomach, her hair damp beneath my sticky hands.

"I'll help you, Diana," I say. "We can do it together."

"You?" She sits up so fast she cracks her head against my chin.

"Ow! Yes, *me*. I could stay off school. At the beginning anyway, and I could look after it in the evenings so that you could still go out sometimes. We could keep it in our room and take it in turns in the night, y'know if it's crying, if it needs feeding or changing or whatever."

Could we do it? I'm wondering. *Could we really?* I'm excited suddenly, the words are pouring out. I can hardly hear what I'm saying. I can still hardly believe it, that she's pregnant, and yet I can see it now, so clearly. A little round blonde thing bundled in a crib between our beds, or stretched out on a blanket on the beach. In a sunhat. In a pram. I'm going to save her; her and the baby. I can't stop seeing it now.

"Diana," I say. "It's going to be alright. Really."

But the way she's looking at me stops me before I can explain. She isn't crying anymore and her face has lost that battered softness. It's hard now, hard and flushed. Her cheeks are bright with blood as if she's being stripped down, towards the bone. It's the way she looks at Rene sometimes; it's the way she looked at Pete.

"Diana, what's wrong?"

I actually raise my fingers to my face, wondering if there's something horrible there, a splash of vomit or a smear of bird blood. She snatches my hand away from my cheek so that there's nothing between us. Nothing to shield me from her cool, dark gaze. Her fingernails dig deep into my wrist.

"Diana, please, what have I done?"

"You," she breathes. "You're just like all the rest."

And then before I know what's happening, she's rising and dragging me up with her. My arm twists sharply in the socket as she yanks me to my feet.

"Stop it, you're hurting me."

But she doesn't answer. She won't look at me, not anymore. She's turning me, pulling me, towards the door. When I manage to squirm out of her grip, she seizes my shoulders and pushes me instead. I stumble into the wall and she catches me, grabbing the back of my T-shirt only to propel me heavily before her, into the hall.

"Diana!" I twist to look at her over my shoulder. "Diana, please."

She pushes me again and then again, harder, her palm smacking between my shoulder blades and then against the back of my neck. She's muttering too, but she isn't talking to me, but about me.

"Little bitch - I'd forgotten. Little cow."

"Diana…"

With both hands, she knocks me through our bedroom

door and then stands there panting, her eyes black and blazing, her arms swinging as if she can't wait to grab me again. As if she can't wait to hit me, bite me, pin me down. Sniffling and trembling, I back away from her, my left foot skidding on a magazine and then becoming tangled in our piles of discarded clothes. I look around, dazed, at the mess and the open window, at Diana's pillow dropped among the debris on the floor. My nose is running. My wrist is throbbing. There's the ache of her handprint in my back.

"What? Diana, what?"

And that's when I see my things, strewn across her sheets. There's my pencil case and my science textbook; my school bag's been torn open on her bed. And there, with its lid gaping, spilling photographs among my open folders and my dried up pens, is her little metal box.

Twenty-Two

"Oh God, Diana..."

She walks slowly towards me, so slowly she seems to float. Her feet barely skim the junk across the floor. She looks calmer now. The colour's settling in her cheeks and her eyes are softening, but I can still feel her anger and her passion; an electricity that's almost visible, flickering against the cooped up air. As she steps slowly closer, I watch my right hand rise between us. I don't know what I'm doing, or what I want. I have no idea whether I'm trying to reach out to her or hold her back. The window's behind me, but the wall beyond her is yellow, hot with sun. She comes right up to me so that she's standing, with her head bowed, just inches from my face. My hand drops like a weight against my side. We're breathing heavily. A warm breeze from the garden stirs against my back. I'm sweating all over; my T-shirt's sticking to me, my underwear too. Diana's chin is glistening, covered in tiny, dew-like beads. Somewhere outside, a car starts and stops and starts again. Birds are singing and there's a man whistling as he walks lightly along the road beside the house.

In here, the air is throbbing.

Diana shakes her head. A small, light shake. Her curls whisper, but barely move.

"I thought I could trust you, Janie. You, at least." And there's something so sad and final about the way she says this that I actually wish she had raised her arm and smacked me, that she'd hurt me in some simple, straightforward way.

"Diana, I'm so, so sorry. I don't know what I was thinking, what I'm doing. I don't know why..."

But she's not looking at me now. Her head's inclined and I know that she's gazing at the pictures spread across her bed. I can't turn with her. I don't want to look at them. They're the last thing in the universe I want to see right now.

"I didn't look at them. Honestly. I took the box, but I didn't look inside."

"Janie..." Her voice is still empty. Her eyes crawl back across my face. "You found the key."

"I know! I know I did, but I didn't actually open it. Maybe I was going to, but I didn't get that far - Rene shouted for me - I didn't do it. I don't even know why I wanted to. Diana, I'm sorry. I'm so sorry." But she isn't listening.

"Well," she says, very quietly. "I hope you're happy now, Janie. I hope you're satisfied."

"Diana, I didn't look, you've got to believe me."

But she's turning away from me now, walking past me. I make myself follow her. She stops, head bowed, over her bed. I still can't look.

"All I've ever done, Janie, is watch out for you. For a long time, that's all I wanted; to keep you safe." I suppose her words should be reassuring, but there's something about my sister's tone as she says this that pinches at the skin on the back of my neck. It makes me shudder. It's the growing chilliness in that small, bare voice, and it's the way she's just standing there with her shoulders bent and the sunlight swimming across her hair. For a moment she could be an old, old woman. She could be anyone.

"Diana. Please." Standing just behind her, I reach out to touch her shoulder, my fingers trembling. She doesn't shake me off, but she doesn't seem to feel me either. Through the gauzy cotton of her top, I can see the little blue smudge of her flower tattoo. I want to run my fingers over it. I want to press my face to it, my lips, but I'm scared to get much closer. Her shoulder feels so stiff and still that she could be hollow, made of wax. She's like the pirate models they used to have down by the arcades, the ones that used to terrify me when I was little because they were so life-like, but *empty*. "Diana..." I want to explain, I need her to understand, or to turn around and look at me, at least. "I only wanted to see what she looked like, and maybe, for a little while, I did start wondering what happened to her, where she went, but I don't care about any of that anymore. None of it matters, Diana. Are you listening to me? It doesn't even matter anymore..."

But even as I'm protesting, I catch myself wondering all over again. I'm picturing the white heath criss-crossed with police tape, that spaceman with his bag, and then, despite myself, I'm asking her. I'm almost shouting:

"What did happen to our mother, Diana? Where did she go?"

And at last she turns to face me. As she swings around, she knocks my fingers from her shoulder. She's blinking and her mouth's stretched open as if she's screaming, except not one word comes out. But I'm still shouting. I'm babbling. Something's burst inside me and I'm yelling at her now.

"They found bones, Diana. They found a body on the heath. Is it her? I keep thinking, *what if it's her?* But there's no one who will tell me because no one ever tells me anything. Not even you, Diana. Because I don't matter. Because nobody, nobody cares."

"Fine," says Diana. "You want to know, then take them."

She snatches at the pile of papers and pictures on her bed and starts throwing them at me. She throws whatever she can grab hold of, not just the photographs, but my schoolbooks too, and pens. My science textbook hits me squarely on the chin and as I stumble back there are pictures raining down around me. Beyond them, Diana's still grasping things and throwing things. With a flash of anxiety I remember her knife, hoping that it won't come flying at me next. I glance at the bed, but I can't see it anywhere among the mess of sheets and papers. She's probably buried it already, I think. Somewhere truly secret this time, truly safe...

I stare at my sister, at her hair, whirling witchlike around her taut and shining face, and a bitter taste floods my mouth. A taste like rust and rain and dirty skin. And for a second time, I find myself wondering who she is. Not just this woman she's turned into, but the little girl she was before. But then I notice how her hands are shaking. How she can scarcely hold the pictures, how she has to fight to let them go.

"I'm through protecting you," she snaps. "You want to know the truth? Then take it. Take it."

She kicks at the layers of paper already fallen to the floor. I catch a blur of colour beneath her foot, but that's all. I still can't look. *She's right*, I think. She's always been right. I should never have wanted to know, but it's too late now. Finally, she picks up the box and jams it up against my chest.

"Take it," she hisses.

I glance down at it and then quickly away. Although she seems to have been throwing stuff at me forever, there's still something in there, something caught. My hands don't move. I shake my head. I will not look.

"Go on, Janie!" Her mouth twists, she's barely pretty anymore. I step back and she comes right after me through the thick air, across the tangled floor. The box is wedged between us so that it's almost like a dance as she presses into me and I shuffle towards the door.

"No! I'm sorry. I don't want it. I don't care."

"Yes you do care, Janie, so stop lying. You care more about this than anything else, though why you care's beyond me. After all, our mother didn't care, Janie. Don't kid yourself about that. Our mother hated us. The pair of us, but most especially she hated you."

"No," I whisper. "No, that isn't true."

It's not just the box pushing against me; her face is thrusting towards mine. She's so close that I can taste the vomit on her breath. Her eyes are huge. I'm pulled up short. The doorframe's hard against my back.

"Yes it's true! Things were bad enough before you came along, but when she was pregnant and then, after, after you were born... It's your fault, Janie. It's all your fault."

I break away and fall breathlessly sideways through the doorway into the hall. I see Diana's face, her shouting mouth, and then black. And I could keep falling deeper, part of me longs to fall deeper, to slip under into darkness and nothingness, to faint and dream and disappear. But I drag myself back into reality. I see my sister standing over me. She's shaking and crying again now. Still shouting. But I don't hear her. I won't hear her. I duck out from underneath her. I scramble to my feet. I turn and go racing down the stairs, taking them two at a time, tiny dark red bloodspots whirling past. I'm running because it's the only thing I can do, the only thing I ever do. I run and run, away.

And then I'm on the beach. I'm down on West Beach, hardly recalling how I got there. Our dusty road and the High Street, the tourists drifting by in their yellows and pale pinks, all the tattered flowers - it's just a blur of the same old things. Running through our little town's become a recurrent dream; the arcades and the tea shops and the tourists washing over me day after stifling day... There's even something tired about my panic; the way my heartbeat keeps on banging, the blood hissing through my veins. The buzzing in my head I can't escape. It's only when I reach the beach steps that I realise that the sky has changed. I look up expecting flawless blue and it's a shock to see the clouds. It's a struggle to believe in them, a dirty sheet stretched taut across the sky. They seem to grow a little darker, a little closer, with each stone step I take.

When I reach the bottom, I slip off my baseball boots so

that I can move more nimbly between the buckets and the blankets and the deckchairs. As I run, I stare down at my white bony ankles and pretend the tourists aren't here. Out of the corner of my eye, they're just a blur of white or pink or browning flesh, merging with the rubbish and the sand. I can't see them and they can't see me; we're in our own separate, opposite worlds. While they play, I'm heading straight towards the sea. It's what I need more than anything right now; the crash and surge of the waves, that enormous, oblivious beauty. It's the only thing that I can think of that might give me any peace. I stop running when I get to the edge. The sand is damp and surprisingly cool between my toes. I stand very still and breathe in. The water is filled with darkness, filled with sky. A thin, warm wind tugs the hair away from my face and then there's thunder. It's not loud yet, it's not close. Nevertheless it goes rumbling on for a while and beneath the salt and suntan lotion, there's a familiar metallic, earthy smell. It won't be long before there's rain. My heart's still racing, but it seems like I'm the only person in the Universe who isn't moving now. At the sound of thunder, the tourists have immediately roused themselves into a flurry of activity. I glance back at them, from a distance, as they round up their scattered books and clothes and kids. Picnic baskets are packed back up and lilos hastily deflated. There's a rapid series of clacking sounds like gunfire, as deckchairs are slammed shut.

"Watch your fingers!" someone calls.

And suddenly, all around me, there are mothers. There are mothers rolling up sandy towels and shaking out wet swimming things, mothers calling to their children to '*hurry up now, come right back. We should be home by now.'*

I turn back again quickly, towards the sea, the sky. The clouds are hanging close over the water. A great grey sack, heaving gently, with things caught deep inside. In the distance, there's a single surfer, a small brown shape in bright red trunks, bobbing on his stomach with the waves. He's the only person out there now. Every now and then he rocks more violently and almost disappears amidst the swell. Lightning cracks the horizon, a perfect blazing-white fork. It's so quick I almost miss it, though when I blink it's still there, a silver scratch behind my lids. For a moment the air is flooded with the sounds of the children on the beach behind me. They're laughing, screaming, shouting helplessly, wordlessly, as they gather up their toys and run. The surfer turns around. Still lying on his front, his arm curves. He's using long, sweeping strokes to ride his board back towards the beach, but a great black shadow seems to be gathering in the water underneath him. Everything is growing darker. Even the glittering patches on the surface are looking tarnished. For a second or two, I consider the possibility that he isn't going to make it, that the sea will suck him back and pull him under, but he's fast out there. He's young and strong. There's more thunder and then a second flash. As the lightning fades, he reaches the sand and staggers out, shaking his shaggy blonde head like a dog. While he hefts his board up beneath one arm and begins to stride away across the beach, I take a step forward, a small careful step, and then another, and another that carries me straight into the white horses.

The water's freezing and, as the froth parts, mostly clear.

I watch my feet through it. They're as pale as fish. They vanish and then return through flurries of sand and tiny stones, those creamy milkshake suds. I take another two steps and the cold water rushes up my calves and over my knees. There are icy fingers snatching at my thighs, sliding away and grasping again.

I could keep going, I think. *I could just keep walking. Out and out and out.*

There's more thunder. I glance nervously over my shoulder to see if anybody's watching me, but mostly, the beach is empty. It's amazing how quickly tourists can disappear. *Like lemmings*, I think. Over at the steps, there's a line of figures marching steadily away. There are more people crowded around the bottom waiting to go up and only a few stragglers left on the beach closer by, still collecting up their mats and bottles and camera cases or waving their arms, frantically directing.

An empty plastic carrier bag dances gracelessly across the sand.

And then I notice them. Two young girls, dressed almost identically in green bikini tops and shorts. Their hips bump together as they bend over their stuff. Their brownish-blondish hair lifts and turns with the rising breeze. As they stand, they lean in towards each other. They're talking so intimately that their faces almost touch, and then one girl, the prettier girl, steps back and laughs. The other girl shakes her head, but in a matter of seconds, they're both giggling. They jog away from me with their beach bags bunched against their chests and though it hasn't rained a drop yet, the prettier one holds a magazine over her head as if it's pouring.

From here, their long bare backs look smooth and soft and flawless. Even in the dull light, the girls are honey coloured. Touched with gold.

I take one last glance back out towards the horizon. Far out, where the sea's deepest and coldest, there's a breaking line of glimmering light, but the shadows in the lurching waves are growing denser, closer. The tide creaks and crashes. There are little bubbles tugging at my feet like tiny mouths. With an effort I turn my back on all of it. I step away. I face the beach. I'm going to follow those brownish-blondish girls, I'm going to trace their *last known steps* just one more time. It isn't much of a thing to do, I know. But what else, I wonder, do I have left?

The girls are hurrying. They're already growing small and blurry. Soon they'll join the crowd at the foot of the steps and then I'll lose them. They'll vanish. I find myself jogging to catch up with them. My feet are bright pink now from the freezing water. I stumble across the uneven sand and career into the trench of a collapsing castle, scattering lovingly collected shells and bluish pebbles. A little plastic flag snaps beneath my heel. The sand rises indignantly around me, mustard that sticks when it hits my wet knees, my skinny thighs. I imagine that the criss-crossed footprints I'm running in belong to them - *those girls* - although I know this isn't likely.

There's another flash of lightning. For a moment, the beach turns bone-white, then arctic blue. The sand is snow. It's followed almost straight away by thunder, cracking and exploding as though in jubilation. I put my head down and run faster, but by the time I've reached the cliff steps, the girls are gone. Everyone's gone. I think I'm too late, but then there's laughter, young girls' laughter, caught between the roaring, rushing waves and the sound of the wind, that's gathering strength; a thirsty whining whistle in my ears.

The steps rise almost vertically against the rusty cliff, so I have to step back to get a better look. I peel the hair away from my eyes and sure enough, the girls are there. I see them where the steps turn - a flicker of green cotton, a smudge of honey-coloured skin. I start climbing fast, taking long stretching strides, although beneath my bare soles the steps are sharp with grit. I should put my boots back on, they're still hanging by their laces from my hand, but I can't afford to stop. The lightning breaks over us again, and then the thunder. My own body blazes underneath me, a photograph in black and white. I watch my bony knees rising and sinking and try to concentrate on reaching the girls, and nothing else. I try not to think about what will happen when I do catch up with them, what I'll say or do. I don't want to imagine their expressions when I face them. When I grab them. My witchlike fingers their perfect skin.

And then there's a sound, a roar, but not of thunder. It comes as if from nowhere, or from everywhere. From the sheer red cliff face rising above me and from the sky, beyond. It comes from the beach behind me too. It ricochets out of the carved rock steps beneath my feet. Even the shards of stone, pressing into my soles like broken glass, seem to vibrate with the sound. For a moment, they press deeper. It's a roar of rage. A man's roar. I think of the car park at the top of the steps. Of the man who will have returned there from the heath, to go on selling tourists all his sweet and sticky things. I picture him smiling his gap-toothed smile even as he gazes beyond his customers to the darkening sky. He's been waiting, I think. Waiting for the storm to begin, for the crowds to disperse. He's been waiting for an opportunity - a girl. A fair and freckled skinny type, with brownish-blondish hair.

I think of the girls up ahead of me. Just out of sight. Just out of reach. I want to stop. I want to turn around and run away, back down the steps to the cold damp comfort of the sand. To the forgiving indifference of the sea. Instead I keep watching my knees. I keep on going, up and up, until suddenly the rock face falls away from me, and my body - the whole world - changes. I've reached the top. The sky pours outwards, all around me, rushing and glowering on every side. The wind whips closer, colder, scuffing my arms with goose bumps. Straight ahead, the road is empty. A little way along, there's the arcade, but it has its shutters down already. I can't see anyone about. The car park lies in the other direction. Well, where else, I think, will the girls have gone?

I take a sharp, reckless turn but I keep my head bowed as I hurry towards it. I concentrate on the uneven paving stones and the potholes, on the clouds of gnats that come and go. If it weren't for the rocks and heather, I tell myself, I could be anywhere. But then the heather turns white, skeletal, with lightning. The thunder rolls back, and just beneath it, there's that roar again. His voice. I'm closer now, it's clearer.

"Fuckers, fuckers!"

At least, I think that's what he's saying. My gut clenches. The heather darkens, and ripples. What have they done, I wonder, to make him so angry? I sprint forward, just as a stronger gust of wind comes at me from nowhere, shoving me backwards and throwing salt into my eyes. It pushes its way inside my head too, the way his voice has.

"Fuckers! Fuckers!"

Wind and words jumble together and rush right through me, tearing at my thoughts. Making me shiver, suddenly sick with fear.

But I won't run away. Not this time. This time, I'll save them.

I'll make something better. Do something right. And so I keep going, though I still don't look up until my bare feet hit the gravel, and when I do, I have to rub my eyes. I can't see the girls anywhere, but along with the ice-cream van, there's one other car up here, parked at an angle across the stones. It's long and white and shining. Through the back window, there's a square of shadow, a square of black.

My breath catches in my throat. My stomach contracts. There's something hard, a little rock, wedged inside me. I rub my eyes more forcefully, pressing my thumbs into my sockets. When I open them, the car's still here, but it isn't what I thought. There are blocks of dark colour on it that I somehow missed or blotted out. There's a row of unlit lights across the roof and writing on the bonnet.

There's no woman here. No blue-eyed, blonde woman dressed in a creamy blouse and a floating skirt. There's no new kidnapping. It's just the police. They've got here first. The breath pours out of me, but even when I see two uniformed officers rounding the van with the ice-cream man cuffed and stooped between them, the relief I thought I'd feel is hardly there.

As they cross the gravel, the wind lifts the men's hair and ruffles their shirts. The air is rich with the stink of tin and dirt, and just as they reach the police car, the first drops of rain begin to fall. I feel them break icily in my hair. They slither down my back. The gravel jumps and then darkens, marked as though with scattered pennies. The men keep moving. Not one of them looks over.

It seems that the girls I was following have vanished. Perhaps it doesn't matter; perhaps they were never even here. I could have made them up.

I don't know anything.

As the police manoeuvre the ice-cream man towards their car, pressing down on his fat, red head as he slides into the back, I'm fully expecting him to look at me the way he did at the heath. I'm waiting for him to shout something, or at least mouth something, or show that grin again, perhaps? But he doesn't do any of these things. He doesn't so much as glance in my direction.

There's another flash of lightning. Thunder bellows directly overhead, so I don't hear the car doors slam. They don't bother with the siren, but the blue lights come on and begin to turn. They look soft, unthreatening, against the shadowy sky. On the other side of the car park, on the ice-cream van, Donald Duck is also watching with that single, maniac eye. Even through the mist of rain, you can see gravel rising in powdery clouds around the tyres.

He's gone, I think, *it's over.*

But as I watch the police car turn away, its blue lights blurring through the hazy rain, I know that I am wrong. It comes to me that nothing's ever simple, that nothing here is done. After all, aren't the Missing Girls still missing? Isn't the emptiness inside me still right there? I sink down on to the damp grey gravel. I sit with my ankles crossed and my arms clasped around my clammy white knees. The rain is coming down faster, but it doesn't matter. It doesn't make any difference. I don't have anywhere to go. I watch it fall, a silver web. I watch puddles forming in the dips and tyre tracks between the stones, drops spreading and exploding. Tiny stars. I wipe the water from my eyes and then I go on watching. I go on waiting. I wait and wait and after a little while, I realise what it is that I'm still waiting for. Hoping for. I'm waiting for a car to pull up, for a door to open. I'm waiting for someone to find me. To take me with them. To take me home.

Twenty-Three

I don't realise how dark the house is until I'm stumbling inside. It's darker than the night I've left behind, where the rain's whirling silver through the shadows and crashing down in sheets of glass that shatter before they've even hit the ground. When I slam the front door closed, it's like pulling a black hood over my face. The darkness in our hallway is so complete that when I glance down at my hands and my torn, wet feet, they're no longer there.

I stand for a moment in the nothing, listening to the quick soft drip of water tapping against the floorboards from my hair and sodden clothes, and to the deeper, denser drumming of the rain still falling relentlessly on the door and walls outside. My breathing sounds hoarse and laboured like the gasps of someone old, or drowning. I don't think I've ever felt so drenched in my whole life, not swimming in the local pool or floating in the rolling sea, not even going under. There's rain still streaming down my back and hanging in threads from my nose and chin, and the skin on my arms feels swollen, spongy with water. I wipe my wet palms over my wet cheeks. I don't know why. Even if the house wasn't pitch-black, I'm so soaked that no one would be able to tell how hard I've been crying. My breath's still catching, but I can't feel the tears anymore. I can't feel anything, not the cold, although I'm shivering, not the little cuts and grazes that split the soles of my invisible feet. I slip and stumble heavily through the shadows, fumbling my way inside, clutching at the walls and bundled coats. My body's not my body, it's waterlogged and numb.

By the time I've reached the staircase, my eyes have adjusted so that I can just about make out the open doorways to the living room and the dining room. They're deeper velvet squares. I pause, squinting, at the bottom of the staircase, trying to locate the edges of the steps before I climb them. I've already skidded twice in the pools of water I'm trailing through the hall. Of course, I could just switch on the lights, but in a way, I like the dark. I can pretend that the house doesn't belong to us, but to another family entirely. I grope for the banister, but stop with one foot raised, convinced suddenly that there's someone in the hallway with me. Someone hiding in the shadows, watching, reading my thoughts.

"Diana?" I whisper.

It's like being small again. Like games of Hide and Seek when I'd search for hours it seemed, and never find her.

Except it's not really Hide and Seek I'm thinking of. It's 'Terrorists'. There's that same sense of waiting and not-knowing. A tension in the dark itself. I'm just as scared as I was back then. The shadows aren't so friendly anymore; the house shifts and creaks around me. The sketchy ceiling's floating closer. I can smell my own sweat, and the dampness in the floorboards. Sweet musty layers of warped and wilting wood.

Then I don't so much see, as sense, a movement. Something flickering near the kitchen. I step back and skid again. As I regain my footing, I glance up. There's a pair of yellow eyes, glittering softly through the black.

It's just the cat again, *the stupid cat.* I feel dumber than ever, as if somebody has put him there deliberately, a cheap trick at my expense. Quickly, I turn away and move on. The banister's back beneath my hand and as I climb I try to shake away my paranoia, this sense of foolishness and fear, but I only succeed in scattering more drops of icy water. Vaguely, I find myself wondering if anyone's bothered washing the bird blood from the stairs.

On the landing, it's not so dark. There's a pool of light burning gently from the gap under Rene's bedroom door, though from the other doors there's nothing. I walk quietly past them, still unable to completely shrug off the feeling that this isn't my house, that I'm trespassing. Or playing secret games.

Maybe I am, I think. *Maybe that's what this is.*

I stand in the hallway, breathing noisily despite myself, with my fingertips resting on Rene's door. My bare feet are startling in the pool of yellow light. They're rubbery and shrivelled. Fish-skin feet, with mud and blood all over them. It doesn't matter. I flatten my palm against the panelling and step inside.

The whole room stinks of lavender. Of lavender bags and

Rene's perfume, of the fabric softener she uses on her clothes. Rene's bent over the bed with her back to me, sorting and folding laundry into great piles across her sheets. I'm sure she's heard the door opening behind her, I'm sure she knows I'm here, but she doesn't turn around. She just keeps going, shaking out a tangled ball of tights and brushing off a skirt, her movements sharp, but regular, like she's part of some machine.

"Rene, where is everyone? Why's the house so dark?" The sound of my own voice startles me; it sounds so normal.

Rene doesn't answer. She doesn't even look at me, she just goes on rolling and smoothing and folding. She doesn't miss a beat. I gaze around the room as if in a dream. Perhaps I've slipped into one of Rene's dreams, I think, and that's why I don't exist. In the floor length mirror, I glimpse her face as her head bobs and turns. She's looking only at her hands and at the things she's holding, lifting, folding. I see the familiar lines set into her forehead like cracks in concrete, and the circles beneath her eyes. I see her small thin mouth. Her lips are pressed together so tightly that you know that her teeth are gritted underneath. That she's locked in under there.

I catch myself in the glass behind her. Glistening and dishevelled, I look like something dragged up from the sea. There ought to be bits of net clinging to me, seaweed hanging from my bony limbs. What little colour I have has been washed completely from my skin, and even in the dim light, my ribs stand out in ugly bars where they're sticking to my T-shirt. Like some *disaster victim*. I look away. Only the bedside lamps are lit and so it should be cosy in here, with the thick curtains drawn against the beating rain, but there's something stark about the room instead. Perhaps it's the shadows growing from the darkest corners of the ceiling, stretching overhead like inky hands. Perhaps it's the way that all the drawers are hanging open, or the ghostly pile of crisp white shirts heaped in a mound across the sheets.

Rene pads over to the wardrobe, while I stand very still, listening to the rain and my own ragged breathing. To the gentle rustle of her long cotton skirt. There's a jangle of hangers as she reaches inside and pulls out a coat, her winter coat. She carries it back with her like a parcel, clasped tightly to her chest. My eyes flicker back towards the bed before she gets there. I see a dark red suitcase lying open beneath that heap of ironed clothes. My breath catches. It feels like there's a sharp little pebble embedded in my throat. My voice cracks around it.

"So, you're really going then?" I say.

She turns to look at me at last, and for a moment, in the lamplight, her eyes flash as brightly as the cat's. Her shoulders stiffen - it's not quite a sigh and not quite a shrug - but she doesn't say a word. She doesn't even snap at me for dripping all over her spotless floor. She's already moving again, gliding and rustling between the wardrobe, drawers and bed. She's folding and packing, folding and packing, as if that's all that she can do. I watch her. With the cold sea taste of pebbles in the back of my mouth I stand and watch until it occurs to me that if I go on standing here, listening to the rain and the constant hush and whisper of her skirt much longer, I will go mad.

I will go madder.

So I go over to the bed and start picking up her clothes. As Rene shakes out jumpers and underwear and folds a dress against its hanger, I lift the packed things from her case. I carry them carefully back to her wardrobe and her drawers, one garment at a time. I work slowly, methodically. I'm just as careful as Rene, preserving all her neat, sharp creases - I only wish I wasn't so wet. I'm dripping in her drawers. Of course she can't let this carry on.

"Janie," she says at last, "Janie, please."

But now, I'm ignoring her. She reaches for the blouse I'm holding, a peach-coloured thing that's shaking in my hands, but I duck away from her, and step back. She follows me to the wardrobe, but I don't let her have it. The hangers are cold against my palms. Before I can slip the blouse inside, she reaches for me. She grabs my wrist and pulls me around to face her.

"Give me my blouse."

I shake my head. Water sparkles through the air. Rene lets go of my arm and grabs the blouse instead, but I don't let go. Her face is grim with determination. Her skin is sallow and exhausted-looking, and her jaw is set, but there's a new glitter to her eyes.

"Give it to me!"

She pulls and pulls, but I hold on tighter, enjoying the way the silk crumples in my fists. She's got both hands on it as well; her fingers are claws, her knuckles white. Neither one of us is worrying about her pristine creases anymore. We don't say anything as we tussle, but Rene's chest is heaving, her breath is battering noisily out of her - I can't tell hers from mine. There's a soft tearing sound and buttons fly, but still we don't let go. It occurs to me even as I attempt to grip the fabric more securely, how stupid this is, how funny we must look, fighting over rags and scraps like gulls. Panting, I glare into Rene's glaring face and I think how you can never really imagine what's going to happen. In all my fantasies I could never have foreseen this, this tug of war over a blouse. Scuffling like dogs. And I think how I've never honestly considered the possibility of Rene truly leaving us. Or how strongly I might feel it, running way down deep inside...

It *is* funny, I think. It's ridiculous. Madness. And then, I can't help it, I laugh, a short, barking laugh, like one of Diana's laughs that comes from nowhere. Loud and final and dismissive. Rene drops her hands immediately. In her eyes, the light goes out. After a moment I let go too and the blouse slithers, sad and broken, to the floor.

"I have to go," she says.

"You can't." I hear the words spill out of me as if they're being said by someone else, a little girl perhaps, on the verge of tears, of a tantrum. "You can't go too, Rene. It isn't fair."

She shakes her head and steps back over to her suitcase. Her small white slippers are lying between the piles of skirts and shirts on top of the bed, tucked neatly, carefully, one inside the other. I watch from over her shoulder as she picks them up and pushes them quickly down the side of the case, between the layers of packed things, and the lining.

Outside, the rain keeps falling.

"You weren't even going to say goodbye?"

She sighs, her shoulders slump and then she turns to me as though I've actually grabbed hold of her, physically forced her face-to-face. It's so obvious how much she doesn't want me here - how the last thing she wants to do is deal with me right now - that I almost walk straight out of her bedroom door. I almost save us both.

But I'm not going anywhere, not yet. Something like remorse rises inside me, a warm, muffling sensation, clouding my head, but beneath it, there's another brighter heat. The first sparks of anger, turning and smouldering deep down inside my stomach. I can taste it too. Dirt and ashes on my tongue.

Behind the heavy curtains, the window rattles and shakes, rain knocks against the glass. Rene looks down at her own feet and then across, at the puddles and mud I've streaked across her carpet, and at her own blouse lying in its fleshy little pool. When I'm sure she's looking back at me again, I grind my torn, dirty heels into her pristine, vacuumed floor.

"Janie…" she says. She shakes her head and starts again. Her voice is softer now: "Janie. Of course I would have said goodbye. I'd have come back and explained."

But from the way she's saying it, I can tell it hasn't even occurred to her to do this till right now. I press my heels down harder and roll the side of one muddy foot slowly and deliberately back and forth.

"I was coming back anyway," she insists. "I can't carry everything tonight. There's stuff all over the house, and there's my furniture."

"Your furniture?"

I can't believe we're having this conversation, that we're talking about things. But then abruptly, I'm picturing our kitchen without the sideboard and empty spaces in the living room where the high backed armchairs have always been. It's bewildering. The embers in my belly are pricking at me like tiny needles.

"You don't understand, Janie, I have to get out. I've already called Pete. He's coming over to pick me up. I can't do this any longer, I can't stay under the same roof as your sister another night. Another minute."

"My sister?" I say it slowly, but then the words are coming out so hot and fast, I'm almost choking:

"*My sister* told me what you said to her. About her not being a fit mother, a fit person even. About how she was selfish and how she'd never cope. She said you wanted to take the baby! That it would be better off with anyone but her. How can you think that, Rene? How could you say it? Don't you think that Diana isn't scared enough already? She's terrified! She needs us more than ever, don't you get it, Rene? Don't you care?"

"She can't do it, Janie."

Her voice is gentle, her arms are crossed beneath her breasts. She looks like she could just go on standing there while I fume at her, for hours and hours, unflinching, unblinking, her eyes cold and hard in slitted lids.

"Your sister isn't capable of bringing up a child, Janie. She isn't right."

I'm not empty anymore. My head is raging; the words are burning in my throat. I march right up to Rene and spit them at her. I want to shake her and shake her. I want to knock her narrowing eyes wide open and tear her pursed pale lips apart. There's ice water crashing, burning, through my veins, rain hammering my head, and I think that this is how Diana must feel when she looks at Rene. I can't stop thinking about Diana. She drives me on.

"She'd be a better mother than you ever were!" I yell. "At least she'd stand by her kid. At least she'd be there. She wouldn't be like you, Rene, running away the minute things get hard. At least Diana loves people, at least she'd try. She wouldn't just bitch and criticise the way you do Rene... We knew you never wanted us. Some days, a lot of days, we didn't even know why you were here. At least Diana would hug her baby, she'd touch her baby. You could hardly bear to touch us. You wouldn't even look at us some days!"

"How dare you?" Rene roars.

And I realise that I've done it. I've knocked her sideways. She's looming over me, her hands are rising and her eyes and mouth are gouged wide open, dark and glistening as holes. The air seems to crackle between us and for a moment, we're flying together and there's something wild, almost joyful, in our fury, our release, but then her hand comes crashing down. She hits me hard across the face and in that instance makes me nothing. There's nothing in me but white noise.

"After all I've done for you," she hisses. "After all I've given, all I've given up for all these years. After all the clothes I've washed and meals I've cooked. After the way that I've protected you, and what have any of you ever given me in return, except your messes and your whining? Your ingratitude. You imagine I didn't care because I couldn't pretend to be some touchy-feely auntie, playing games with you and cuddling? As if those are the only things that matter. You have no idea, Janie. You have no idea you're even born."

As she shouts, she leans in closer, and closer, until she's right on top of me. I can see the powder in her pores and the gleam across her teeth. Her breath is warm and stinks of orange juice. I cringe beneath her, half expecting her to strike me again, but what she actually does is worse. She starts to cry ; thin fast tears that turn milky with her make-up.

"You think you had it hard, Janie?" she says. "When I was a kid, there was discipline. True discipline. Our mother used her belt on us and if she didn't have her belt, she'd use whatever came to hand - a wooden scrubbing brush, a broom pole... Once she took the shoe off her own foot and wore it like a glove. I still see that sometimes. Too often I see it... the way her arm went up and smashed back down. That pointed heel. You never forget a thing like that. My sister - my little sister - curled up beneath her in a ball... You think I didn't love you because I didn't kiss your grazes better, because I didn't tuck you in at night? Well, I did my best, Janie. I did my best with what I had."

She steps sharply away from me, bumps awkwardly against the bed.

I don't know what to say. I'm breathing fast, as fast as her. For a moment there's only my heartbeat and the thumping rain. There's nothing else. Nothing's real. But then gradually, piece-by-piece, I start to picture it; a woman wielding a shoe, the two children sobbing at her feet... And the littlest one, the one hunched up into a ball, is Rene's sister, my own mother.

And suddenly I can't stop seeing her.

A little girl with fierce dark eyes like smashed black glass.

A little girl with golden bunches.

Again and again, I picture her, not just cowering on the kitchen tiles, but bent across a bed, huddled in our bathroom, between the toilet and the sink. She's in the back seat of a car, grappling with a seatbelt. The metal clip flashes like a knife between her hands.

And wherever I see her, she's murmuring the same words, over and over.

"Run," she's saying. "Hide."

And though her voice is almost normal, the place where her mouth usually is, that 'Hollywood smile', has disappeared completely behind a fat red flower of blood.

I open my eyes wide, I don't want to see these pictures anymore. But I have to put my hands up to my face, I have to dig my nails right in to make them stop.

Behind the curtains, the windowpanes are shuddering in their frame. Rain smashes into the glass like shingle and Rene, I realise, is still talking. Telling me things I no longer want to hear.

"You don't know anything, Janie," she's saying. "You don't know what it was like for me to come here. How bad things were back then. You have no idea what I've done for this family. How I held you all together, and with practically the whole town against us. If it wasn't for me..."

She stops. She shakes her head.

"What do you mean?" I ask, but my voice is weak.

I'm barely listening. I'm still thinking about Rene's mother, my grandmother. And I'm wondering at the way Rene swapped one violent relationship for another when she married Uncle Pete.

Pete, I think, and a whole new wave of panic goes shuddering through me.

"Oh, I know what people were saying." Rene murmurs, her voice cooler now, detached. She's distracted by her suitcase, I think, or by the slippery, lacy thing - some kind of camisole - that she's balling in her hands.

"As soon as I arrived here, they made sure to let me know. A small town like this you couldn't not hear them. Whispering, gossiping. All those silly theories about how she wasn't alone, how he might have been involved in some way too. And, to be honest, he didn't help matters. All over the place, he was. It didn't look right. Not to them."

And I can't believe what I am hearing, or the blank mask of her face. I can hardly get the words out, I'm so stunned.

"What? What are you saying? Are you actually admitting that Pete had something to do with it? With the way my mother disappeared?"

But she doesn't reply. She looks frozen, caught. Her long fingers are locked together on that beaten silken thing. Her mouth's a narrow square. She's peering at me warily with frightened, shadowed eyes.

Inside my head, the tide's still rising. I hear my voice from far away.

"And you're actually going back to him?"

I watch her come undone. Her hands open first. Her underwear wafts to the floor, and then fierce colour comes bursting back into her cheeks. Her eyes gape and her mouth twists, forming a ghoulish almost-smile.

"What are you on about Janie? I'm not talking about Pete. No one's talking about Pete. It's your father they were worried about. He was the one who was acting so funny. More relieved than shocked, than sad…"

I break.

I'm on my feet. I've got my hands on her and I'm pushing her backwards on to the bed. I'm screaming.

"I don't understand you. What are you saying! What happened to my mother?"

I know that she won't answer me, but I don't let go of her. She's reeling back and forth beneath my hands like an old rag doll, full of sawdust, full of nothing. I can't bear to look at her, but when I close my eyes there's the heath and that spaceman with his body bags. An old forgotten grave…

And there's my father too. He's walking away the way he always does, his shoulders stooped, his grey head bowed. A quiet man. A shattered man.

And then, even with my eyes wide open, Rene's disappearing. I shake her and shake her, but it doesn't make any difference. I can hardly see her anymore. She's lost between all the other pictures, between the large dark spots like blood.

I throw her away from me. She grunts as she rolls on the bed beside her case. And I'm out of her room and back in the hall before I even know what I'm doing. I'm running, with the dark house crowding in around me. Shadows fill my mouth like dirty wool, but I won't be sick. *I won't be sick*, not like poor Diana, bitch Diana.

My blood is thundering in my ears. *Diana*, I think. I want Diana. *I need you right away.*

I grab at the door to our room and almost swing right past, my feet stumbling over one another as I cry out for her.

"Diana! Diana..."

Our bedroom's black, it's rocking back and forth. I slap the wall inside, groping for the light switch as I squint towards her bed, though I see nothing. The switch slips beneath my fingers. I fumble. Sobbing, I turn it on. In the glaring white, there's no relief. I blink and swipe my hands through the cool, damp air. It makes no difference. This isn't our room. This isn't our house. Our beds are here and my things are here, slid up against one wall, but the floor is clear, completely clear.

All Diana's things are gone. I rush over to the window. Of course she's left it open. The carpet beneath it is sodden with rain. It squelches gently beneath my feet. I lean out into the night. It's black and close, still raining hard. It's too dark to see the trees, too dark to see anything or anyone, but you can hear the trees and you can feel them out there; the wind and rain thrashing through the leaves and the great heavy branches swaying and creaking like masts on an ancient ship. In seconds, my face is soaked again. I'm battered, blinking away rain. It fills the world around me with a thousand separate heartbeats and beneath them, there's this other sound. Like children splashing, stamping and jumping, dancing joyfully through the dark. And I know there isn't any point in calling anymore. *I know that you are gone.*

It takes a long time to step away from the window, to step back into the light. It takes even longer for me to notice the gift she's left behind, that little metal box, sunk into the centre of the pillow on my bed. And even when I see it, I can't go to it, not right away. I need all my strength and several more minutes just to walk back across the empty room and when I do, I tread slowly, cautiously, as if the floor is made of glass.

In my hands, the box is heavier than I remember. You can tell it's full before you open it. And against my palms, there's something rigid, wrapped in tissue, wedged across the base.

I start to think of Diana on her hands and knees - she's already found the knife and now she's gathering up the pictures and the papers that she threw - she's shuffling them all together and fitting them back inside the box... She hasn't bothered with the padlock so when I push open the dented lid I know that it's exactly what she wants. And when I take out the newspaper article folded neatly on the top, my breathing's almost even. My heart has slowed.

But still, as I smooth open the soft, yellowed page (folded neatly, deliberately, on top), I have to fight the urge to shut my eyes. As if that will make any difference. After all, I think, isn't she here anyway? Even in the darkness of my head - especially in the darkness of my head? Hasn't our mother always been here, looking just as she does in this old news picture?

A pale blonde woman beside a long white car.

It takes every last bit of courage to lift the article closer, to start to read. And even then, after a minute, or maybe it's less than a minute, the paper's started shaking and the words are melting together so that I can hardly carry on. But I won't cry. I refuse to cry. I won't give in.

Instead I hold on tightly to the edges of the box and I think of Diana, of my Diana, as I fumble underneath it for the knife.

Twenty-Four

The car park is a different place this morning. Last night's storm has changed everything. The few trees and shrubs that clung around the edge are now mostly driftwood. After I've slipped between the railings and away from the white gravel, I have to pick my way around broken branches and uprooted trunks. There are shaggy roots strewn across the rocks and heather like strands of dirty hair. But despite everything, it's a beautiful day. The sun's shining, but the heat has lifted. Although the storm's devastated the skinny bushes, the heather's thriving. It's full of colour now, blues and purples and deep misty pinks. There are butterflies too, dozens of them, flitting among the flowers on milky wings. Some of the rocks are still damp and slippery, so I watch my feet. I don't want to fall and drop the box I'm clasping tight against my ribs. I want to do this right.

There's a cool, clean wind tugging at my T-shirt and drying out my eyes and mouth. I find myself blinking as I gaze up towards the wide, blue sky, licking my lips and tasting salt. The sky is full of seagulls. They're everywhere, wheeling and diving, whiter than snow. Their cries fade and return with the rolling wind and beyond them, there are clouds racing through the blue. These aren't storm clouds, but tatters; wisps of smoke and shredded paper that fall apart before your eyes.

I don't stop until I've shuffled along the edge about as far as you can go before the cliff drops down almost vertically to West Beach. The railing's not far behind me, but I don't look back over my shoulder at the car park. I'm not really interested in it anymore. I no longer care about the bonelike stones or billowing dust or who is parked there. None of it matters. I've come here because it's the highest point that I can think of. And that is all.

I teeter on the edge, staring out across the bay.

In the distance, the ridge opposite looks almost soft from over here. It doesn't plunge, but seems to billow down towards the beach, the deep orange rock melting gently into the golden sand below.

West Beach is packed, of course. Despite the storm last night and this morning's news, nothing has changed down there. Deckchairs and windbreakers ripple with the breeze. The tourists scurry about like colourful insects, in their lemon-yellows and their pastel blues, in their vivid sunburnt pinks. The teenage girls are still screaming and the children still play, building castles and digging trenches, flying back and forth with buckets, trailing water through the sand. No one seems to have noticed the drop in temperature. They're still stripping off and flapping towels, careering recklessly into the sea.

With one hand to my forehead to shield my eyes from the glare, I stare out across the water. I watch the waves as they rise and fall and shatter, the suds coming apart like the ragged clouds above. Further out, the light turns like knives beneath the surface, flashing silver, and then that dark.

That's where they've been hiding. My Missing Girls.

They found them this morning, washed up further down the coast. As far as anyone can tell at this early stage, there isn't any evidence of foul play. It was on the television breakfast news - *"breaking news just in"* - so perhaps that was why they didn't give the discovery much airtime. The girls had simply drowned and hadn't been kidnapped or murdered the way everyone was expecting.

The reporter didn't even bother interviewing the dead girls' mothers. It was just that same picture shown all over again, the one with the guide uniforms; the girls looking somehow more ordinary than ever, despite how pretty they both were, with their smiles and their freckles and their brownish-blondish hair. They were just girls again, girls you wouldn't give a second glance to if they were to pass you on the street. Girls like so many other girls; interchangeable, forgettable.

One of the coastguards came onscreen briefly to stress the importance of warning signs, and that however experienced a swimmer you think you are, you must never, never swim beyond those flags. No one knew why those girls might have done that. In the end, no one seemed to know much about them at all. *'A simple tragedy,'* the reporter had called it, but he barely sounded sorry.

"In other news," he went on gleefully, "parents and the

community at large have been scandalised following the arrest of a local man on drug dealing charges. Edward Lloyd, who was familiar to many as the face behind Kiddies Kornets, had been under police surveillance for several months..."

And then there he was, in a sun-drenched snapshot, leaning out over the counter of his van, one eye winking (or perhaps just squinting) above that familiar gap-toothed grin. Our local ice-cream man. Our local dealer. Of course Diana knew him. And I thought how if she'd been sitting there beside me watching the news, I could have told her what I'd believed about him. Quite probably she would have laughed. We'd both have laughed, we'd have giggled into our cornflakes until we gagged. But Diana wasn't there, so I'd reached instead for the remote and snapped the television off. I went upstairs and fetched her box. I came out here.

And now I'm all alone and feeling it as I stare out over the glittering water. I watch the waves swell and break, and swell and break, and I think how, once a story's over, no one cares. The story ends, the people in it disappear, and then there are other stories and that's all.

I open the box.

I gaze at the page of newsprint for a moment, at the picture of a woman who doesn't exist, who has never really existed, not for me. In order to take it out, to tear it up, I have to put the box down on the ground. I crouch beside it among the broken branches and the butterflies. When I take the cutting out, the wind tries to snatch it from my hand.

I don't let it go just yet though. Starting with the headline at the top, 'Local Woman's Suicide', I begin to read it through once more, but then I stop. After poring over it for half the night, I already know it off by heart. I don't need to read it to know that when I was three years old, my mother drove her white Rover estate out of town 'to a well-known picnic spot' further down the coast. I don't need to read again how she took an overdose of prescribed antidepressants and over-the-counter painkillers, washed down with a half bottle of vodka, and how they found her, still 'sitting' in the driver's seat, at least four hours later.

I no longer want to ponder the list of reasons why my mother should want to do such a thing. As if her 'long term mental ill health' wasn't enough, there was the fact of social services recent involvement with the family; the claim from 'a close friend' that teachers at the eldest daughter's infant school had been concerned about abuse.

And I certainly don't want to think about the way my mother wasn't alone in the car when she drank her booze and swallowed her pills. I don't want to imagine what secrets she might have whispered to the toddler they found safe and well and strapped securely in the car's back seat. I don't want to know why my mother decided to take me with her on that day, or why, eventually, she left me behind.

It doesn't matter. It's just a story. That little kid isn't real to me any more than this woman is, this mother. None of it's real in the way my bedroom was this morning, when I woke to find all over again that Diana's bed was empty, that all her things are gone. It's this hole in me that matters, this sadness, a longing that's so deep it feels physical, like a hunger, a craving. It's Diana who matters, who has always mattered, not some pale blonde woman with her long white car. Not some mother who doesn't actually exist.

I rise to my feet now as if Diana's standing right here beside me, as if she's smiling at me and nodding, understanding, urging me on. I rip the cutting in half and then in half again. I keep tearing until it's unreadable, almost nothing, and then I lean out over the edge, over West Beach and the sea, raising my hands towards the gulls and the little zipping clouds. I open my fingers and watch the pieces fly.

When they're gone - and they're gone so fast, bursting for barely a moment like a blizzard against the blue, like a flash of hard white winter - I pick up the box. A part of me had been planning to hold on to the other photos - the wedding photos and family photos; the normal smiling snapshots - for another time, another year maybe, another life, but now I see it's pointless. I don't bother ripping up these pictures. I simply upturn the box and shake them loose, thinking of whirling blossom and then of movies in which dark clothed mourners scatter ashes to the sky.

Briefly, I catch myself thinking of the old bones they found buried on the heath, still in the process of being identified as far as I'm aware. I think how there's probably someone else out there about to learn of an ending they could never have imagined. I wonder if the truth will finally come to mean as little to them as it does to me? But then I shrug, dismissing the idea. That's their story, not mine.

For just a moment, I watch the pictures dance against the wind, but then I turn away. I don't try to follow them. I'm not worried where they'll end up, whether far out to sea or bobbing with the lolly sticks in the white horses, or stuck in someone's sandcastle along with all the other makeshift flags, I just don't care. They're gone.

She's gone.

I'm about to let the box fall, empty, to the ground, when I remember the knife, wedged back into the base. After last night, I told myself that I wouldn't look at the knife ever again. I wouldn't touch it. But this is different.

I know what to do. Impatiently, trying not to focus on it, I tug it out from the metal seams with sweating fingers and hold it high above my head. I hold it there just long enough to glimpse the yellowing bone handle and the leftover tissue still clinging to the blade in dirty shreds. I pull my elbow back and throw it hard.

It spins against the sky and in the instant when the sun catches it and makes it blaze, I see that girl again.

That little girl with blonde bunches and crushed-glass eyes.

The girl who shut me in a wardrobe and tried to pull our front door shut, the one who was always pushing at me or pulling me, who buried me in coats. The girl who hid me repeatedly, shielding my body with her own.

But as soon as I blink she vanishes, like the knife has vanished. The sky is blue and empty once more. There are only the birds, the scudding clouds. My heart is banging and my hands are shaking. Around the edges of the gap that yawns inside me, I'm as cold and hard as ice.

You can come back now, Diana, I think. *I've set us free.*

As I turn and walk back along the railings towards the car park, kicking the box away, scattering twigs and stones and butterflies, I find myself picturing my sister sitting at the kitchen table when I get in. She's smoking a roll up and drinking a coffee laced with whisky; all her things spread out in front of her. I know what will happen next. She's been waiting.

"Jesus," she'll say when she sees me. "What's up with you?"

But then I don't allow myself to imagine anymore. I know it isn't really about to happen like that, that it's a waste of time to fantasise. And there are plenty of real things I need to be getting on with. First, I should try to find Carl, if he's still about. I'll talk to his family if he's gone too. And then there are Diana's drinking friends and her biker friends. There are lots of people who could help. And I need to go to the police station too and file a report. I need to start doing all the things you need to do to bring a person back.

She's coming back.

I know this as well as I know the little blue flower on her shoulder blade and the fine blonde roots in her thick black hair. All I have to do is find her.

Megan Taylor was born in 1973 in Greenwich in South London where she stayed, more or less, for the next thirty years, working, studying, having children and writing.

She has had stories short-listed in several competitions, including the London Writers Competition and the Asham Award. In 2006, her first novel 'How We Were Lost' was placed second in the Yeovil Prize (the Betty Bolingbroke-Kent award).

Megan currently lives in Nottingham with her young family, where she is studying for an MA in Creative Writing with Manchester Metropolitan University and working on her next novel.

www.flamebooks.com

Acknowledgements

With thanks to Dan for all his love and help, and for always being there, and to Fred and Lola for putting up so brilliantly with their writer Mum.

Thank you to Mike Carden for his time and advice and encouragement throughout, and to all the other people who have supported 'How We Were Lost'; to John Beevers and Robert Cockburn for their enthusiasm at the start, to Catherine and Aaron for reading early chapters, and to Sean Wood (www.perfectwork.co.uk) for his amazing editing.

Also available from Flame Books:

A Dangerous Man - *Anne Brooke*

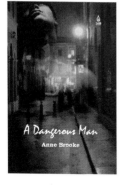

Michael Jones, a young gay artist and part-time prostitute will do anything to stage his first exhibition. When he falls in love with rich financier, Jack Hutchinson, he seems set to achieve his goal. But as Mikey becomes caught between the unforgiving territory of smoky-bar Hackney and the green-garden luxury of upper class London, we discover the intense mindscape of a man obsessed with his dreams as he attempts to free himself of his past. When a net of antagonistic relationships and inner battles encroaches upon him, the consequences of Mikey's uncompromising pursuit emerge in thrilling tragedy, leaving him having to fight for all he holds dear, and in the only way he knows how.

Within a plot thick with the flesh of individual struggle, a backbone of page-turning tension carries Mikey's plight through the charcoal grey London which rubs itself so close to his skin, entrapping him in a dark kaleidoscope of sex and crime. Pushing him to the full expression of his haunting richness, Brooke alerts us to the psychological discourse and emotional minefield of a troubled man struggling to establish a sense of self and place in urban England.

"I loved it, it had me gripped. Everyone go out and buy this book!" - Paul Burston (Gay Section Editor, *Time Out*).

The novel is available now at **www.flamebooks.com** and from selected booksellers and online retailers. ISBN: 0 9545945 6 8

FLAME BOOKS

Flame Books is an innovative new publisher established upon ethical foundations. We aim to publish the most exciting contemporary English-language fiction by excellent new authors, and wish to offer fair contracts and royalties to authors whilst also supporting numerous worthwhile charitable projects. We seek to be closely involved in the writing community and to use the internet to establish new relationships between ourselves, authors, readers, and all involved in producing and distributing quality publications.

All titles published by Flame Books can be purchased direct from our website and international delivery is available on all orders. Our titles can also be bought at selected bookstores and via online retailers.

www.flamebooks.com